# OPERATION LIGHTNING BOLT

An absolutely gripping historical murder
mystery full of twists

## HILARY GREEN

JOFFE
BOOKS

Joffe Books, London
www.joffebooks.com

First published in Great Britain in 2022

© Hilary Green

Cover art by Jarmila Takač


ISBN: 978-1-80405-528-1

## AUTHOR'S NOTE

The main characters in this story are fictional but some of the supporting characters really existed. One of these was Brigadier Colin Gubbins, one of the senior officers in charge of the Special Operations Executive. In SOE circles his code name was 'M'. Ian Fleming knew him and it is thought that he was the inspiration for 'M' in the James Bond novels.

# PROLOGUE

*August 1942*

In what had once been the salon of Grendon Hall, a nine-teenth-century stately home in the village of Grendon Underwood, some two dozen young women sat in front of two-way radio sets with headphones clamped to their ears. One of them glanced at a schedule pinned above her desk, tuned her set to a particular wavelength and waited, pen at the ready. At exactly 21.35, a series of bleeps transmitted a recognition signal in Morse code, followed by a message. The young woman diligently transcribed the dots and dashes into five-letter groups, until she heard the recognized signal for *message ends*. She returned with *message received* and broke the connection with a sense of relief. She knew the sender only by the code name 'Fisher', but she had been picking up his transmissions for several weeks and had come to recognize his 'fist', the characteristic style of transmission that was unique to each operator.

She looked at what she had written. The transmission had been short and clear with no need to ask for a repeat. It had been forcefully impressed on her that every extra second spent on air exposed the agent at the other end to the risk

1

of being located by one of the German detector vans, with grim results.

The five-letter words meant nothing to her. She tore the sheet on which they were written off her message pad and handed it to a colleague, who carried it up to the decoding department on the floor above.

Twenty minutes later, the commanding officer of Station 35a, as Grendon was known to the Special Operations Executive, put through a call via a scrambler phone to an office in Baker Street, London.

'We've just received a message from Fisher. It reads, *Urgent exfiltration required.*'

'Who do they want picked up?'

'It doesn't say, but I think we can presume whoever it is, is in a pretty desperate situation.'

That night a Lysander aircraft took off from an airfield in South East England. Arriving over the target area in occupied France, the pilot picked out the expected pattern of fires laid out on the ground below, two in a line and the third at right angles, and flashed a recognition code. When someone on the ground flashed the agreed code in return, he circled, losing height, and brought the plane in to land on a strip of open ground marked out by torches. The plane bumped over the uneven surface, came to a stop and then swung round to taxi back to the point where it had landed, turning again with the nose into the wind ready for a quick take off. Even before it had come to a standstill a little group of men emerged from the surrounding trees and ran towards it, carrying a stretcher. The pilot opened the cover of the rear cockpit and the men manhandled the stretcher into the plane.

The pilot looked down at the upturned face of one of the men. 'Who is it?'

'It's Max. She's in a bad way. The bastards have tortured her.'

# CHAPTER 1

*July 1943, Beaulieu, Hampshire*

The woman had been dead for at least two days, Inspector Wilson reckoned. The blood that had soaked into the bed-clothes had dried to a rust-coloured crust and attracted a hoard of flies, which rose in a buzzing mass when he waved his hand over them but returned as soon as he stepped back. The room stank of blood and excrement and decomposition. A bloodied kitchen knife lay on the floor. He looked down at the body.

'Terrible waste! She must have been a real looker before . . .'

'Yeah, I guess she must,' his sergeant agreed. 'What do you reckon? Suicide?'

'Looks like it, from the cuts to her wrists. If it is, we can expect to find a note.'

'No sign of one so far.'

'Well, have a thorough search and see if you come up with anything. Do we have a name?'

The sergeant consulted his notebook. 'Mrs Lillian Harvey, according to the lady next door.'

'Who found the body?'

'She did, she and her husband. Seems the deceased had a cat. She heard it mewing outside the door and thought it was odd that it wasn't let in.'

'What's the neighbour's name?'

'Mrs Janice Godley.'

'Where is she now?'

'I got PC Francis to take her back to her house. She's a bit shaken up.'

'Not surprising. OK.' The inspector turned to the door. 'There's nothing more we can do here until forensics have finished. I'll go and have a chat with Mr and Mrs Godley. In the meantime, organize a house-to-house. See what the other neighbours can tell us. Who were her friends? Did anyone have any reason to think she might top herself? You know the sort of thing.'

In the sitting room of the cottage next door, Inspector Wilson found an elderly woman sitting with a blanket round her shoulders, clutching a mug of tea between her hands. A man of a similar age, but with an upright, soldierly bearing stood nearby. The police constable introduced Wilson.

'Take a seat, Inspector,' said Mr Godley. 'Can we offer you a cup of tea?'

'Thank you, no. I won't keep you long. I can see your wife has had a nasty shock. Can you tell me exactly what happened this morning?'

'It was the cat — Buffy, she called it,' the woman began. 'I heard it mewing and mewing and I thought it was strange because she — Mrs Harvey — she's very fond of it. She wouldn't have gone away and left it. So I went and rang the bell, but there was no answer. I thought perhaps she'd been taken ill, or had a fall. So I looked through the windows . . . I wouldn't normally do that. I mean, I'm not the sort of nosy neighbour who'd make a habit of that sort of thing . . .'

'No, no. I quite understand,' the inspector said. 'Go on, please.'

'Well, I couldn't see any sign of Mrs Harvey. I don't know if she keeps a spare key anywhere and there was no sign of her downstairs, so I called Peter — that's my husband — and he got a ladder and climbed up to the bedroom window — just to make sure she was all right, you know, but . . .' she trailed off into silence.

'Well, I don't have to tell you what I saw. You've seen for yourself,' her husband said. 'So we dialled 999.'

'Quite right,' the inspector said.

'But what happened?' asked Mrs Godley tremulously. 'Peter said there was blood everywhere.'

'We don't know for sure, madam. We have to wait for the post-mortem. But what can you tell me about Mrs Harvey? It would help us to fill in the background.'

'Very little, I'm afraid,' said Godley. 'She liked to keep herself to herself. Always very polite, but, well, she didn't seem to want to socialize. But then, she was so much younger than us. It's not surprising.'

Wilson thanked them for their help and took his leave. Pausing outside on the pavement he took in the row of neat cottages with their carefully tended gardens and shook his head sadly. In a village like Beaulieu, you could almost forget there was a war on — forget rationing and the Blitz and the threat of invasion — until something like this happened. As if to reinforce the thought, three Spitfires roared low overhead, shattering the peace.

* * *

At Palace House, the luxurious mansion of the Barons Montagu of Beaulieu, currently the home of the Special Operations Executive's 'finishing school', Caroline Grayson, one of the support staff from the First Aid Nursing Yeomanry, knocked on the door of the commanding officer.

'Yes, Grayson, what is it?'

'I thought I should let you know, sir. Something has happened to Lily.'

'Happened? What do you mean?'

'I'm not sure. She didn't come into work yesterday and she didn't show up this morning, so I walked down to the village to check in on her. When I got there, I saw a police car parked outside her house and the police were putting up tapes to keep people away. There was a little group hanging around in the street — mostly neighbours, I think. I asked one of them what was going on and he said he'd heard she was found dead. Then a police inspector came out of the house next door, so perhaps they were the ones who discovered her — but that's just a guess. Anyway, sir, I thought you should be informed.'

'Quite right. Did you have any reason to suspect she was ill, apart from the fact that she didn't show up this morning?'

'No, sir. She was here the day before yesterday and she seemed fine.'

'Very well. Thank you for letting me know. I'll take it from here.'

As the door closed behind Grayson, the CO picked up a scrambler phone and put through a call to a London number.

* * *

In his office at 64 Baker Street, Brigadier Colin Gubbins, known to his colleagues in SOE as 'M.', picked up a phone and put through a long-distance call to a number in the remote Scottish Highlands.

'Fergus? I need an immediate and up-to-date report on Maxwell. What can you tell me about her current state of health?'

'In a word? Robust.' The Scotsman rolled out the word with relish.

'Robust? Really?'

'Aye. She's made a remarkable recovery, considering what she went through. But she's worked hard at getting fit again and I reckon she's in peak condition now.'

'And psychologically?'

'Ah, well, that's a different story. But the problem is less to do with what happened in France than what has happened since. The lass is close to going out of her mind with boredom.'

'Are you sure that's what it is?'

'Quite sure. That girl's got a fine brain, but it needs stimulation. Sending her up here to do the kind of menial routine work we do is a terrible punishment.'

'It wasn't intended as punishment! You know that. But when an agent knows as much as she does about our operations, she can't just be turned out into the wider community. A spell in the "cooler" was intended to give her time to recuperate — and give us a chance to assess her suitability for further deployments.'

'Well, that's as may be, but to a girl like that being shut away up here is just another form of torture.'

'So, in your judgment, she's ready to return to active service?'

'You're no thinking of sending her back to France, are you?'

'Not at present, but I do have an important job for her.'

'Well, that's what she needs. You'll have no reason to regret your decision.'

'Excellent! Get her on the first train back to London.'

# CHAPTER 2

Twenty-four hours later, Lieutenant Katherine Maxwell, Kim to her friends, Max to her colleagues in the First Aid Nursing Yeomanry, presented herself at 64 Baker Street and was told to go up to the first floor. In M.'s office she came smartly to attention.

'Lieutenant Maxwell reporting for duty, sir.'

The brigadier rose from behind his desk and crossed the room to greet her.

'It's good to see you, Max. Are you well?'

'No problems that a hot bath and a couple of hours sleep won't cure, sir,' she replied with a grin. 'Calling that train the overnight sleeper is a joke.'

He smiled. 'I'm sorry to drag you straight in here after the journey, but what I have in mind won't wait.'

'Are you sending me back into the field?'

He looked at her and saw no trace of fear in her expression. She was a slight figure, no more than five feet four inches tall, but he knew from the reports of her preliminary training that the slender form was capable of feats of strength and endurance that would put many male athletes to shame. Her face, framed by unfashionably short dark hair, was elfin, with its pointed chin and high cheekbones, and dominated by a pair of grey-green eyes that could sparkle with amusement but which could also sustain a calm, assessing gaze that many people found disconcerting. There were no signs, that he could see, of the appalling treatment she had received at the hands of the Gestapo torturers, except for a faint scar running from the corner of her right eyebrow to her lip. The main damage was hidden under a smart uniform that seemed to have survived a night on the train remarkably uncreased. But he had seen the medics' report — the toes devoid of toenails, the feet swollen to twice their normal size, the marks of the lash on her back, the wrists swollen and abraded by the manacles from which she had been hung for who knew how many hours. And now she was facing the prospect of being sent back to face a similar fate without a flicker of hesitation.

'No,' he said gently. 'Not yet, at least. I'm sending you to Beaulieu.'

Was she relieved or disappointed? He could not tell from her expression. 'As a conducting officer?'

Every agent preparing to be sent overseas was given a mentor, someone who had been in the field and could tell them what to expect, and what to look out for. They were called conducting officers.

'No. I need you to have a wider remit than that. Officially, you are going as a lecturer in fieldcraft — for which you are well qualified.'

'Officially?'

'Yes. In a sense, I am asking you to go undercover again.'

'Undercover — among our own people?'

'I know it sounds bizarre, but there are cogent reasons. Why are we still standing up? Have a seat. Would you like a cup of what passes these days for coffee?'

'No, I'm fine, thank you. I had breakfast on the train.' They sat and she fixed him with those remarkable eyes. 'So what is this all about, sir?'

'You will remember Lily, from your time at the finishing school?'

'Yes, of course.'

'Did you ever work out what her real function there was?'

'To seduce any susceptible male agents and report if alcohol or sex loosened their tongues — pillow talk, if you like — and also whether they talked in their sleep and if so in what language.'

'You seem to have a fairly comprehensive picture. Were you shocked?'

'Initially, perhaps, but I could see the rationale behind it, and Lily is very pragmatic about it. We had some friendly chats and she could tell some very funny stories.'

M. was silent for a moment. Then he said, 'Lily was found dead yesterday morning.'

'Dead! How?'

'I have no further information at the moment, except that the police were called and appear to be treating the house as a crime scene. So it is obviously not natural causes. Is there any chance it might be suicide?'

'Suicide? Lily? Never!'

'What makes you so sure?'

'I told you, she was very pragmatic — and very patriotic. She knew that however sleazy the job might look to an outsider, she was doing her bit, in an important way, towards the ultimate victory. I simply can't imagine her killing herself.'

'That was my reaction, too. That's why I sent for you. We can't be seen to be conducting a separate investigation to the police, but neither can we be entirely open with them about Lily's function. Nonetheless, I want you to make some enquiries on my behalf. Was there someone at Beaulieu who might have had a reason to kill her? Could it possibly have been a foreign agent? Has someone infiltrated the organization? You can see the vital importance of getting answers to those questions.'

'Yes, I can.' Kim was silent for a moment, then she looked up. 'Why me, sir? I'm not a cop, or a private investigator. What makes you think I've got the qualifications, or the experience for the job?'

'It depends what you mean by qualifications. You have a brain that is capable of solving complex problems. When you were at Grendon you were the best decoder in the place. No matter how garbled or incomplete the message, you would manage to make sense of it — even if you had to sit up all night to do it.'

'We all did that if necessary.'

'But you were better at it than any of the others. Then, when you volunteered to be trained as an agent yourself, your superiors commended your propensity to probe every scenario with a forensic eye for detail. You know most of the lecturers at Beaulieu and they will accept your presence at face value, but at the same time you are accustomed to operating undercover. I can't think of anyone better qualified.'

Kim hesitated briefly. Then she said, 'All right. If you think I'm the right person for the job, I'll do my best. But do you really believe we might have a mole at Beaulieu?'

'I don't know.' M. sighed and spread his hands. 'But if Lily was murdered, we can't have the civilian police grubbing around in our dirty linen.'

'I understand that,' responded Kim. She was silent for a moment. 'Did Lily have any family?'

'Not according to her file.'

'What do we know about her life before she came to work for us?'

'Born Lillian Baker to a single mother in the backstreets of Liverpool. A bright kid. She managed to get into the local grammar school and was doing well. Then, when she was sixteen, she ran away to London, though it's not clear why. Exactly where she was for the next ten years is a bit vague, but she re-emerges as a high-end call girl married to a pimp who went by the name of Carl Harvey. He disappeared when war broke out, leaving her to fend for herself, and someone — I won't say who — who had made use of her "professional services" suggested that we recruit her. That was two years ago. So far, I would have said she's been a valuable asset.'

'Any chance it could be someone from her past with a score to settle? What about this Carl character?'

'I've initiated some enquiries as to his whereabouts, but so far nothing has come up.'

'I'm thinking,' said Kim slowly, 'that if I'm going to have any access to the police enquiry, I can't do it as myself. I shall need an alter ego, someone with reason to be asking questions. A newspaper reporter, perhaps, or a long-lost relative — but why would a relative suddenly reappear, unless she heard something about what's happened?'

'The death might be reported in the local rag, possibly.'

'Good point. Maybe we could offer the paper an anonymous tip-off?'

'I'm sure that could be arranged.'

'Right. I'll need the relevant paperwork, and a change of appearance.'

'Well, you know the appropriate departments. Tell them you have authorization from me and it's top priority.'

'Thank you. As soon as I get that organized, I'll get myself down to Beaulieu and suss out the reaction to the news there.'

'One more thing,' said M. 'I want you to keep in touch, but we can't trust an open phone line. The best answer seems to be a dead letter drop.'

'Very well. Where?'

He scribbled a note. 'This is the address of a house in Hythe. It was damaged in the bombing of Southampton across the water. It's empty but more or less intact. Put your reports through the letter box. There's a tub of geraniums on the left of the front door. When you leave a letter move it to the right. Someone will know then to pick it up and will put the tub back on the left so you know it's been collected. Understood?'

'Of course.' Kim paused. 'Should I have a code name, in case I need to make direct contact with you? Something fairly ordinary, but not so common that it's likely to be anyone else.'

'That makes sense. Let me think. How about Morag? There aren't a lot of girls with that name in this part of the world.'

'Fine, Morag it shall be.'

'Excellent!' M. stood up. 'I'm delighted to have you on board for this.'

She rose too. 'And I'm grateful for the chance to be useful, sir. I'll try not to let you down.' She came to attention. 'Will that be all, sir?'

'Yes, for now. Thank you — and, Lieutenant . . .'

'Sir?'

'Take care. This may not be France, but if our suspicions are correct, it could be just as dangerous.'

'Don't worry, sir. I'll be careful.'

\* \* \*

The pathologist drew back the sheet covering Lily's body and looked up at Inspector Wilson.

'I'm sorry, Inspector. You're not looking at a suicide here. You're looking for a murderer — and a particularly nasty one.'

Wilson clenched his jaw. 'Tell me the worst.'

'For a start, I found traces on the thorax and both arms of restraints — rope by the look of it — and similar marks on the ankles. It's consistent with the victim having been tied down to a surface, probably to the bed where you found her. There were also marks on the back of the skull consistent with a blow from a blunt instrument, not enough to kill but probably enough to induce temporary unconsciousness. Taken together, these suggest to me that the victim was first stunned, then tied down to the bed.'

'She wasn't tied when we found her.'

'No. When the perpetrator had finished what he intended to do, he slit her wrists, presumably in an attempt to make it look like suicide, and when the victim was sufficiently immobilized by loss of blood, he removed the ropes and left her to die.'

'Finished what he intended to do?'

'Look here.'

The pathologist turned the corpse's head to one side and shone a light into the ear. Leaning closer Wilson saw that the passage was blocked by some red substance.

'And here.'

He turned the head the other way and shone his light into the other ear.

'What is it?' asked Wilson.

'I shall have to remove it to be sure, but it looks to me like sealing wax.'

Wilson swallowed. 'Please tell me this was done after she was dead.'

'I'm afraid not. This poor woman was deliberately immobilized and tortured and then left to die.'

'Dear God! Why do such a thing?'

'I couldn't tell you. But the sealing up of the ears suggests to me that perhaps she heard — or overheard — something she was not supposed to.'

Wilson digested this for a moment. Then he said, 'You said he waited till she was sufficiently immobilized before he removed the ropes and left her to die. What makes you think he didn't wait until she was dead?'

'Because of something I noticed when I examined the scene before the body was removed. Most of the blood was on the bed or on the carpet but there were also streaks of blood on the headboard. Not the sort of splashes you might get when an artery is punctured. Perhaps she tried to pull herself up, to call for help?'

'Maybe. I have to admit I didn't spot anything at the time.'

'Well, you had no reason then to think you were looking at a murder.'

'No, true. Plenty of reason now, though. The scene is still left undisturbed. I'll take another look. Thank you, doctor. You'll let me have a written report?'

'Of course.'

Back in his office Wilson described the pathologist's finding to his sergeant.

'Why would anyone do such a thing? I can't fathom it.'

'Maybe the pathologist's got a point — she overheard something she shouldn't have done,' the sergeant suggested.

'What could a woman like that overhear to warrant being tortured?'

'I dunno.' The sergeant shrugged. 'But sometimes a bit of local gossip can get blown up out of all proportion. Maybe she was given to tittle-tattling and caused some trouble.'

The inspector stood up. 'Go back to the house-to-house. See what you can find out. Was she known as a gossip? Has there been any kind of scandal that she might have been mixed up in?'

CHAPTER 3

Kim Maxwell paused outside the gates of Palace House and looked up the drive at the magnificent building. With its turrets and gables and mullioned windows it was a perfect example of Victorian Gothic. She knew some people despised that style as inauthentic but she liked its romantic associations, and with its grey stones set off by the surrounding sweep of green lawns it was beautiful. Not that the gardens were at their best now. Gardeners were hard to find, and much of the land had been turned over to growing potatoes and other crops. Her previous time here, at the end of her training, had been tense and fraught with the anticipation of danger to come, but even then, the house and its grounds had given her comfort. Seeing it now gave her a sense, almost, of homecoming.

She was warmly welcomed. No one knew the details of what had happened to her in France, though rumours had inevitably circulated; and she was well remembered from the time when she had attended the 'finishing school' as an agent in training. No one seemed to find it odd that she had been sent back as a tutor. As M. had said, she was extremely well qualified to teach the finer points of fieldcraft. It did not take long for her to pick up the buzz of curiosity around

Lily's disappearance and the involvement of the police. A discreet watch by some of the staff on the cottage had seen the stretcher being carried out with its burden covered from view, and speculation was rife about the possible cause of death, especially among the personnel of the First Aid Nursing Yeomanry, widely known as FANYs.

Kim made no attempt to conceal her interest. 'I got to know Lily quite well when I was here before. I hate to think that something bad has happened to her.'

'So do we all,' said Catherine Grayson. 'It must be someone unconnected to us. But no one here would hurt her, surely.'

'I don't know,' murmured Kim thoughtfully. 'All we really know about the men and women being trained here is that they have been selected because they have the skills and characters that will make them good secret agents. And that they have already been through a very tough preliminary training. And I can tell you, once you've been through that, any finer feelings you might have thought you had have been well and truly crushed.'

'I can understand that,' said Catherine. 'I mean, we FANY girls only see the nicer side of them, but I have to admit sometimes it makes my blood run cold, knowing that you all have to be prepared to kill without thinking twice if necessary. But why Lily? She may have been a tart, but I can't think of a kinder, more harmless creature.'

'You don't think it could have been some sort of sex game gone horribly wrong, do you?'

Catherine looked both shocked and slightly puzzled. 'I'm not sure I know what you mean.'

Kim regarded her with a hint of amusement. She had forgotten what sheltered lives some of her FANY colleagues had led until the outbreak of war.

'Oh, I'm just speculating. Do you know who her last "client" was?'

'As it happens, I do. It was the boy we called Lucien. I saw him go off in her car.'

'When would that have been?'

'Let me think. It must be nearly a week ago now.'

'Do we know when she died?'

'No. But I saw her the next day, so it must have been after that. You know, I remember her telling me she was worried about him.'

'About Lucien? Why?'

'She said he seemed upset, on edge. He was very restless all night and kept talking in his sleep.'

'Did she say what about?'

'He kept rambling on about a storm and being struck by lightning. I told her she should inform his conducting officer.'

'Who is that?'

'It's Raoul.'

'Raoul? He's here?' This was a surprise. Before being dropped into France every agent was given a new identity, with a new French name. Kim had trained with a man who was subsequently given the name Raoul. They were dropped to different circuits when their training ended and had inevitably lost touch. Until now, she'd thought he was still on active service somewhere in France. She felt a small tremor of excitement. Any romantic or emotional attachment between trainees was severely discouraged, for obvious reasons, but she could not deny that she had been attracted to Raoul. If this was the same man, this new posting had an added bonus.

'You know him, then?'

'Yes. I'd love to have a chat with him. Is he around or is he out on an exercise? Do you know?'

'I think I saw him heading for the library about half an hour ago.'

'Right. I'll pop along there and see if I can catch him.'

The man who looked up from his newspaper as she entered the library was the same man she had trained with, but she was aware at once of a subtle change in him. He looked older, for one thing. Not surprising, perhaps, but after all it was only two years since they last met.

'Hello, Johnny,' she said, using the name she had first known him by.

'It's Raoul,' he said sharply. Then he recognized her. 'Kim! Good lord! Talk about a blast from the past!'

He stood up and they moved towards each other. She would have hugged him, but something in his eyes stopped her and they shook hands formally.

'How are you?' he asked, 'I heard . . .'

'I'm fine,' she assured him. 'What about you?'

'Oh, I'm OK. What brings you here?'

'I've been posted. I'm to teach our little lambs fieldcraft in the hopes of keeping them from the slaughter.'

He did not smile. She remembered him as someone with a mischievous grin, always ready to see the funny side of things. Something was wrong.

'I thought you'd been confined to the cooler.'

'I've been reprieved — time off for good conduct. How about you? I thought you were still in France.'

'No. I had a couple of near misses and Baker Street decided it was time to pull me out.'

'Near misses?'

'Nothing . . . nothing compared to what happened to you. Just . . . scares, you know.'

'But you're OK, really?'

'I told you. Never better.'

It was clear that neither of them wanted to talk about their experiences, so Kim changed the subject. 'What do you make of this awful business with Lily?'

He shrugged. 'I know no more than you do. I've been away for the last couple of days, only heard about it when I got back last night.'

'Away?'

'Taking one of my trainees to Gaynes Hall ready to be dispatched.'

'Oh. Was that Lucien?'

'How do you know that?' The question was a little too sharp to be casual.

'I was talking to Catherine. She reckons he was the last person to see Lily alive.'

He turned away and sat down. 'I don't know what makes her think that.'

She took the chair opposite him.

'Well, she saw them go off together, and then next morning Lily told her she was worried about him.'

'Lily had no business to gossip to one of the FANYs. What did she say?'

'That he'd been very restless and kept talking in his sleep about storms and lightning.'

He looked at her and for a split second there was something in his gaze that disturbed her. Then he relaxed and smiled. 'Oh, that! Yes, she told me about that, but I was able to reassure her. Apparently, he had a frightening experience before the war. He was studying at the Sorbonne in Paris and he decided to fly home instead of taking the train. They flew into a storm and the plane was struck by lightning. He thought they were going to crash. He told me he still has nightmares about it. He was dreading the flight out when he was deployed.'

'Not ideal, for someone who's going to have to parachute into enemy territory.'

'It wasn't the jump that was worrying him, just the flight.'

'Whose idea was it to put him into Lily's tender care?'

'It was Dr Kline. He had made his usual assessment of the agent's fitness for deployment and decided the boy was a bit keyed up and needed something to take his mind off things.'

'Kline?'

'Oh, of course, you wouldn't have come across him. He only arrived a few months ago. Apparently, someone at head office thought it would be a good idea to have a psychiatric assessment before any agent was sent into the field.'

'So he's a psychiatrist?'

'With a flourishing practice in Harley Street, I'm told.'

'What's he like?'

'Austrian Jew, brilliant man. Can be a bit gruff, doesn't suffer fools gladly, but very sound.'

'Did you agree — with what he said about Lucien?'

'Yes, I did. Lucien is one of the quiet ones but he's very able. He showed courage and initiative in his earlier training, but he has a tendency to overthink things. I thought a bit of physical release would be good for him.'

'How did it go — apart from the sleep talking?'

'Not too well, I gather. Lily said he was a virgin and in spite of her best efforts he couldn't get it up.'

'Did you report all this to Kline?'

'Of course.'

'What did he make of it — talking in his sleep, particularly?'

'I explained about the previous incident and he decided it wasn't significant.'

'So where is Lucien now?'

'Somewhere in France by now, I hope. Kline signed him off as fit, and I escorted him to Gaynes Hall the following day to await a flight. He trained as a radio operator and "Grocer" circuit was desperate for one. Turns out their own "pianist" is sick and out of action. The conditions were right so he went off the following night.'

'And Kline signed him off so quickly? Even after Lily's report?'

'Yes, I know what you mean. But Kline reckoned it was the waiting that was getting him down and he'd be better getting off asap.'

'Really?' Kim mused for a moment. 'Well, I suppose Kline knows what he's doing.'

'Are you thinking Lucien could have had something to do with Lily being killed?'

'I don't see how. When did you say he left?'

'The evening after he spent the night with her.'

'Hmm. We don't know exactly when she died, do we?'

'She was alive the morning before he left.' Raoul shrugged. 'But nobody has seen her since.'

'And her body was discovered . . . ?'

'Yesterday morning.'

'When did you leave for Gaynes?'

'On the five thirty train.'

'And what was Lucien doing earlier that afternoon?'

'Packing, I suppose.'

'So he could have gone into the village . . .'

'And bumped her off? It's possible, I suppose. But I can't see him doing it. Not the type.'

'Well, as someone reminded me not long ago, we're all trained to kill without a second thought if the occasion demands it. And we know things didn't go well the night before, sexually. Perhaps that made him feel humiliated or inadequate . . . I'm just groping in the dark. Maybe it has nothing to do with what goes on here. Maybe it was someone from her past.'

'Much more likely, I should say.'

Kim changed the subject after that and a few minutes later the gong sounded for dinner, but the conversation left her with a nagging feeling that she had missed something. The change in Raoul disturbed her. Something had happened to him in France that he did not want to talk about. What were the 'near misses' he had spoken of?

Later that night Kim opened one of the two cases she had brought with her and took out a pair of black trousers, a black roll-neck sweater and a black balaclava. She waited until the great house was silent and dark and slipped out of a side door. With blackout regulations in force, not a gleam of light showed from any of the windows, but there was an almost full moon and once her eyes had adjusted, she was able to make her way down the drive, keeping to the grass verge so that her footsteps made no noise. The impressive gates were shut and locked, but she sprang and caught the top of the wall, hauled herself up and dropped down into the road beyond. From there it was only a short walk into the village.

The police tape was still in place round Lily's cottage and a solitary constable stood hunched outside the front door.

Kim knew every inch of the surrounding countryside from exercises undertaken during her previous stay and she knew that the cottages along that lane backed onto woods with a public footpath running through them. She flitted on silent feet across the road and swung herself over the stile at the beginning of the path.

The night was very still, with scarcely a breath of wind, and for a moment she stood still, listening. Experience in the field had taught her never to take it for granted that she was the only person out and about. As her ears became attuned to the sounds of the woods, she heard faint scufflings in the undergrowth and somewhere not far away an owl hooted, but there was nothing to alarm her and she began to make her way along the path.

Very soon she was standing behind the fence of Lily's back garden. It was a simple picket fence and she vaulted it easily, ducked under the police tape and crept up to the back door. Here she paused to put on a pair of thin cotton gloves. Lock-picking was part of the SOE curriculum and the lock on the cottage door was of a simple design. It took her less than a minute to open it.

She padded silently up the stairs and reached the door that she guessed must open into the main bedroom. Again she stood still, listening. Satisfied that the house was empty and her arrival had not triggered any alarm bells, actual or metaphorical, she turned the knob and pushed the door open.

The stench caught her by surprise, and for a moment she stood paralysed, pressing her hand over her mouth to quell the urge to vomit. When it subsided, she entered the room.

She had noted from outside on an earlier reconnaissance that the curtains had been closed, presumably to deter snoopers or press photographers. This meant that she was able to switch on the small torch she carried in her pocket without fear of alerting the policeman on duty outside. She shone the light around the room, suppressing a new wave of nausea. She had not expected there to be so much blood.

The bed had been left as it was when Lily's body had been removed, and her outline was still visible, defined by a dark stain. The sheet was black with dried blood and it had pooled on the carpet.

There was evidence of the police investigation, in the shape of numbered markers and the residue of fingerprint powder, and the drawers of the dressing table had been pulled open and their contents tumbled. Kim rummaged through them and peered under the bed. She checked the wardrobe, catching a whiff of perfume which overlaid the prevailing stench. Lily had always dressed attractively but respectably, and there was nothing to suggest to anyone who did not know her what her previous profession had been. Kim felt in the pockets of her jackets and ran her hands inside the shoes.

There was nothing of any help.

If there had ever been any useful evidence it was now in the hands of the police. She moved closer to the bed and her torch picked out streaks of blood on the bedhead. Puzzled, she examined them more closely. They were not random. One clear outline had been repeated several times. She pulled a notepad from her pocket and, holding the torch between her teeth, copied it. That done, she took a final look around the room, noting Lily's hairbrush and powder bowl still on the dressing table, her dressing gown hanging behind the door, pathetic reminders of a vibrant personality. Then she switched off the torch and made her way back the way she had come.

By the time Kim got back to her room it was late and she was exhausted. She had slept little the previous night. She put her notebook away in a drawer, pulled off her clothes and climbed into bed. But weary as she was, sleep would not come. Her sudden transition from the mind-numbingly boring routine of the Scottish 'cooler' to the middle of this tragic scenario had come about so fast her brain was still trying to catch up.

It was bizarre to find herself back here at Beaulieu and she had a strong sense of déjà vu — but then, she had had difficulty believing what was happening to her the first time she came here. Up to that point her life had been following such a mundane course that she had given up expecting any excitement.

It had not always been like that. There had been times when she had very different expectations.

Her childhood had been nomadic. Her father was a civil servant who worked for the Foreign Office and was frequently posted to different embassies round Europe. By the time she was twelve she had lived and gone to school in France, Belgium, Italy and Austria and spoke the languages of those countries so naturally that sometimes she found it hard to distinguish between them. From that age onwards, she was sent to a boarding school in England, which provided both stability and the sort of education regarded as befitting a young woman of a certain class — which was to say, she was prepared for marriage to a gentleman who would have the means to support her and her children and who would expect in return a wife with certain accomplishments. She learned to ride and play the piano and paint a little. A high standard of academic achievement was not seen as requisite. The curriculum offered the usual basic subjects — English literature, history, geography, biology (chemistry and physics were regarded as being beyond the scope of girls) and mathematics, at which Kim excelled, and crucially it included Latin, without which entry to Oxford or Cambridge Universities was impossible. Kim liked Latin, enjoying the challenge of its complex grammar. She read voraciously and learned reams of poetry by heart, played chess and developed a taste for crossword puzzles. It was an enlightened maths teacher who saw her potential and persuaded her parents that she should sit the entrance exam for Cambridge University. She passed and embarked on the three most enjoyable years of her life.

As well as delighting in the rigour of studying maths at degree level, she joined a number of societies, including the mountaineering club. She was already an accomplished skier, having spent school holidays in Geneva, where her father was now based. She soon developed a passion for the mountains, revelling in the challenge of a dangerous ascent. A fellow member of the club was a young man called Simon Calloway. He was very good-looking, a daring mountaineer and an amusing and empathetic companion — with the added bonus that his family owned large tracts of Yorkshire. The pair fell deeply in love and got engaged on Kim's twenty-first birthday. They planned to travel the world after graduation, and climb as many mountains as possible. But two months later he was killed by an avalanche while attempting the north face of the Eiger. The only reason why Kim did not suffer the same fate was that she had remained at base camp with a heavy cold.

Broken in spirit, she graduated with an upper second instead of the first-class degree everyone predicted. The only career open to a woman with a maths degree seemed to be as a teacher, so she took up a position at the North London Collegiate School for Girls and resigned herself to a life without excitement. The next three years passed pleasantly enough. Most of the girls were intelligent and she enjoyed teaching them. She spent her holidays in Switzerland or going on walking expeditions with colleagues in France and Austria. There were one or two romantic encounters — a brief affair with a Swiss ski instructor, a more or less platonic relationship with the brother of one of her friends — but no one sparked the passion she had felt for Simon.

Overshadowing every activity at the time was the growing prospect of war. When it was finally declared, Kim volunteered as an air raid warden and contemplated going into one of the women's services. It was around that point that an old acquaintance from Cambridge asked her if she would consider taking up some top-secret work that would be a great value to the war effort. And so she found herself recruited into the First Aid Nursing Yeomanry. She protested that she had no interest in nursing, but it was made clear to her that this was no longer the corps' main focus and she was taken aside and asked to sign the Official Secrets Act.

There was, she was told, a branch of the organization that had refused to be co-opted into the army like the main body, and it was these 'free FANYs' that she was joining. They were in all ways a law unto themselves, owing no allegiance to any official military hierarchy, and as such were seen as perfect adjuncts to a new and very secret organization, the Special Operations Executive, whose remit was to encourage resistance and carry out acts of sabotage behind enemy lines.

She signed immediately, and was sent to Grendon Underwood to learn to code and decode messages to and from agents in the field. Her background in maths and talent for spotting patterns meant that she was ideally suited to the job, but after a year, she grew bored with being confined to an office. By that time, she had formed a fairly accurate idea of what the men sending and receiving the messages were doing. So she applied to train as an agent herself.

There followed the most demanding months she had ever experienced. At Arisaig, SOE's training ground in Scotland, she was in her element scaling rock faces and abseiling down, crossing rivers on makeshift rafts, and surviving in the open with the minimum of food and shelter. Unarmed combat came less naturally, as did weapons training and the use of plastic explosives. By the end of the course, however, she had shown herself adept at all of them.

Later, at the Beaulieu 'finishing school' came instruction in breaking and entering, disguise and deception, how to set an ambush or disable a vehicle, how to tell if she was being followed and lose the 'tail', and a dozen other elements of what was known as 'fieldcraft'. Finally, after a week of parachute training, she was dropped behind enemy lines to join an existing circuit as their courier.

As with all agents, before leaving she was given a new identity. She was now Maxine Dubois. She had a birth certificate and identity documents in that name; she also had the names and photographs of her parents and the address of the house where she had grown up and the school she had attended. There were even photographs of her as a child. In this new life, her mother was dead and her father, a black-smith, was now a POW. She had a fiancé who had been killed at the battle of Sedan. She loved animals and now worked for the local vet, which gave her a reason for moving around the countryside.

For four months, everything went well. She cycled around the area, carrying messages or supplies in her bicycle basket. Then, one day, she was on a particularly dangerous mission. The circuit was planning to sabotage a local railway junction and she was carrying plastic explosive, wrapped up to look like the week's meat ration and hidden among other groceries, when she was stopped at a checkpoint and searched. She might have got away with it, but the soldiers had a dog with them, trained to pick out the characteristic almond-paste smell of *plastique*.

She had never told anyone the full extent of what had been done to her in the next ten or twelve days.

She tried to erase the memory.

All she knew was that somehow she withstood the questioning without revealing the identities of the rest of the group, or where they could be found. Eventually, word got out that she would be transferred to Gestapo headquarters in Paris and her colleagues saw an opportunity. The convoy was ambushed, her guards shot and she was freed, unable to stand and barely conscious.

She had a dim recollection of being lifted into the plane but her next clear memory was of coming round in a hospital in England. Weeks of slow recuperation followed and then the transfer to the cooler, the SOE base in Scotland to which agents who were no longer operational but knew too much were sent.

# CHAPTER 4

*France, the hills of the Morvan*

Lucien finished stringing his aerial around the beams supporting the roof of the barn and tuned the dial on the wireless set to the correct wavelength. He had dropped into France three days earlier and everything had gone according to plan. The pilot had located the signal flares without any trouble and he and his radio set had landed unscathed.

The leader of the circuit, a chap going by the name of Gregoire, had been there to meet him and take him to the remote cottage where he had based himself.

'I am glad to see you,' Gregoire had told him on the way. 'I had not expected to get a replacement for my ailing operator so quickly.'

The following day had been occupied getting to know his surroundings and being introduced to the local *maquis*, Frenchmen who had taken to the hills rather than work for the Germans.

Now he had a carefully encoded message to send, reporting that he was operational and including a request for some essential supplies. He glanced at his watch. His scheduled transmission time had arrived.

He had just sent the recognition code that would identify him to the operator at the other end when he heard vehicles roaring into the farmyard. Brakes squealed, doors slammed and German voices shouted.

One thought flashed through Lucien's mind. How could they have picked up his signal so quickly? Somehow they must have known he was here.

The wireless pipped. The operator back in England was ready and receiving him. There was no time to encode a new message.

He tapped out a single word.

Then boots shook the ladder leading up to his position and a rifle was pointed at his face.

* * *

*England, Lyndhurst Police Station*

Inspector Wilson looked up as his sergeant came into the office.

'Well?'

'I went round all the neighbours, boss, and had a good chat but I'm afraid I haven't come up with anything very useful.'

'What have you got?'

The sergeant referred to his notebook. 'Seems the deceased was a widow. Husband was killed at Dunkirk. She came down here to escape the bombing. Very quiet, apparently very respectable, but kept herself to herself.'

'Did she have a job, or was she living on her widow's pension?' the inspector asked.

'She told people she had a position as a sales lady in one of the big department stores in Bournemouth. Went off every morning, came home at teatime, just as you'd expect. But I did learn one thing that doesn't fit the picture. Apparently, she had "gentlemen callers". Usually young chaps, who came in the evening and were not seen to leave again till next morning.'

Wilson sat back. 'Now we're getting somewhere. How did the neighbours square that with her "respectable" image?'

'She told one of them that they were men who'd been wounded on active service and were recuperating at one of the convalescent homes on the coast. Said she'd been asked by the Red Cross to entertain them, show them a bit of "home comfort".'

'Home comfort?' The inspector guffawed. 'That's a new name for it.' He became serous again. 'When was the last one?'

'The Godleys clammed up when I asked them — didn't like to talk about it. But the lady who lives two doors down had been keeping an eye open. I don't think she bought the convalescent home story. According to her, there was one last Wednesday night — that's two days before the body was discovered. He stayed all night. There was another one, an older chap, who called in later that day, but he didn't stay.'

'That looks like our man, then. Did you get a description?'

'Not a very clear one. A bit older, like I said. Quite tall. In civvies. Had a hat on, so she didn't get a good look at his face.'

'OK.' The inspector nodded. 'We'll need to check with all the convalescent homes and see if the story stands up. See if we can get a list of names — if they did come from one of the homes, they must keep records.' He paused, frowning. 'But none of that explains the sealing wax. Did you get anywhere with that?'

The sergeant shook his head. 'Not really. There was no suggestion that she was in the habit of eavesdropping or passing on gossip. Quite the opposite, really. Didn't want to be drawn into conversation, refused invitations to come in for a cup of tea and so on.'

'Hmm.' The inspector got to his feet and began pacing round the room. 'Forensics haven't come up with anything useful. The only fingerprints on the knife were her own and the same goes for the rest of the house. Any progress on finding relatives?'

'None at all.' He lifted his shoulders helplessly. 'There was nothing in the house — no letters, no will, no photographs. It's like she dropped from heaven. No one knows what part of London she'd lived in. No one ever saw a visitor — except the young men.'

'The pathologist says she'd never had children, so there's no point in looking in that direction.' The inspector rubbed his hand over his face. 'There's the house to be disposed of, and all her possessions. Who's going to get all that? Who's going to pay for the funeral? There must be someone — a brother or a sister or a second cousin twice removed.'

'We could try getting the BBC to broadcast an appeal.'

'Good idea, sergeant! I'll get onto them at once.'

* * *

Kim had almost forgotten that she had been sent to Beaulieu, officially, to teach fieldcraft, so it came as a shock when the CO introduced her to the four would-be agents she was to train. There were three men and a young woman, and like all those being prepared to go into France, they had been given new identities. The woman was Jacqueline and the men were Jean-Jacques, Pierre and Roland.

In keeping with the same security protocols, Kim introduced herself as Maxine — shortening it to Max.

According to their files the girl was from the Women's Auxiliary Air Force and Jean-Jacques and Pierre came from prestigious army regiments. Roland was the odd one out. He was slightly older than the others, in his early thirties, she guessed. He was not a career soldier but had volunteered in the Sussex Yeomanry and before being recruited by SOE had risen to the rank of sergeant. To her intense disapproval Kim saw that the other men regarded him as an inferior because he was not an officer. She could see no justification for this. In every respect, he exhibited the manners and bearing that would, to the socially conscious, mark him out as a 'gentleman', and since all were speaking French the usual

English markers of accent and phraseology were absent. She was curious about his background, but to inquire further would be a breach of SOE training. At this stage, all agents were expected to live their 'legend', the background cover story they had been given. Their past history was irrelevant. All that mattered was that each had performed well in their earlier training and came with glowing reports from their teachers.

Kim spent the morning going through the basics of shadowing a quarry without being observed and how to lose your 'tail' if you were being followed. Then she put them in pairs and gave one of each pair a quest, to bring back a particular object which could be found locally, without being observed by their partner, while the other was to follow and provide a detailed report of exactly where their quarry had gone.

Jacqueline returned triumphant with her 'treasure' while Jean-Jacques arrived hot and frustrated, having lost her within the first half hour. Pierre had also found his object, but Roland reported with a shrug that he had followed him every step of the way without being seen, and he was able to prove it.

Dinner was a formal affair, with the men in uniform or dinner jackets and the women in long dresses. This was the first time Kim had seen Dr Kline. He was easy to spot as he was one of the few in civvies. She observed him with curiosity. He was a small man with a rather large head and an oddly triangular face, broad at the brow, emphasized by heavily rimmed glasses and tapering to a pointed chin with a little goatee beard. As the diners mingled over pre-dinner sherry and cocktails, she made a point of introducing herself. It quickly became clear that he had no interest in small talk, but after a few anodyne exchanges he fixed her with a look of an intensity she found disconcerting.

'Tell me, Lieutenant Maxwell, do you think Britain can win this war?'

'Yes,' she responded emphatically. 'Of course I do.'

'Why?'

'Because we are already winning it. We've driven the Huns out of North Africa, and out of Sicily. Besides, we cannot allow that monster Hitler to overrun the whole of Europe.'

'You see Hitler as a monster?'

'Don't you?'

'It is a rather emotional term. I would rather take a more reasoned approach. So you believe Britain should continue the fight, whatever the cost?'

'Yes, to the last ditch.'

'Ah, Winston Churchill's famous "we will fight them on the beaches, on the landing grounds," et cetera, et cetera . . . So you agree with that?'

'Of course. Don't you?'

'I look at the terrible damage being done to London, and to the other major cities, and I compare it with Paris, where the beautiful buildings remain untouched because the French preferred to yield to overwhelming force rather than see them destroyed.'

'The French government did. There are plenty of Frenchmen and women who are still ready to fight for freedom.'

'Ah, freedom. Another emotional term which is rarely rigorously defined. But of course, you have good reason to be emotionally involved. I know a little of what happened to you in France. It might help you to talk about it, perhaps?'

*Not to you!* was Kim's immediate reaction. Aloud she said, 'Thank you, doctor, but I have already had the opportunity to discuss what happened with some very highly qualified people.'

'Well, if you should change your mind, my door is always open.'

To Kim's relief, dinner was announced and she was able to make her excuses. She found a place at the table well away from him. The tone of the conversation puzzled her. Was he sounding her out for possible defeatist tendencies? Or was he actually trying to put ideas into her head?

\* \* \*

Every evening when dinner was over the carpet in the great hall was rolled back and a gramophone was brought out so the trainee agents, their tutors and the FANY staff could dance. It was a welcome opportunity for all concerned to take their minds off the grim reality they faced every day. It was taken for granted by the men who were at the top of the organization that for the people they recruited an evening spent dancing represented normality, though Kim knew that for some it was as exotic as life on a South Sea Island.

But the nine o'clock news was sacrosanct, and everyone gathered in the drawing room to listen to the latest reports from the Front. That night there was nothing of special interest, and Kim was about to retire to her room when the announcer said, '*I have been asked to broadcast the following appeal for information. Will anyone related to, or having any knowledge of, Mrs Lillian Mary Harvey, believed to have been living in London until recently but currently in Beaulieu, Hampshire, please contact Hampshire Police on . . .*'

'Bingo!' Kim muttered under her breath.

## CHAPTER 5

The following afternoon a young woman with faded blonde hair and grey-green eyes, wearing a cardigan over a cheap 'utility' summer dress, knocked at the door of the cottage occupied by Mr and Mrs Godley.

'Excuse me for bothering you,' she said hesitantly, 'but I'm looking for Lillian Harvey, do you know where she is? My name's Sally Baker. Lillian Harvey's my sister. There was an announcement on the wireless asking anyone who knew her to contact the police, so I came straightaway, but there's a policeman at her door and he won't tell me anything.' The accent was trying to conform to what was known as BBC English but still had unmistakable traces of South London.

'Her sister! Oh goodness!' Mrs Godley pressed her hand to her throat. 'We didn't know she had a sister. But you haven't heard? You don't know?'

'Know what?'

'Oh, you'd better come in. Would you like a cup of tea?'

'That's terribly kind of you. I could do with a drink.'

Mrs Godley led Kim into the sitting room. It was a small room and the upholstery on the three-piece suite was faded, but the impression Kim got was one of comfort and security. It made a sharp contrast to the events she was investigating.

Mr Godley was reading the newspaper. He put it down and stood up.

His wife said, 'This is Miss Baker. She's Lillian Harvey's sister. Now, do sit down, my dear. I'll just go and put the kettle on.'

'Her sister?' said Godley, resuming his seat.

'Yes. We haven't been in touch much lately. It's . . . well, you know, one of those family disagreements. But when I heard the announcement on the wireless, I felt I had to come and see her.'

'Why didn't you contact the police, like it said on the wireless?'

'Well, I thought I'd better talk to Lil first, find out what it's all about. I had her address but no phone number, so I came down to see her. But there's a policeman on the door and he wouldn't let me in. What's going on? Where is she?'

'Oh dear. You haven't heard?'

'Heard what?'

'Look, I'm terribly sorry. It really would be better if you'd spoken to the police first. But the fact is, your sister is dead.'

'Dead! Oh my goodness! How?' The young woman clasped her hand over her mouth and swayed as if about to crumple to the floor. Mr Godley jumped up and helped her to a chair.

'We . . . we're not . . .' He struggled for words. 'You really need to ask the police. But it seems she may have taken her own life.'

'Taken her own life? Why would she do a thing like that? Oh dear, oh dear! I don't know what to say.' The young woman pulled a clean hankie from her bag and held it to her eyes.

Mrs Godley came back with a tray of tea. 'Here, you've had a nasty shock. Just take a moment and drink this. I'm afraid there's no sugar — the rationing, you know.'

The young woman took the offered cup and thanked her, sniffing back tears. 'Oh, this is awful. How could she do such a thing?'

'I'm afraid we can't be much help there,' Mr Godley said. 'As we told the police sergeant, we didn't know your sister very well.'

'The police? Have they been asking questions, then?'

'Oh yes.' Mrs Godley responded readily. 'The sergeant was here again yesterday.'

'What sort of questions?'

'Oh, how well did we know her, did she have many visitors, that sort of thing.'

'Did she? Have visitors?'

'Well—'

Mr Godley cut in, slightly too quickly, 'Not that we saw.'

His wife flushed and rattled on. 'They asked funny questions too. They wanted to know if she enjoyed a *gossip*.' Her voice dropped to a whisper, as if shocked by the very idea. 'Or whether she might have overheard something — something other people wouldn't want known. I thought that was a very odd thing to ask about, didn't you, Peter?'

'I suppose the police have their reasons,' replied her husband heavily.

'How peculiar,' agreed the young woman. 'So can you tell me how she died?'

Mr Godley caught his wife's eye and shook his head. He stood up. 'You really should be putting these questions to the police, not to us. Do you have a car?'

'No, I took a taxi from the station.'

'Well, there is a bus that will take you into Lyndhurst. That's where the police station is.' He looked rather pointedly at his watch. 'There's one in just over five minutes, if that's what you want to do.'

The visitor put down her teacup. 'Oh, yes. That would be the best thing, wouldn't it? I'd better be on my way, then. Thank you ever so much for the tea.'

On the bus Kim considered what she had just been told. It was a pity she couldn't have spoken to Mrs Godley on her own, she mused. She was sure she would have got a lot more information from her, but her husband was obviously much more cautious — quite rightly, of course, but not very helpful in the circumstances. She puzzled over Mrs Godley's last remarks.

*They wanted to know if she enjoyed a gossip.*

Why would the police ask if Lillian was a gossip? The implication that she might have overheard something was worrying, since that was her principal function at Beaulieu. But it was not a topic they wanted the civilian police delving into. A sudden recollection flashed into Kim's mind, causing her to shiver in spite of the warm sun streaming through the bus windows. In France, during her last mission, she heard that a young woman who was sleeping with one of the Resistance fighters was thought to have passed on information she had overheard to the Germans. She was found dead, strangled, and both her ears had been cut off as a warning to others.

Twenty minutes later the faded blonde with a worried expression presented herself at the enquires desk at Lyndhurst police station.

''Scuse me. I'm Lillian Harvey's sister. I believe you're looking for me.'

Very quickly she found herself seated in Inspector Wilson's office.

'Thank you for coming in, Miss . . .'

'Baker, Sally Baker. There was this announcement on the wireless, saying you were looking for relatives of Lilian Harvey. I tried to go and see her but the next-door neighbours told me she was dead. Is that true?'

'Who did you speak to?'

'I don't know.' The young woman shook her head. 'They didn't give me a name. They seemed a nice old couple.'

'But why didn't you come straight here, as the appeal asked?'

'Well, I didn't know she was dead, did I?' The woman's tone was defensive. 'Fact is, we haven't seen each other for several years. My mother didn't approve of the man she married, so we fell out. But we've kept in touch — Christmas cards, the odd postcard, that sort of thing. Last thing I heard she'd moved down here to get away from the Blitz. When I heard the appeal on the wireless, I knew something must be wrong, so I thought I'd best have a word with her for a start. Then, when I got there . . .' She paused to dab at her eyes with a handkerchief. 'When I got there the policeman wouldn't let me in, and he wouldn't tell me why not, so I knocked next door and they told me. They said she killed herself. Is that true?'

Wilson sighed. 'I'm sorry,' he said. 'I'm afraid I can't go into details at the moment. It's under investigation. What can you tell me about your sister's friends and associates?'

'Nothing, really. I told you, we don't keep in touch.'

'Is there anyone in her past life who might wish to harm her?'

'Harm her?' The young woman gasped. 'You don't think she was murdered, do you?'

'As I said, it's under investigation. Anything you can tell us about your sister's past might be useful.'

'There's nothing I can think of. Everyone loved Lil — until she went off with that man. And he's dead, isn't he? Killed in the fighting?'

'So I understand, though as yet we haven't been able to trace any record of him.'

The woman nodded. 'I wouldn't be surprised if Harvey wasn't his real name. He was a bad sort all round.' There was a pause, as if she was steeling herself. 'Can I see her, please? I need to see her, to say goodbye, like.'

Inspector Wilson hesitated briefly. Then he nodded. 'If you can wait a little while, I'll put a call through to the mortuary. I expect it can be arranged.'

Twenty minutes later, an attendant led the way into a small room, bare except for the table on which a body lay, covered by a white sheet. He drew the sheet back far enough to expose the face. The woman beside him drew back, a hand pressed to her lips.

'Oh no! Oh my dear God! Lil, what ever happened to you?'

She groped for her handkerchief and looked around for support. 'Oh my goodness, I feel a bit funny. I've come over all dizzy. Do you think I could have a seat — and a glass of water, perhaps?'

'I'll fetch you a chair.'

The attendant left the room and Kim quickly leaned over the table. Her reaction had not been entirely false. She had truly liked and admired Lillian for her warmth and good nature. It had been a shock to see that beautiful face frozen in death. But this was far from the first dead body she had encountered. Suppressing her natural feelings, she took Lillian's head in her hands, turning it gently to one side and then the other. Her ears were intact, but something caught her eye. A spot of vivid red against the dead white skin. She peered more closely and then drew back, swallowing genuine nausea.

When the attendant returned, she was standing back against the wall and Lillian's head was straight. He set a chair for her and gave her a glass of lukewarm water. She sat and sipped, then asked, 'Can I hold her hand for a minute?'

The attendant retrieved a hand from under the sheet and Kim took hold of it, noting the stitches closing a wound in the wrist. She bent her head and sat silent for a few minutes, mentally promising that the perpetrator of this cruel death would be hunted down and brought to justice. Then she thanked the attendant and left the police station, without leaving an address.

In a nearby café she pulled out a notepad and composed a letter to Brigadier M.

*Imperative police investigation closed down asap. Could result in serious embarrassment.*

She took another bus into Hythe, found the address M. had given her and posted her note through the letter box. Then she left, remembering to move the pot of wilted geraniums from one side of the door to the other.

Back at the great house she found her four students waiting for her. She had set them another challenge, instructing

Jacqueline and Jean-Jacques to set up a secret meeting somewhere in Bournemouth, which was the nearest large town. The other two were to attempt to follow them and note the location if they found it. On this occasion Pierre had not succeeded, but Roland, again, had shown an aptitude for this work.

'Well done, Roland,' she congratulated him. He smiled and gave that slight lift of the shoulders she was coming to recognize, as if what he was being asked to do was so easy it did not warrant praise.

Kim found herself noticing that he was extremely good-looking. His eyes were a striking blue and the sunshine had brought out chestnut highlights in his hair. She appreciated that he was careful not to exhibit any sense of triumph in front of the others, in spite of the off-hand attitude of the other men. A man with a lot of self-confidence, she noted, and perceptive enough not to antagonise his colleagues

On the way back from Hythe she'd had time to think through what she had discovered. She had no doubt that Brigadier M. would be able to employ emergency wartime regulations to lean on the Hampshire police and get them to put the investigation on the back burner. But she was no nearer to formulating a working theory for Lily's murder or the identity of a possible perpetrator. Clearly someone was worried that she had revealed a secret of some sort, but what was it and where had she heard it?

A second, minor problem was also worrying her, but she did not wish to arouse suspicion by seeming too concerned. She sought out Catherine and said, 'I've been thinking. Has Lily got any family?'

'Not to my knowledge.'

'Well, someone has to arrange a funeral for her. After all, she was one of us. We can't let her go to a pauper's grave.'

'I see your point,' responded Catherine. 'But we can't actually acknowledge her. I'll have a word with the CO and see what he suggests.'

Three days later, a solicitor arrived at the police station with the information that he was acting on behalf of an anonymous donor who was prepared to offer sufficient money for a respectable funeral, and by that time the inspector and his superiors had been warned not to ask too many questions.

# CHAPTER 6

Kim recalled what Raoul had told her about Lily's last report and Lucien's ramblings about a storm. There was something odd about the way Professor Kline had brushed the information aside and the sudden urgency with which Lucien had been dispatched to France. It seemed that he might hold the clue to the mystery, but to communicate with him would be difficult, if not impossible. She did not want to go through official channels, which would mean involving Maurice Buckmaster, the head of F Section, which dealt with agents in France. She had no reason to think that there had been any leakage of information there. She knew Buckmaster from her own experiences and trusted him implicitly, but she wanted to keep the investigation within the closed circle of Beaulieu as far as possible. Another field of enquiry occurred to her. On the pretext of an appointment with a specialist in London, not likely to be disbelieved in view of what she had suffered at the hands of the Gestapo, she took a day off. But instead of staying in London she changed trains and made her way to Grendon Underwood.

The old mansion was not as grand as Palace House but it had much in common with its architecture, with its gables and mullioned windows. Kim approached it with the same sense of nostalgia she had experienced on her return to Beaulieu. Her time here had been demanding, but she had made some good friends.

After reporting to the commanding officer and exchanging greetings with old colleagues, she made her way up to the decoding room. Pauline Clayton, the FANY in charge, jumped up from behind her desk.

'Max! How good to see you! How are you?' Pauline stopped suddenly with a grimace of embarrassment. She had heard the story of Kim's capture and escape but had no wish to bring up painful memories.

Kim grinned to put her at her ease. 'I'm fine. It's amazing what a few weeks in the Highlands can do for a girl.'

'So what brings you here? Don't tell me you're coming back to work with us. We could certainly do with your brilliant knack with corrupted codes.'

''Fraid not,' Kim said. 'I'm just after a bit of information. I'm following up on an agent who was dropped into France a couple of weeks ago. I think he was given the code name Farmer. Do you have the decrypts of his messages?'

'Farmer?' queried Pauline. 'But he's been blown, hasn't he?'

'Blown? What makes you say that?'

'Hang on. I'll look up his file and you'll see what I mean.'

She came back with a buff folder marked *Top Secret*. 'He was dropped on the fifth of August. We didn't hear from him until the seventh. His call sign came over correctly but then the message broke off. He managed to send just one word: in clear, not in code. We haven't heard from him since, so I assume he was caught while he was sending.'

'One word?' asked Kim. 'What was it?'

'It's strange. It was *Blitzschlag*. I looked it up. It's German for "lightning bolt".'

'Why would he send in German? It couldn't have been one of them, using his set?'

'Unlikely, unless they already had his call sign.'

'He would have had to tell them,' mused Kim. 'If he was taken the moment he dropped, I suppose he might have cracked in one day and given it to them, but most people hold out longer than that — unless he was working for them all along . . .'

'Is that likely?'

'I wouldn't have thought so, but we know they have managed to infiltrate double agents once or twice. But *lightning*?' Kim thought for a moment. Lucien did have some kind of obsession about thunderstorms. It seemed in character.

'Any idea what it means?'

'Search me. But it's given me a lot to think about.' She went on, with a deliberate change of subject. 'Anyway, forget that for now. What's been going on here? Tell me the latest gossip.' They chatted for a while and then Kim thanked her colleague and made her farewells. By evening she was back in Beaulieu.

\* \* \*

The train journey was long and uncomfortable. The carriages were crowded with men in uniform either going on leave or returning from it, the air thick with cigarette smoke and the smell of sweat. They were held up for nearly an hour because of an unexploded bomb on one of the bridges. By the time she reached Palace House dinner was over and she had to make do with a rather dry ham sandwich from the kitchen.

Afterwards, she showered and crawled into bed, but once again her brain was too busy to allow her to sleep.

Lucien had been captured within two days of his arrival. Had someone alerted the Gestapo? If so, who? Raoul knew he had been dispatched, of course, but she could not believe that he was a traitor, and besides, as far as she knew, he had no means of communicating with the enemy. F Section HQ knew too. Someone there could be a double agent. But one question nagged at her. Why had he been sent off with such haste? Why had Dr Kline been prepared to sign him off when Lucien had given every indication that he was not in the right state of mind?

*Blitzschlag? Why would he send that one word?*

Some subtle interaction of neurons triggered an association. She climbed out of bed and took her notebook from the drawer. Those marks on the headboard, scrawled in Lily's blood — they looked like vertical lines with a jagged bend in the middle. Wasn't that a common symbol for lightning? Had Lucien's ramblings included the word *Blitzschlag*? And where had he heard it? Had Lily made those marks in the last moments of her life, as a warning? Or had the murderer left them as some kind of signature?

The next day had to be given over to her students. She dressed, thinking about what she should try to teach them. It occurred to her that this part of the job was taking up more time than she had expected. M. was asking a lot, expecting her to do a full-time job as well as investigating Lily's death, but she understood the need for some kind of cover for her activities. She decided to concentrate on showing the four trainees how they could easily change their appearance if they were in danger or being followed by adding a few simple accessories. There was a cupboard up on the top floor that reminded her of childhood games, holding as it did a treasure trove of items for 'dressing up'. She took her students to it and they spent an amusing morning trying on different disguises.

'Think about it this way,' she said. 'You are a Gestapo agent following someone you suspect may be carrying a secret message. All you know about her is that she is wearing a blue dress and has fair hair. She ducks into a department store and for a moment you lose sight of her. You wait for her to reappear. A woman comes out of the shop, wearing a dark raincoat and with a headscarf covering her hair. Is that the one you were following? Without seeing her face you can't be sure. To make it more difficult, this woman seems much shorter. The one you want was wearing high heels, perhaps, and this one has on flat shoes.' Kim kicked off her shoes and pinned a scarf in place to demonstrate. 'See what I mean? So you don't know whether to follow her or not.

And of course, it works both ways. If you're trailing a mark, it can be useful to change your appearance. Some things you can always carry with you — a scarf, a change of shoes, a light coat rolled up in a pocket. Others you might buy, if you can be out of sight of your pursuer for long enough. If circumstances require it, you might even indulge in a bit of shop-lifting.'

Jacqueline's eyes twinkled and Kim winked at her, then turned to the men.

'A man can do similar things, of course — add a hat and scarf, take off a jacket, put on glasses, ditch something you were carrying, like a briefcase, or conceal it inside a shopping bag. You can also confuse a follower by blending into a group. Mix with factory workers just coming off shift, or office workers heading for the train or the bus. Finally, don't forget you can do a lot just by changing the way you walk. Slump your shoulders, add a limp, put your hands in your pockets.' She looked at Pierre and Jean-Jacques. 'This particularly applies to you two. Anyone can tell at a glance that you're soldiers. You're going to have to learn to slouch, to stroll rather than march. Do you follow me?'

At lunch she told them, 'I'm going to set you another test. I shall go into Bournemouth this afternoon. I shall take the 1.45 train and take a stroll on the promenade, do some shopping and treat myself to afternoon tea. Your job is to follow me and keep a record of where I go and what I do, without me recognizing you. If I catch sight of you, I shall make a note of when and where. You are at liberty to change your appearance as often as you like and if anyone is able to get close enough to ask me if I have seen a small brown dog without me spotting you first — well, I'll buy that person an ice cream. Understood? Oh, and for the purposes of this exercise you are free to revert to speaking English.'

She took the train as she had promised, but on the journey she took off her navy jacket, stowed it in her shopping bag, and replaced it with a sky-blue cardigan, switched her heeled shoes for sandals and donned a large-brimmed sun hat. At the station she took a taxi, stopped it after a short distance and jumped on a bus just as it was moving away. In this way she reached the promenade.

It was a beautiful summer day, and for a while she allowed herself to simply enjoy the warmth and the fresh sea air. But reminders of the war were never far away. The beach was fenced off with barbed wire and notices warning of land mines, and the peace was often shattered by the drone of low-flying aircraft as formations of bombers headed for the Continent. She found a seat and pretended to read a book, as she waited for the game to begin.

It was not long before she spotted Jean-Jacques, looking out of place in a dark suit. She almost missed Jacqueline, who had also acquired a sun hat and had somehow attached herself to a pair of women pushing prams with toddlers at their sides. She was chatting away with them and even holding one of the children by the hand.

After a while Kim closed her book and headed for Plummer Roddis, the largest department store, and almost bumped into Pierre in white shorts and shirt, carrying a tennis racquet. In the shop she saw Jacqueline again, lingering by the perfume counter in a green jacket she had not been wearing before and a matching beret. Kim went into one of the changing rooms and when she came out, she had pulled on a navy skirt and added a headscarf and dark glasses. Outside the store, Jean-Jacques, in a striped blazer now, was gazing into a jeweller's window, using the reflection to watch for her. She walked away on the opposite side of the road and left him still watching.

She bought a copy of the evening paper from a seller at the corner of the street and headed to the Highcliffe Hotel for tea. As she walked it occurred to her that she had not seen any sign of Roland. She wondered briefly if he had decided that the whole exercise was pointless and taken the afternoon off.

Tables were set for tea in the gardens of the hotel and she seated herself at one of them. It was a while before she was served. With all the younger men away in the forces, or doing war work, hotels had to rely on a much older workforce, who were not as quick on their feet as the younger waiters. At length a menu was placed before her. She scrutinized it briefly. 'I suppose all the cakes are made with dried egg and reek of baking powder, and there will only be marge to spread on the scones.'

'The exigencies of war, I fear, madam,' the waiter wheezed.

'I'll have a pot of tea and a toasted tea cake, please.'

'Very good, madam.'

Kim looked around her. There was no sign of any of her students. She read her paper, happy to relax for a few minutes.

'Your tea, madam.'

A silver teapot, milk jug and sugar bowl were set on the table and a toasted tea cake was placed in front of her.'

'Will that be all, madam?' The effort seemed to have made the waiter wheeze more than ever.

'Yes, thank you.'

'Very good, madam. And, by the way, you don't happen to have seen a small brown dog, do you?'

Kim sat back and looked properly at him for the first time. He had greyed his hair with talcum powder and had a grey moustache. In his white waiter's jacket and dark trousers he looked no different from any of the others. But if she had looked at him properly, she would have recognized those blue eyes.

'Roland, I owe you an ice cream. Well done!'

He smiled and gave her a small bow. 'Thank you, madam.' He kept his voice in character. 'Happy to oblige. I hope you're enjoying your newspaper.'

She stared at him again. 'That was you, the newspaper seller?'

'Yes, madam.'

'You must have run all the way here! And how did you manage in that time to persuade the hotel to let you dress up as one of their waiters?'

'I guessed this was where you would come for tea, so I had a good look round earlier. It wasn't hard to arrange an exchange with one of the real waiters. I told him it was for a bet. The thing is, no one ever really looks at waiters.'

'Suppose I had gone somewhere else?'

'I'd made my preparations at three other hotels as well. I felt sure you would want to go somewhere like this, rather than a Lyons teashop.'

She shook her head, laughing. 'Well, I take my hat off to you. It was brilliant.'

\* \* \*

On her return to Palace House Kim made up her mind to challenge Dr Kline about why he had sent Lucien into the field so precipitously, but there was no reply when she knocked on the door of his office and he was not in the canteen or the library or any of the likely places she could think of. Bumping into Raoul in the corridor leading to the library she asked if he knew where to find him.

'Kline? You won't find him this evening. It's Thursday. He goes up to town every Thursday. When he joined us, he insisted on keeping his private practice going — said he couldn't leave his vulnerable patients in the lurch — so he goes up on Thursday evening, holds his clinic on Friday and then has the weekend off. He won't be back till Sunday night.'

She thanked him and turned to head for her own room to find Roland waiting for her.

'Could we talk privately for a few minutes?' he asked.

'Of course. Shall we go and sit in the garden?'

They found a bench on the far side of the mill pond, which lay close to the rear of the house. It was a lovely summer's evening. The gardens were bathed in soft sunlight and the grey stone walls of the mansion were reflected in the still water of the pond. For once, there was no noise of aircraft passing overhead, not even a contrail in the cloudless sky. Kim looked at Roland with curiosity. The more she saw of him the more she felt that he was different from all the other would-be agents she had met, and this request for a private conversation reinforced that sense.

'So, what's the problem?'

'Not a problem, exactly. It's . . . difficult. We're not supposed to know anything about each other's past lives, are we?'

'No. The less you know the less you can give away if . . . if it comes to the crunch. Why? Whose previous life do you want to know about?'

'It's not that. I'm not asking you to tell me anything. I just feel you ought to know something about me.'

'Know what?'

He hesitated, chewing the corner of a fingernail. 'I won't go into detail. It's just that before . . . before the war, I had to live on my wits, and it's given me certain skills. Well, you've seen that to some extent.'

'You certainly have a talent for assuming different characters — and for persuading people to become part of your deception. And you're good at fading into the background when necessary.'

'That's right. You might want to ask yourself how and why I acquired those skills.' He looked at her and then away, and she thought she saw the colour rising in his cheek. 'I'm telling you this because I don't think it's fair to let you take me at face value. I heard . . . someone told me a bit about what happened to you in France, and I respect that enormously. So I want to be honest with you — as honest as I can be.'

Kim touched his sleeve, and when he looked back at her she held his gaze. She could make a guess about what he was not telling her. At Arisaig they had been taught to pick locks by a convicted burglar and how to gain access to buildings in other ways by a man who had served a prison sentence for breaking and entering. SOE was not fussy about where it obtained the skills it required.

'Look,' she said, 'I don't care what you did before the war. What matters is what you're doing now, and I trust the people who recruited you to know what they're doing. In my book, you possess ideal qualifications for the job in hand. But I really appreciate your honesty, and I respect you for it.'

The relief on his face was touching, and for an instant she saw a vulnerability that she not suspected.

'Thank you,' he said.

'No, thank you. It's best if we understand each other.' She smiled at him. 'We shall both end up doing things we would be ashamed to admit in polite company, but we are doing them from the best motives and if we have any feelings of guilt, we just have to live with it.'

'You're very kind,' he said. 'And if there is ever anything I can do — perhaps something you couldn't ask the others to do . . .'

'I'll remember that,' she said. 'Now, we'd better go in or we shall miss dinner.'

The conversation left her with a pleasant feeling of warmth. She had to admit to herself that, whatever his past misdemeanours, she found Roland very attractive and she was glad he had felt able to confide in her. Nevertheless, by the time dinner was over her thoughts had reverted once again to Dr Kline.

She was convinced that Lily's death and Lucien's capture were linked and that Kline was involved. He had suggested sending Lucien to spend the night with Lily. He had then dispatched him into the field although he had shown obvious signs that he was psychologically unready. Lucien had been picked up by the Germans so quickly that it was impossible for him to have been tracked down in the normal way. Someone, for some reason, had set him up, and Kline seemed the obvious candidate.

That implied that he was in touch with German intelligence — a double agent, in fact. But he was Jewish. Surely no Jew would be working for the Nazis?

She needed more than just a gut feeling to proceed any further. She needed evidence.

As she brooded over the problem an idea occurred to her, so daring that she almost discounted it out of hand. And yet . . . it might actually be worth consideration. If it worked, it just might give her the lead she needed. If it didn't, at worst it would be a waste of time. Of course, if it went wrong she could find herself in all sorts of trouble. She decided it was a gamble, but one worth taking. Having come to a decision, she went in search of Roland.

She found him in the shooting gallery, practising his marksmanship with a Smith and Wesson revolver. Seeing her come in he removed his ear defenders and came to join her.

'Can I help you?' he asked.

'You said earlier that you would be prepared to help me with things I couldn't ask the others to do.'

He looked at her with a new interest. 'Yes, and I meant it.'

'I'm going to take a big risk and confide something to you that could get us both into trouble if I'm wrong. So I'm trusting you to keep it under your hat.'

'I won't breathe a word. I swear.'

'I have reason to believe that Dr Kline may not be what he seems and I want to find out more about him. He has a clinic in Harley Street where he sees patients every Friday. I want to know who they are. It may be perfectly innocent. They may really be in need of psychiatric help. But it could be a cover for him to meet people he doesn't want us to know about. Are you willing to help me find out?'

'Absolutely. How do you want to go about it?' His lack of hesitation was encouraging.

'We'll go up to London tomorrow. I'll find an excuse to tell the CO. Once we get to the clinic, we need to find a way to get in there and if possible look at his appointments for the day. If we can't find a way to do that, we shall just have to watch who comes and goes. I'm not sure what I'm expecting to find. It may all be a waste of time, but I want to give it a try.'

'OK,' he said. 'You square things with the CO and I'll have a think about the best approach. What train do you want to catch?'

'The first train's at six thirty-five. That should get us there in time to find the place and get an idea of the surroundings before he starts his clinic. I'll arrange for us to have an early breakfast. See you in the morning.'

'I'll be there!'

## CHAPTER 7

All agents were supplied with a suit made from French cloth by French tailors and with the labels of French manufacturers. Kim told the CO that the suit provided for Roland was too tight, suggesting with a wink that perhaps the food at Beaulieu was too tempting. She needed to take him to London to be measured for a new pair of trousers. She told the same story to her other three students and set them to memorize maps of France and plan routes between some of the major cities which would avoid likely check points. She also gave them a manual of French etiquette so they would not give themselves away by having the wrong table manners.

When she came down next morning, Roland was already eating breakfast. She had put on the blonde wig and the dowdy summer dress she had assumed as Sally Baker and for a moment he frowned at her as if she was a stranger unexpectedly intruding on his solitude. Then recognition dawned and he smiled, the wry self-mocking smile she was coming to know.

'Very good. You nearly had me fooled. By contrast, I've reverted to a previous incarnation.' He was wearing his army uniform with his sergeant's stripes and looking, it struck Kim, happier than she had ever seen him.

As she started on her breakfast, he leaned towards her. 'I've been thinking. The best way to have a chance of looking at Kline's appointments is if we pretend we have one — an appointment, I mean.'

'Both of us?' she queried with a lift of her brows.

'No, just me. I'm suffering from shell shock after being caught up in the Dunkirk catastrophe. It's gone on all this time and finally the medics have referred me to Kline — or that's what we believe.'

'So we turn up at his clinic and the receptionist checks her book and says we don't have an appointment and while we're arguing with her, we hope to get a look at the book. But she's not going to show it to us. It's confidential information.'

'I know. We shall need to create a distraction of some sort. We shall just have to improvise on the spot.'

'OK. It might work,' agreed Kim. 'So, if you're the patient, who am I?'

He put his head on one side. 'My wife?'

'All right. That makes sense.' She found herself smiling.

He put his hand in his pocket and produced a ring. 'You'd better put this on.'

She slipped it onto her finger. It was a good fit and it looked like real gold. 'You've really thought this through, haven't you?'

'Spent most of the night doing it,' he agreed.

'Do you make a habit of carrying a wedding ring around with you?'

'You know the Scout's motto. Be prepared.'

'So what are we called?'

'I thought Mr and Mrs Barton. I'm Ronald. What about you?'

'Katherine,' she said.

'Right!' He grinned suddenly. 'Please to meet you, Mrs Katherine Barton.'

'You're looking forward to this,' she said.

'I love a challenge,' he replied.

'Well, don't get carried away,' she warned him, but she could not deny the stirring of an excitement she had not felt since she was dropped into France.

As they left the house, Kim said, 'If that's our story, we'd better revert to speaking English.'

'Good point! I'm so used to French I almost forget which language I'm speaking.'

It was the first time she had heard him speak their native language in his natural voice and there was a definite hint of East London cockney in his accent. It fitted the uniform and his non-commissioned rank, but for some reason she was slightly surprised.

As they walked to the station they discussed the details of their assumed characters, constructing a back story that would withstand interrogation, just as she had been taught when she became Maxine Dubois. He had already thought out the basic facts and had created an imaginary life that had the ring of truth. This man, she reflected, already had all the skills a secret agent needed. No wonder he had treated the exercises she had given him with that air of amused contempt.

She asked. 'Were you, by any chance, an actor in a previous existence?'

He gave her a sideways look. 'In a sense but not . . . not professionally. Perhaps I should have been.'

The train was crowded with men in uniform mixing with civilians on their way to work. Roland, in his khaki battledress, blended in perfectly. They found seats in opposite corners but it was impossible to continue a conversation. As they neared London, they picked up more passengers, men with bowler hats and rolled umbrellas, heading for work in the City. Kim looked at them, in their clean white shirts and black jackets and striped trousers, and reflected that most of them had probably spent part of the night in the Observer Corps or as air raid wardens, or even as members of the Home Guard. Yet here they were, prepared to negotiate the rubble and the bomb craters to get to work, determined it should be business as usual. It gave you hope for the future.

The train pulled into Waterloo more or less on time and they took the tube to Regent's Park station.

'What number Harley Street?' asked Roland.

'I don't know. We'll just have to look for his brass plate.'

As it happened, they were just beginning their search when a taxi pulled up a short distance ahead and Kline got out and went into one of the buildings. As they reached it, Kim saw the brass plate bearing Kline's name and the initials denoting his qualifications.

'OK, so now we know,' said Roland.

'Keep walking,' she replied. 'We need to give him time to be occupied with his first patient before we go in.'

They strolled to the end of the street, and as they reached the corner a well-dressed man in a dark suit passed them. Kim had a fleeting impression of a fine-boned, well-bred face. Looking back she saw him go into the same building. They waited a short while, then strolled back again. There was very little bomb damage here, except for boarded up windows in one or two houses, blown out by a blast. When they reached the house again, Kim said, 'Right. In we go.'

'Over the top,' he said, and she saw his face suddenly twitch. A chill ran through her veins. *He's scared!* They had not even begun and he was frightened. It was surprising, and very worrying, but it was too late to turn back now. She led the way up to the door and rang the bell. As they waited the twitch transferred itself to Roland's left arm and he hunched his shoulders as if expecting a blow. Suddenly, she understood.

The man who answered the door looked more like a bouncer at a nightclub than a doctor's manservant, but Kim said confidently, 'We have an appointment with Dr Kline.'

They were admitted to a waiting room furnished with leather armchairs and a circular table covered with magazines. A middle-aged receptionist sat behind a desk at one side. Kim went over and repeated what she had said. Roland lurked behind, chewing his thumbnail and glancing nervously about him.

'What name?' the receptionist asked.

'Barton. It's for my husband, Ronald.'

'I'm sorry. There's nothing down here for that name.'

'Oh, there must be. Our doctor at home told us he'd made the appointment.'

'I'm afraid there must be some mistake.'

'But we need to see Dr Kline. My husband,' Kim lowered her voice and leaned towards the receptionist, 'he's in a bad way. It's what they call shell shock. It's been going on for months and we're at the end of our tether. Are you sure we're not in your book?'

She made to pull the book towards her but the receptionist kept a firm grip on it. 'I'm sorry. I'm afraid there's no appointment for a Mr Barton. Now, if you don't mind . . .'

'Oh, don't tell me we've come all this way for nothing! Perhaps we've got the wrong day. Maybe it's next week.'

The other woman reluctantly turned the pages. Kim was beginning to feel their plan was not going to succeed when the distraction they needed occurred — an air raid signal began its unearthly wail. Roland gave a howl like an animal in pain, threw himself to the floor and crawled under the table, huddling there with his arms over his head, and continuing to howl and call out unintelligible words.

'Oh my goodness!' exclaimed the receptionist. 'Oh, the poor chap!'

Kim waved her arms helplessly. 'Now you see? You see how bad he is.'

'Can't you do anything? Can't you stop him? Dr Kline will be livid if his consultation is interrupted.'

'I don't know what to do! He won't listen to me when he's like this.'

'Oh dear, oh dear!' The woman came round from behind her desk and crouched beside Roland, patting his arm and crooning, 'There, there. It's all right. You'll be all right.'

Roland seized his opportunity and grabbed her wrist. 'Mum! Mum! Don't leave me!'

Kim spun the appointment book to face her and was scanning the pages. There wasn't time for pen and paper but she had always had a good memory and training had made it sharper. It took less than a minute to memorize the names on the page. She glanced quickly at the entries for the following week and saw that they were almost the same. She straightened the book and turned back to look under the table.

'Come along, Ronnie. That's enough.' Her voice now had a ring of authority. 'There's been a mess up. We'll just have to go home.'

At that moment the all-clear sounded and the receptionist exclaimed, 'There, it was a false alarm. I told you there was nothing to worry about.'

Kim reached under the table and Roland allowed himself to be pulled to his feet. She drew herself up with an expression of righteous indignation. 'I'm sorry you've been troubled. We shall just have to find someone who cares enough to help a poor soldier who's fought for his country.'

So saying, she took her husband's arm and marched him out into the street. They kept up the act until they were round the corner into Cavendish Road and then they stopped and looked at each other, breathless.

'Are you sure you're not an actor?' she asked.

'Missed my vocation,' he replied. 'Did you get the names?'

'Yes. Don't talk to me for a minute.'

She pulled a notebook and pencil out of her handbag and scribbled rapidly. 'There.'

He looked at what she had written. 'Are these your abbreviations?'

'No. That's how it was written in the book. Hast, Lyn, P.LL. Hast at ten o'clock, Lyn at eleven. Then a Mrs Carter at two, and P.LL at three. These other names are written in full, but I reckon those are in code, an extra layer of secrecy.'

'I can't say they mean much to me.'

'No, nor to me at the moment, but it's a start.'

'What now?'

'It seems Kline allows an hour for each patient, so we've got . . .' she consulted her watch, 'nearly forty minutes before anything's likely to happen. I think it's time for a cup of tea and a change of appearance.'

They found a small café just round the corner and ordered tea and rock buns, which turned out to live up to their name.

'So, what's the plan?' he asked.

'I want to see who goes in to see Kline next. When the first man comes out, you follow him. See what you can find out about him. I'll hold on and follow the second patient. But we can't keep walking up and down the street. We need to find somewhere we can keep watch without being conspicuous.'

'Agreed. Any ideas?'

'I noticed the windows of the house opposite are boarded up. I wonder if it's occupied.'

'Only one way to find out, I guess,' he said. 'Ring the doorbell.'

'On what pretext — assuming someone answers?'

'Looking for a room to rent?' he suggested. 'There are plenty of folk made homeless by the Blitz.'

'OK. We can try that.'

She noticed that he had lost the cockney accent. He sounded like an American. Not the American of the cowboy westerns she had loved as a teenager, more the tones of the educated east coast. *The man's a chameleon*, she thought.

They had both brought overnight bags with them, and when she had finished her tea, Kim went to the ladies. When she returned, she had covered her hair with a silk scarf and was wearing a blue coat and dark glasses. Roland in his turn made a more radical transformation, exchanging his khaki uniform for grey flannels, a navy blazer and a straw boater.

'Ready to go?' he asked.

'You sound different,' she said. 'It goes with the outfit.'

'Suit the action to the words, the words to the action, as the Bard tells us. Or, if you prefer Gilbert's version, "merely corroborative detail, intended to give artistic verisimilitude to an otherwise bald and unconvincing narrative".'

She laughed out loud. 'I didn't take you for a Gilbert and Sullivan fan.'

'I'm a magpie,' he said. 'I pick things up.'

'"A snapper-up of unconsidered trifles",' she suggested.

He grinned. 'Look, we could go on swapping quotations all day, but perhaps there are more important things to do.'

'Quite right,' she said soberly, aware that for a few minutes she had allowed her pleasure in his company to distract her from the business in hand.

They made their way back along Harley Street, and as they approached another man rang the bell beside the brass plate and was admitted. This man was shorter but equally well-dressed, and that was all Kim could see.

'The first chap will be out any minute,' she said. 'You keep an eye out for him. I'll scout the building opposite. Meet back at the café between one and two.'

'OK,' he agreed and she saw him take up a position leaning on a lamp post, glancing at his watch as if waiting for someone.

The house with the boarded-up windows showed no sign of life. Kim rang the bell but there was no reply. Steps led down to an open area allowing light into a basement and a door, probably intended as the servants' entrance. At one time the drop would have been protected by metal railings, but as with so many other places, they had been taken away to be melted down for the war effort. The area was littered with scraps of wastepaper and other debris, suggesting that no one had been down there recently.

Kim looked up and down the street to make sure she wasn't seen. Then she made her way down the steps and knocked at the door. Once again there was no reply. A glance upwards showed her that she was out of sight unless someone was standing directly above her on the pavement.

She delved into her pocket for her lock-picking equipment.

The door gave easily.

Inside, she stood still, listening, but the only sound was a rustling as some small animal, probably a rat, scuttled for safety. She was standing in a kitchen. Another door gave onto a flight of stairs. Kim climbed silently. The house smelled dank and musty, as if it had been unoccupied for some time. At the front of the house two rooms led off the main hall.

The first was furnished as a sitting room, but all the furniture was draped with sheets. Obviously, the owners had vacated the place deliberately, to get away from the Blitz. Kim crossed to the boarded-up window. The glass was broken, as she had expected, and a gap between the planks gave her a limited view of the street. She searched about the room, lifting some of the covers, for something she could use as a tool. A sideboard drawer yielded a carving knife and a steel for sharpening it. Inserted into the crack between the boards, it gave her enough leverage to prise them slightly apart.

Now she could see the street and, immediately opposite, the front door of Kline's surgery. Moments later, the door opened and the tall, aristocratic-looking man came out and walked away in the direction he had come from. To her left, Roland glanced once more at his watch, shrugged, peeled himself away from the lamp post and strolled off after him.

The next hour passed slowly. Kim was tempted to explore the rest of the house but she confined herself to her position by the window. When her watch showed her that the hour was almost up, she went back down the stairs and let herself out of the basement door.

It was harder to see from here but she wanted to be in a position to follow when the moment came. She ducked back into the kitchen and grabbed a broom she had seen standing in a corner and began sweeping the rubbish into a pile. A position halfway up the steps allowed her to watch the feet of passers-by and between them to see the steps leading up to Kline's door. She leaned on her broom and lit a cigarette, and almost at once the door opposite opened and the small man came out. She waited for him to start walking up the road. When he was at a safe distance, she abandoned the broom, stubbed out the cigarette and put the dog end in her pocket — cigarettes were far too valuable in these days of rationing to throw away half smoked — and climbed up to street level. Her quarry was heading for Marylebone High Street.

\* \* \*

It was almost 1.45 p.m. when Kim arrived at the café. Roland looked up from his newspaper with an expression of relief.

'Everything OK?'

'Yes, fine. Sorry I've been so long. My target led me quite a dance.'

'So? Where did he take you?'

'No, you first. Have you eaten?'

'Pie and mash. It was . . . edible.'

A waitress was hovering nearby, so Kim ordered the same thing. As the girl left them, she looked at Roland. 'Tell me.'

'You're not going to believe this.'

'Try me.'

'Our friend headed straight for Holloway Prison.'

Kim stared at him. 'You're joking!'

'No, I know it sounds unlikely, but—'

'No, you don't understand,' she interrupted. 'Mine went prison visiting too — only to Brixton.'

'Brixton?' For a fleeting moment a new expression crossed Roland's face. It was almost as if he had suddenly scented danger. If he had been an animal, she thought, his ears would have pricked up and his nose would have lifted to test the air. It was gone in an instant and he said, 'Well, this is getting very strange.'

'You reckon — what was he called — Hast was visiting someone in Holloway?' she said.

'Well, he went in and was there for half an hour.'

'Ditto Lyn. So two men have a consultation with Kline and then each go off to visit someone in prison. What do you think? Carrying a message of some sort?'

'That seems the most likely explanation.'

'Holloway is a women's prison. I wonder who he was visiting there.'

'I don't see any way to find out. But Brixton — there are some hard cases in that place. Looks like Kline is involved with some pretty dubious characters.'

'But his actual clients looked eminently respectable.'

'True.'

'What about his third appointment?'

'Mother and teenage son. I got back just in time to see them leave. They went straight to Marylebone Station and took the train to Beaconsfield. I think they were genuine.'

'I suppose he has to have a few like that to keep up his cover.' Her food arrived and she ate quickly. 'If we're going to check out the rest of the list, we don't have much time. I've found a way into the house opposite. We can watch from there.'

As soon as she had swallowed her meal and paid the bill they headed back to the empty house.

'Make it look as if we have every right to be here,' she said. 'If anyone queries it, we're thinking of renting the place.' She let them both into the basement and led the way up to the front room. 'Kline's next patient must be in there already if they're on time, but we can see who comes out through this gap in the planks.'

Kline's two o'clock appointment proved to be an elderly lady in a wheelchair, accompanied by a uniformed nurse, and they decided they could discount her, but his last client, identified in the appointments book simply as P.LL, seemed to fit the same mould as the first man: middle-aged, smartly dressed, giving no suggestion in his bearing that he was in need of psychiatric help.

'Because a man can put on a smart suit and comb his hair it doesn't mean his mental state isn't in chaos, I suppose,' remarked Kim. 'But it is odd that three such men are in need of urgent attention from Kline.'

'I wonder which prison he's headed for,' commented Roland dryly.

In the event, a taxi was summoned by Kline's muscular manservant and P.LL got into it and disappeared.

'Well, we can't follow him now, even if we wanted to. There's no chance of getting another taxi to follow him.' Kim straightened up and stretched. 'I think we've done all we can for today. It's time we were getting back.'

As they climbed the basement steps the manservant appeared again and headed towards Marylebone High Road, presumably in search of another taxi. Kim just had to time to register the fact that this must mean Kline was ready to leave when the man himself appeared on the doorstep. In the hot and stuffy confines of the shuttered house, her wig had become increasingly uncomfortable and she had pulled it off. Now Kline was literally just across the road from them. For the moment he was busy pulling on his gloves and not looking in their direction, so she said the first thing that came into her head.

'Kiss me!'

Roland reacted immediately. He pulled her into his arms and held her close, turning so that his back was to Kline and she was shielded by his body. His lips were pressed firmly to a point on her chin, just below her own, but some visceral reaction caused her to move her head so that their lips met. The kiss that had begun as a theatrical illusion became the real thing and she felt her body respond eagerly. It was more than a year since she had last kissed a man and she was suddenly aware of a hunger she had been ignoring.

A car door slammed and the taxi drew away. Roland lifted his head and looked into her eyes.

'Well, that was a surprise.'

She dropped her eyes. 'Merely intended to give artistic verisimilitude . . .' she murmured.

'Ah, right,' he said, and they both laughed.

* * *

The train back to Beaulieu was crowded, as before, so there was no chance of private conversation, for which Kim was very grateful. She spent the journey berating herself for a shameful loss of control. True, Roland was a year or two older than she was and obviously a man of experience; but she was in the position of tutor and she had woefully failed to live up to the standards that imposed. She had put them both in an invidious position and she did not know how to remedy it.

As they walked from the station to Palace House, Roland said, 'Look, I want to say something but I'm not sure how to put it.'

Kim's felt colour rising to her face. Here it was. He was going to say, very politely, that the kiss had been a mistake and he did not want it to lead to anything further . . . not that it could anyway, of course.

'Yes?' she said, keeping her voice as neutral as possible.

'I just want to say *be careful*. I told you I've had a bit of a rackety life, and I've met a few pretty undesirable characters. If Kline is involved in some way with men in Brixton prison . . . Well, I just think that makes him a very dangerous man. I'm not sure what your object was in today's exercise, but I'm afraid you may be putting yourself in harm's way.'

Relief surged through Kim's nerves, but she kept it out of her voice. 'Isn't that what we signed up for — both of us?'

'But the danger came from out there,' he gestured in the direction of occupied France, 'not from within.'

She hesitated. Her impulse was to tell him about her suspicions, but an ingrained habit of secrecy where operational matters were concerned prevented her. 'I'm just following up some . . . irregularities. I think you're right. Kline is dangerous. But I don't have enough information yet to take it any further.'

'I see,' he said, noncommittally. 'Well, I've said my piece. Just let me know if there is anything more I can do to help.'

They had reached the gate leading into the grounds of the great house and had to show their passes to gain entry. Once back inside it was natural to slip back into the routine and their places within it.

Kim dressed for dinner rather more carefully than before. Her wardrobe was limited in the circumstances, but she had brought with her a dress of turquoise silk that she knew suited her colouring very well. She decided this was the night to put it on.

That night she did not feel like dancing, but for the sake of form, she accepted invitations from first Raoul and then from Jean-Jacques and Pierre. She knew from previous evenings that Roland was a better dancer than any of them, but she guessed that he felt uncomfortable in his khaki non-commissioned officer garb when all the others were resplendent in their dress uniforms. That evening, she noticed, he did not dance but spent the time smoking and drinking whisky, and she was relieved. Physical proximity would have been a strain for both of them.

Back in her room she took out her notebook and studied the list of names. Who were these men and what was their involvement with Kline? The truncated references meant nothing to her but she wondered if they might to M. She decided that there were two courses of action open to her. As soon as she had the chance she would leave a letter at the house in Hythe, giving M. the list. More immediately, she would seek an interview with Kline and drop a hint of her suspicions. It might be enough to spur him to some action that would provide the evidence she needed, or at the very least his reaction might be revealing.

Next morning, she met her trainees as usual. 'Today,' she told them, 'you are going to learn how to pick someone's pocket.'

'Oh, come on!' objected Pierre. 'We're soldiers, not criminals.'

Kim fixed him with a stony glare. 'Believe me, when you get to France — if you ever do — you will be required to commit deeds that would have your average criminal banged up for years in peace time. If that conflicts with your sense of honour you had better back out now.'

Pierre subsided with muttered apologies and Kim caught Roland's eye. He was smiling sardonically.

After a morning spent trying out different techniques on each other, she set them free to try their luck with members of staff and fellow students. In the afternoon they were all required for firearms training with another expert, so she was free to make her way to Kline's office.

He was interviewing another trainee so she had to wait, but when the man came out, she knocked and entered without waiting for a response.

Kline looked up from his notes with a look of satisfaction. 'Ah, you decided to accept my invitation.'

'No, I'm not here for that. I was wondering if we could have a chat about the students I'm working with.'

He returned his attention to his notes. 'I'm busy. I could give you an appointment for tomorrow sometime.'

'It won't take long. I just want to know what your impressions of them are.'

He put the notes aside reluctantly and took a folder from his desk drawer. 'Very well. Remind me. Who are we talking about?'

For the next few minutes she listened to his assessments, which were insightful and quite revealing. Interestingly, he found Roland the most difficult to analyse, commenting that he hid himself behind a series of alternative personas.

When they had completed the review, she stood up to leave. Then, as if at an afterthought, she turned back.

'Oh, there is one thing you could help me with, as a German speaker. What does the word *Blitzschlag* mean?'

She was watching his eyes and for a split second she saw the same look, as of an animal scenting danger, that she had she seen on Roland's face when she mentioned Brixton prison. It was masked almost immediately and Kline said casually, 'It means "lightning bolt". Why do you ask?'

'It came up in a message from one of our agents in the field. I'm friendly with one of the decoders at Grendon and she asked me if I had ever come across the term.'

'It came up? In what context?'

'Oh, I can't tell you. She didn't give me the whole message, just that one word. Anyway, thank you for translating it for me. Such a powerful word! Much more evocative than the

English. *Blitzschlag!*' She gave it a dramatic emphasis. 'I won't take up any more of your time. Thank you again.'

She closed the door softly behind her. She had sown the seed. Now all she could do was wait to see if it produced any action.

She had told her students to report back to her when they came back from the firing range, and they proudly displayed their haul of cigarette lighters, keys, pocket handkerchiefs and small change. She had made a point that they must remember what they had taken from whom, so they could return their ill-gotten gains. The staff were used to being periodically jostled as they queued in the canteen or finding something missing from their pockets, but some of the other students were less accepting.

One little group of items had caught Kim's eye. It was a small collection of matchbooks, all bearing the names and logos of some of the most exclusive restaurants in London.

'Who did you lift these from?' she asked.

'From Bruno Sykes,' confessed Jacqueline, naming the gardener handyman who had been employed at Palace House after he was invalided out of the army after Dunkirk. It had been generally agreed that Sykes was 'not quite all there', though whether the condition was congenital or the result of shell shock had never been determined.

Kim was puzzled as to how he had come by these exclusive souvenirs.

'OK, Jacqueline. I'll take these back for you,' she said.

The girl looked relieved. 'Oh, thanks. To be honest I was rather dreading it. I gave myself a sort of dare to pick his pocket, because quite honestly he gives me the creeps. I'll be glad not to have to face him to own up.'

Kim found Sykes in his garden shed. 'I believe these are yours.' She held out the matchbooks.

His reaction surprised her. He lunged forward and grabbed them out of her hand.

'What you doing with those? That's private property, that is.'

Kim explained the exercise she has given her trainees.

He glared at her. 'So, who took my things? I'm going to have a word with him.'

'No, Sykes,' she said. 'That isn't necessary. It was just an exercise and there was no harm meant. You've got them back, after all. I was just wondering how you came by them.'

'That's my business,' he muttered sulkily. 'You got no right to enquire into my business.'

'No, you're quite right,' she agreed soothingly. 'I'm sorry. It won't happen again.'

She left him grumbling to himself and went back to the house feeling uneasy. For a moment she had seen a flash of real anger that could easily turn to violence, and she wondered if she should mention it to the CO.

# CHAPTER 8

'*Raus! Raus!* Get up!' The man in the black uniform of the German SS leaned down and shook her. 'Come! Get up now!'

It was the nightmare that had haunted her night after night when she first got back from France.

'Up! Up! Come with us!'

She forced herself to wake up, but the nightmare persisted and she realized that this was not a dream.

This was a real man, shouting at her.

There were two of them. Hands grabbed her and dragged her out of bed, and at last comprehension cut through the haze of sleep. It was a regular part of agent training to wake one of the students in the middle of the night and put them through a mock interrogation. It had happened to her when she was being prepared for the job.

'Stop it, you idiots!' she shouted. 'I'm staff, not one of the students. You've got the wrong room.'

'No talking! Come!'

She was being dragged towards the door.

'Will you listen? This is a mistake. You've got the wrong woman!'

She tried to see behind the SS informs.

It must be some of the staff, dressed up, but she couldn't identify who it was. Still protesting, she was half dragged, half carried down several flights of stairs to the cellar.

She recognized the set-up from her last experience. Two more uniformed figures sat behind a table and in front of the table was a single hard chair. Flood lights lit the chair, leaving the men behind the table in shadow. She was dragged to the chair and forced down onto it, her two guards standing close behind her. She began to tremble. This was how it had begun, when she was arrested in France. This was what had led to the agonies she had suffered at the hands of men dressed like this. As much as her rational mind still protested that this was all a mistake, her subconscious was reliving the trauma of arrest and torture.

The men behind the table began to fire questions at her, sometimes in French, sometimes in English, occasionally in German.

'What is your real name?' 'Why are you here?' 'Who sent you?' 'What is the objective of your mission?' 'Speak! Answer!'

'You know who I am. You know why I'm here.'

'We don't believe you. Tell us the truth.'

'That is the truth. I'm here to do the same job you are doing.'

'Lies! Lies! Stand up.'

She was pulled roughly to her feet.

'Strip!'

This was also a standard part of the mock interrogation, designed to mimic what might happen in reality, but this was no pretence. This was intended to intimidate her. But why?

'No! You've got no right—!'

One of the two men came round from behind the table and slapped her hard across the face. For a moment she saw his face and with a devastating shock she recognized Raoul.

'Strip!' he repeated and grabbed the top of her pyjama jacket, ripping the buttons off and exposing her breasts.

Numbly, unable to comprehend what was happening, she stepped out of her pyjama trousers.

'Get up on the chair.' Her two guards laid hold of her and half lifted her to stand on the chair. It was exactly what had happened to her when she was really in German hands and the memory overwhelmed her. To add to her humiliation, she lost control of her bladder and urine trickled down her thighs. She began to sob uncontrollably.

'Leave me alone! Leave me alone! Please!'

'Then tell us the truth. Why are you here? What have you been sent here to do?'

'I don't know what you're talking about. I don't understand. Let me go!' Her legs gave way under her, and she would have toppled off the chair if one of the guards had not caught hold of her. She found herself on the floor, crouched there with her arms wrapped around herself, still weeping.

'Enough! We have established what we needed to establish.' It was Kline's voice. 'She is not sufficiently recovered to be allowed to work here. She is a security risk. Tomorrow we shall send her back to Scotland. For now, she can be kept in there.'

'In there' was a second cellar, a place she had never seen before. Still naked, she was thrust down two further steps and the door slammed behind her, leaving her in total darkness. She sank to the ground, wrapping her arms round her knees, shaking uncontrollably.

She was back in the hands of the Gestapo. They had beaten her and pulled out all her toenails, one by one; but she had not broken. Now she was in this dark place.

*'Take this bell. When you are ready to speak, ring this. Until we hear that, nobody will come near you. But wait too long and we may already be posted to another town. If that happens no one will ever know where you are.'*

Her groping hands told her that she was in a small, bare room and the only source of light and air was the door that had slammed behind her. She felt around every inch of the walls and floor, hoping to find a loose brick or a crack in the mortar, but there was nothing but smooth stone, slimy with damp. She licked the walls in an effort to assuage the terrible thirst that grew with every passing hour.

By her later calculations she spent three days there. She was tempted many times to ring the bell, but she knew to do so would only condemn her friends to the same misery without giving any guarantee that her sufferings would be at an end. The terror grew in her that even if she did finally give way and ring, no one would come. She would die here without seeing the light of day again.

Then the moment came when the door was thrown open and a voice said, '*Out! There are people who want to talk to you, and I promise you, if you will not speak to us, you will speak to them.*' And she knew she had won. Someone had realized that if they left her much longer she would die, and then there would be no chance to get the information they wanted out of her.

It had not meant freedom, or the end of suffering. That had come when her friends ambushed the convoy in which she was being transferred to Paris. It had been victory of a kind, but its legacy was a recurring nightmare.

*Kline knows this.*

The thought penetrated her terror. Somehow he knew exactly what had happened to her — yet it was something she had never talked about to the officers who had debriefed her on her return. Something she had never confided to anyone in England. His information must have come from contacts in Germany. This was all the proof she needed of his treachery.

That knowledge brought her back to her present situation. She had deliberately sown a seed of suspicion in his mind. This was his reaction. It was far more extreme than she had expected, but it was conclusive as far as she was concerned. Understanding this, she was able to quell her feelings of panic and think logically.

Kline could not have organized the interrogation without the knowledge of higher authority. Therefore, he must have convinced the commanding officer that his assessment of her as a security risk was correct, and her reaction would be seen as proof of that.

Mock interrogations were routine, but normally afterwards the candidate was reassured and taken back to bed, where a cup of hot cocoa and a dram of something stronger awaited them. This final act of incarcerating her in the cellar was pure sadism — in line, if Kim wasn't mistaken, with the treatment of Lily before her murder.

*But Raoul . . .*

The memory of his face flashed before her eyes. Raoul had been party to all this. Kline must have convinced him as he had convinced the CO. But had he gone along with this final cruelty? Kim wondered if he was even now having doubts. Could he come back to release her? The idea was a grain of comfort.

She put the thought aside and forced herself to concentrate on her next steps. Kline had said she was to be sent back to Scotland. Perhaps he believed that he had established her mental fragility sufficiently to ensure that, even if she voiced her suspicions, no one would believe her. But would he stake everything on that?

It was more likely that sometime in the near future an unfortunate 'accident' would befall her. Perhaps on the journey north? She imagined a sudden shove in the small of her back as the train steamed into the platform.

*'She just suddenly jumped! I had no idea she was suicidal . . .'*

No, that was too public, would give rise to too many questions. More probably somewhere in the wilds of Scotland, with few witnesses.

One thing was clear, she had to get away before it happened. The question was, how? If the CO was convinced that Kline was right, her removal would come as an official posting. If she failed to comply, she would be registered as Absent Without Leave, a court martial offence. But going AWOL was far less dangerous than anything she might face when she arrived.

It seemed unlikely that she would be allowed to travel on her own. So the problem was to find a way of evading her escort long enough to disappear.

She forced herself to her feet and engaged on a programme of exercises that left her panting but with blood pumping warmly through her body. By then, she had formulated a plan. So much depended on unknown circumstances, and she would have to improvise, but it was the best she could think of.

She crouched down again on the cold floor wondering what the time was. She had no idea how long she had been asleep before the guards had woken her but guessed it had probably around 2 a.m. The interrogation had lasted — what? — half an hour? And how long had she been here, in the dark? It was impossible to calculate, and that had been part of the terror she had experienced before.

This time, she told herself, there was a limit. Kline would have to report to the CO and get a movement order to send her to Scotland, but then he would have to release her. She wondered if the CO would want to see her for himself. If that happened, was there any point in trying to convince him that the whole situation had been deliberately engineered by Kline? She thought probably not.

Her thoughts returned to her students. *What will they be told?* Anything but the truth, obviously. She had a sudden, vivid memory of feeling Roland's arms around her, his lips on hers. If only she could get a message to him! He knew Kline was involved in something, but what could he possibly do? The whole weight of established authority was against him. But if her plan worked, he could be a useful ally—

The sound of movement on the other side of the door brought her to her feet. The door opened and light streamed in, momentarily blinding her. A female voice said, 'Come out and get dressed.'

She climbed the steps and saw a woman in the uniform and red cap of the military police waiting for her. Her pyjamas were on the chair and a robe hung over the back of it. There was no point in engaging the woman in any discussion, so Kim pulled on the clothes and waited to see what happened next.

'Come along. You need to pack. You're leaving.'

A male officer was waiting outside the cellar door, and the two of them escorted her in silence up to her room. It was light out, but the house was silent and as they passed through the hall Kim saw that the grandfather clock registered 5.15 a.m.

She realised that Kline must have had all the arrangements in place before the interrogation. He'd had no doubts about the outcome. *Cold-blooded bastard*, she thought.

The male officer waited outside her door while she packed her things under the eye of the woman. To Kim's relief, she took no interest in what Kim was packing or which bag she put it in. So she did not query why the blonde wig and the dowdy summer dress went into a small overnight bag along with Kim's purse, her toothbrush and other toiletries. Her only words were, 'Hurry up. We've got a train to catch.'

It was too early for the first train from Beaulieu station, so Kim was not surprised to find a car painted in the regulation olive drab waiting for her. The male officer drove and the woman sat tight-lipped in the back beside her.

'I don't suppose there's any chance of some breakfast, is there?' Kim hazarded.

'When we get to the station, if there's time.'

Kim sat back in her seat. There was nothing she could do now. If her plan worked, her only chance of escape would be on the train.

# CHAPTER 9

Euston Station was a seething mass of people, most of them in uniform. The WRVS had set up a trestle table on the concourse and were dispensing sausage sandwiches and tea from an urn to troops waiting for their train, and the fact that Kim and her escort were in uniform secured them a place in the queue. The tea was sweetened with condensed milk and the sausage was more gristle than meat, but Kim wolfed them down. Dinner last night, with its civilized formality, seemed to belong to another era and she was ravenous.

They had just finished when the tannoy announced that the train to Edinburgh was about to depart. As she expected, it was crammed with passengers. Every carriage was full and soldiers were standing or sitting on their kitbags in the corridor.

Whether it was because two of them were women or whether it was the red berets of the military police Kim did not know, but somehow space was found for them in one of the compartments and a grinning Tommy heaved her suitcase up onto the rack. She kept her overnight bag on her lap, ready for any eventuality. The train pulled out and Kim sat back and let her eyes close. She'd had no sleep for over twenty-four hours and it was going to be a long, slow haul to their destination.

For the next six hours Kim dozed and woke as the train stopped and started. Passenger traffic was subordinate to the need to get essential supplies around the country. Several times they were shunted into a siding to allow a goods train to pass, and at least twice the speed was reduced to a crawl because of bomb damage to the track. As they got further north, she forced herself to wake up and look out of the window. She knew this route well, though mostly she had travelled it at night, and when the train stopped at Durham, she knew that they were getting close to Newcastle. From the chatter of the soldiers in the carriage she had learned that that was where many of them were due to disembark. Timing was now crucial.

As soon as the outskirts of the city appeared through the smoke-grimed windows she nudged her female guard.

'I need to go to the toilet. And I want to freshen up. Is that OK?'

The policewoman hauled herself reluctantly to her feet. 'OK, if you must. Come on.'

It was too much to hope that she might be allowed to go on her own, but Kim had expected that. They struggled down the crowded corridor to the area near the door where the toilet cubicle was situated. There, to her dismay, it proved to be occupied. Of course, she chided herself inwardly, she should have been prepared for that. She waited, gritting her teeth and muttering *sotto voce*, 'Come on! Come on!' Any minute now they would be in Newcastle and she had to be ready by then.

She was on the verge of giving up her plan when the train jolted to a stop. The signal was against it. When the previous occupant came out, she hurried into the cubicle. She performed what was necessary and then placed her overnight bag on the closed toilet seat and began to take off her uniform. It was a struggle in the confined space, but she succeeded at last and pulled on the summer dress. She exchanged her lace-up shoes for a pair of sandals and adjusted the blonde wig. The train was moving again now. Getting her uniform back into the bag was difficult but she

80

stuffed it in somehow. She gave herself a once-over in the scuffed mirror, then, as a final touch, daubed on some scarlet lipstick and put on her sunglasses. Outside, the military policewoman banged on the door.

'Hurry up in there! Get a move on!'

At that moment the train pulled into the station and came to a stop. As Kim had anticipated, the corridor immediately echoed to the tramp of boots and a cacophony of voices as the soldiers fought their way to the exits. She opened the door cautiously and peered out. As she had hoped, the policewoman had been forced away from the door, beyond the exit, and was almost hidden by the throng of khaki-clad bodies and the kitbags held shoulder high.

Kim ducked her head, slipped quickly out of the cubicle and pushed her way back in the opposite direction, towards the front of the train. As she passed the door to the compartment where she had been sitting, she saw the male policeman on his feet staring out of the window, scanning the people who were surging along the platform. Obviously, he had realized something was amiss and was watching for her. She pressed on, squeezing past passengers still standing in the corridor and almost tripping over bags and suitcases, and by the time she reached the first carriage most of the soldiers had disembarked. The last stragglers were making their way down the steps to the platform and another crowd was waiting at the bottom, eager to get on board. Kim followed the last man down and wormed her way through the press until she could see along the platform to the ticket barrier.

Her own ticket was still in the female officer's top pocket, but Kim had been on enough trains during wartime to predict the scene. As she hoped, there was still a throng of soldiers jostling to get through the barrier, and the ticket collector had given up trying to check everyone's ticket. Kim insinuated herself into the middle of the crowd and allowed herself to be propelled out into the concourse.

As the people around her dispersed she paused to look back. The train was now leaving and she could see no sign of her two guards. Perhaps, she thought, they had concluded she must still be on board, but she was taking no chances. She looked up at the departure board. The next train south was not scheduled to leave for fifteen minutes. She dared not risk joining the queue for a ticket until she was sure neither of her guards was still looking for her in the station. She bought a newspaper and stood, pretending to read it, behind a tall stand advertising a brand of soft drink.

A moment later she saw the male policeman at the barrier, questioning the ticket collector. It gave her a brief glimmer of amusement to imagine the conversation. He would be asking if the man had seen a woman in FANY uniform leave the platform. The collector was shrugging and shaking his head. Kim couldn't hear him, but could imagine his retort. *'Adolf bloody Hitler could have come through in the middle of that lot without me spotting him.'*

The policeman gave up and gazed around the concourse without much hope. Then he headed for the ticket office. Kim could guess he would be asking if a FANY had just bought a ticket and he would again be drawing a blank. He came out and looked up at the departure board in his turn. He would need to catch the next train to Edinburgh, where he would have to meet his partner. Finding it was not due for almost an hour he headed for the station buffet and disappeared inside. Kim waited a few minutes longer, then made her way to the booking office. The next train going south was for Birmingham. She bought a ticket and was just in time to board it as the whistle blew.

## CHAPTER 10

Towards lunchtime the following day the internal phone on M.'s desk rang.

'Sorry to bother you, sir, but there's a young woman on the outside line asking to speak to you. She says her name is Morag.'

'Morag! Yes, put her through, please.'

Kim's voice came down the line. 'Can we meet? I'll be in the dining room at Dickens and Jones.'

'I'll be there in ten minutes.'

M. entered the dining room in the upmarket department store and stood for a moment trying to locate the woman who had called him. He had almost given up when a blonde sitting in a corner waved him over.

'Morag! I almost didn't recognize you,' he exclaimed.

She met his eyes uneasily. 'I don't need to explain the reason. I take it you've been contacted by the CO at Bealieu?'

'Indeed. Though I don't fully understand the details. I thought you were back in Scotland.'

'Instead I'm AWOL.' She studied his expression. 'I take it you're not going to hand me over to the military police? There are things I need to tell you.'

'And I have many questions to ask — but not here. Where are you staying?'

'I've checked into a little B and B near King's Cross.'

M. smiled. 'I think we can do better than that.' He produced a card and wrote on the back of it. 'This is the address of a safe house. It's a flat in a block in Kensington. Give this card to the hall porter and he'll let you in. There should be provisions to keep you going for a day or two. Do you have money?'

'Enough to be going on with.'

'Cash only,' he warned her. 'Don't be tempted to use your bank account.'

'Of course not.'

A waitress approached with a menu. Kim ordered a ham salad but M. shook his head. 'I can't stop, I'm afraid.' When the girl had departed, he went on. 'I'll come to the flat this evening. Around six, OK?'

'Yes, of course. I'll be waiting.'

\* \* \*

The flat was comfortably appointed without being luxurious. Kim treated herself to a long, hot bath. She discarded the blonde wig but decided against wearing her FANY uniform. Instead she put on a dark blue linen dress she had bought that morning before leaving the store. A few minutes after six the doorbell rang.

'Good evening, sir.' Her training told her to salute, but she remembered just in time that as she was not in uniform it would not be correct.

'Good evening.' M. had a way of looking at you that was acute without being intimidating. Then he smiled. 'I think we can dispense with the formalities for this evening.'

'Very good . . .' She just stopped herself from adding 'sir'. She found herself in an awkward position as a subordinate but feeling that she should be acting the hostess. 'Shall we sit down? There's a bottle of fairly decent sherry in the kitchen . . . ?'

He opened a bag he was carrying and produced a bottle of Black Label whisky — a rare sight in these days of rationing and shortages. 'I think this might suit the occasion better. Will you join me?'

'Yes, thank you. But I'm afraid there's no soda or ice.'

'A splash of cold water is all that's required,' he said.

When she came back from the kitchen with a jug of water, he had already found two glasses and poured a generous measure into each one.

She said, 'You seem to be quite at home here.'

'I've had occasion to make use of the place once or twice before.'

She recalled the expression on the hall porter's face when she handed him the card and felt emboldened to say, with a roguish lift of her eyebrows, 'I think the porter believes you keep this flat as a place to meet your lady friends.'

He raised a brow in return. 'The last occupant was a man. I wonder what he made of that.' He raised his glass. '*Slàinte.*'

'Cheers,' she responded.

He gestured with his glass towards two easy chairs set on either side of a low table. They seated themselves and he leaned towards her. 'You look as if you've been through the mill. Tell me what's happened.'

As concisely as possible she told him about what she had uncovered: about what had been done to Lily, about the sudden dispatch of Lucien and his one-word message, about her suspicions of Kline and the surveillance she had conducted on his clinic and the strange destinations of his patients, and about her decision to drop a hint to Kline by mentioning the word *Blitzschlag* and its consequences. She left nothing out, and when she finished, she reached for her glass and found her hands were shaking so much that she had to put it down again.

'He knew, you see,' she said. 'He knew exactly what they did to me.'

M.'s face had gone taut with cold fury. 'The man is not only a traitor, he's a sadist, and he will pay for what he's done. I promise you that.' He reached across the table and touched her hand. 'Kim, I'll never forgive myself for putting you through that again.' He caught himself up. 'May I call you Kim?'

She nodded and swallowed. 'Yes, of course, if you like.'

'So how did you get away?' he asked, and she told him how she had evaded her guards, adding with a rueful grin, 'I never expected to use the techniques I learned when I was training in this country, but they came in useful.'

'Thank God they did,' he responded. 'The question now is where do you go from here. We can give you a new cover, a new identity, and find you a safe place to stay. Where do you fancy? The Lake District is pleasant, I'm told.'

She stared at him. 'You're not going to send me away again? Kline tried to make it look as if I'm a hopeless case, half out of my mind because of what happened in France, unable to tell reality from fantasy. I thought you believed me.'

He sat forwards. 'I do believe you! And I'm going to follow it up. But we can't risk you falling into Kline's hands again. This is about keeping you safe until he's out of the way.'

'No!' she said vehemently. 'I need to keep working on this. I couldn't bear to sit around in the Lake District or anywhere else without being involved. It would be worse than that year in the cooler. Please, sir! Don't do that to me.'

For a moment he seemed undecided, then he sighed. 'Very well. If you feel that strongly about it — and I have to admit I would feel the same. Let's discuss the next steps. You say you made a list of the people who visited Kline's clinic. Do you have it?'

Kim produced a sheet of paper from a drawer in the sideboard and handed it to him. 'I wrote it out again from memory. I flushed the original down the loo while I was packing my case to leave Beaulieu. I didn't want to risk it being found if I was searched and I couldn't leave it in the room. But this is an accurate copy.'

M. studied the list in silence for a few minutes. Then he looked up. 'If I'm not much mistaken, what you have here is a list of members of the aristocracy who also happen to be members of the BUF.'

'The BUF?'

'British Union of Fascists.'

'Oswald Mosley's lot?'

'Yes. Many of the most prominent members have been interned for the duration, of course. These are men who have escaped that fate thanks to their elevated social status, but there's no doubt about their affiliation. This first name on the list — Hast. I'm pretty sure that must be Randolph Hastings, aka Duke of Evesham. P.LL. will be Patrick Lloyd, Earl of Cupar. But this last one is the really interesting chap. Lyn — Gerald Weston, Viscount Lyndham. He's a member of English Mistery, later known as English Array.'

'English Mystery?' queried Kim.

'Spelled with an "i" not a "y". It's a medieval term basically meaning a guild. They're a bunch of diehard aristocrats who want to bring back the feudal system. They're reactionary, ultra-royalist, anti-democratic and closely aligned with the BUF.'

'Good lord!' Kim stared at him. 'I had no idea such people still existed.'

'Oh, but they do. MI5 have been keeping a watchful eye on them, but they obviously missed this.'

'So these noble gentlemen are visiting Kline and then trotting off to Holloway and Brixton prisons. It seems a strange place for them to frequent.'

'Not if you know who is incarcerated there,' said M. 'Oswald Mosley and his wife, Lady Diana, are interned in a house in the grounds of Holloway, and Brixton prison is playing host to, among others, Admiral Sir Barry Domville, who belongs to the Right Club and is a council member of the Anglo-German Fellowship, and John Beckett, director of publications for the BUF. All have been interned for the duration under Defence Regulation 18b as posing a threat to national security.'

Kim let out a low whistle. 'This is much more dangerous than I realized. So Kline's "patients" are carrying messages to these men in prison about something that goes by the code name *Blitzschlag*. Yes?'

'Yes.' M.'s expression was grim. 'And *Blitzschlag* means "lightning bolt". Have you ever seen any of the BUF propaganda?'

'Not than I can recall.'

'Their chosen symbol looks like this.' He had been making notes on a pad he took out of his pocket. He turned to a new leaf and drew quickly.

Kim leaned forward to look.

'My God!' She stared at the image. 'It's a lightning bolt. Sir, this is what was drawn on the bedhead in Lily's room. I don't know if she drew it in her own blood as she was dying or the murderer left it there as some kind of warning.'

'You're sure?'

'Yes. It took me a while to realize it but that was definitely what it was.'

'So Lucien may have told her something about *Blitzschlag* — either intentionally or while talking in his sleep. And she reported it to whom?' asked M.

'Initially to Raoul, his conducting officer, who then told Kline.'

'And Lily was then murdered in a brutal manner to punish her for having overheard what she should not have done.' M. sipped his drink thoughtfully. 'Did you discuss this with Raoul?'

Kim nodded.

'I asked him if Lily had said anything significant, but according to him it was just incoherent rambling about a storm.'

'Which he then passed on to Kline. I think we can assume he was just doing his job.'

'That's what I thought, until . . .' Kim stopped, not sure if she wanted to continue.

'Until?'

'He was there, he carried out the interrogation.' M. opened his mouth to speak, but Kim hurried on. 'I mean, he was only doing what is expected in that situation, when it happens to an agent in training. But he must have known it wasn't . . . appropriate for it to happen to me. And he let Kline shut me up in the cellar. I suppose Kline must have convinced him that I really was a security risk, but all the same . . .' She trailed into silence.

'That is certainly a matter for concern,' said M. grimly. 'Raoul has always been considered one of our best agents. He carried out his last assignment in an exemplary manner and I would consider him to be completely trustworthy. But if he has somehow come under Kline's influence, we shall have to watch him very carefully. What concerns us right now is what *Blitzschlag* refers to.'

'If only we knew what Lucien told Lily. He's the man we really need to speak to,' said Kim.

'Unfortunately, he's now in the hands of the Gestapo, so it's highly likely that they now have that information.'

Kim was silent for a moment. Then she said, 'We need to get him away from them.'

'Easier said than done.'

'I was rescued, so we know it's possible,' she pointed out. 'I think it's time I returned the favour.'

M. stared at her. 'You're not suggesting I send you back, are you? After what happened?'

Kim lifted her shoulders. 'Who else can you send?' she asked bleakly.

'No.' M. shook his head. 'No, I can't countenance that. It's asking too much.'

Kim met his gaze and held it. 'It need not be for long. If we can contact the right people I could be in and out quite quickly.' She thought for a moment. 'Do we know what happened to the rest of Lucien's circuit? Were they all picked up, or just him?'

'We would have to refer to your old boss, Buckmaster, for that information.'

'I presume he thinks I'm still in Scotland,' commented Kim. 'He wouldn't know you had sent for me.'

'Yes, I imagine so. But he's the only one who can tell us what the current state of affairs is.'

'There is another way,' suggested Kim. 'I told you I have a friend at Grendon, the one who gave me Lucien's last message. If any of that circuit have managed to get back in touch, she will know about it. I could try her.'

'Very well,' conceded M. 'I'll authorize that, but I'm still not happy at the idea of you going back.'

# CHAPTER 11

Kim travelled to Grendon Underwood with an identity card and travel pass belonging to a fictional FANY lieutenant, but when she presented herself to Hope Gamwell, the commanding officer of Station 35A, she was instantly recognized.

'Max? What are you doing masquerading under an alias?'

'Sorry, ma'am,' responded Kim. 'I'm here on a special mission for Brigadier M. and I'm afraid I can't talk about it. I need to speak to Pauline Clayton, if I may.'

Gamwell looked frosty. 'Well, far be it from me to interfere with the brigadier's plans, though it would be nice to feel I could be trusted. But go ahead. You know where to find her.'

Pauline was pleased to see an old friend again, if reluctant to leave the pile of messages on her desk waiting to be decoded.

'I won't keep you long,' promised Kim. 'Do you remember that strange message you had from Farmer?'

'The one who just sent the one German word? Yes, of course. What happened to him?'

'We presume he's in the hands of the Gestapo. I need to know whether anything has been heard from the other members of his circuit.'

'Grocer, wasn't it, the code name?'

'Yes, that's right.'

'Hang on. It rings a bell.' She opened a locked filing cabinet and rifled through some folders. 'Yes. I thought so. They are still operating.'

'Still operating?' Kim blinked in surprise. 'And in radio contact? How?'

'The boy you asked me about was sent out to replace their pianist because he was sick, yes?'

'That's right.'

'Well, he must have recovered. We had a message a few days ago asking for a drop of supplies.'

'You're sure it was from him, not a German agent using his set?' Kim asked.

'We checked that.' Pauline's tone suggested she was asking the obvious. 'It had all the required identity confirmation codes, and the girl who deals with his messages is sure it was his fist.'

'That's good news! So it was only the new radio operator who was caught?'

Pauline shrugged. 'I can't be sure of that. We only know the circuit is still operational, so some of them must have escaped the cull.'

'And the drop went ahead?'

'We had a message saying thank you, so it must have done.'

'OK.' Kim thought for a few moments. 'So you could get a message out to them to expect another drop?'

'Of course.'

Kim thanked her friend and promised to be in touch again shortly.

By evening she was back in the London flat, and M. arrived soon afterwards.

'It's on,' Kim told him, and summarized what she had learned.

'That's all very well as far as it goes,' he commented. 'But it doesn't mean Lucien is still alive, or if he is that there's any way of getting him out.'

'There's only one way to find out.' Kim met his eyes. 'If we could arrange for me to be dropped, I could find out exactly what the situation is and whether there's any chance of rescuing him. I needn't even be involved in the actual operation.'

M. gave a short laugh. 'I know you well enough not to believe that. You'll be in the thick of it, whatever it turns out to be.' He sat silent for a moment and then sighed. 'You're right, of course. You're the only person I can send, without having to go through usual channels and tell a lot of other people what we're up to. I don't like it, but I can't see an alternative. We must have some idea what the plan is for this enemy operation before we can go any further. I'll have to bring Maurice Buckmaster in, though. I can't start dropping agents into his patch without telling him. Besides which, you need a new cover story and the right documents, et cetera. What happened to the clothes you were given for your first trip?'

'I imagine the Gestapo have got them now,' said Kim dryly. 'Not that they will be much use to anyone else.'

'Of course. Sorry. Thoughtless of me. Well, I'll put all that in train. And I'll get in touch with the boys at RAF Tempsford and ask them to have a Lysander standing by for the next time the moon is right.'

'There's one more thing,' said Kim. 'Someone needs to keep an eye on Kline while I'm away.'

'That hadn't escaped me. I'm wondering who I can trust with the job.'

'I think I can suggest someone.' Kim hesitated. 'I didn't quite tell you all the story of the surveillance I carried out on Kline's surgery. I wasn't alone.'

'You brought someone else in? I didn't sanction that. Who was it?'

Kim sat back in her chair and took another sip of the brigadier's whisky. 'Tell me about the man we call Roland.'

'Roland?' M. gave her an appraising look. He paused, recalling the details. 'Aka the Red Fox, known to his friends as Foxy. Born Renaud Leroux in Cable Street in the East End of London, father French, working here as a chef, mother an English woman from a fairly deprived background. Lately resident at His Majesty's pleasure in Brixton prison.'

'Renaud Leroux, the Red Fox. I get it,' said Kim. 'Why was he in Brixton?'

'Foxy by name, foxy by nature. The father left home when he was about ten and went back to France. Renaud divided his time between his mother in Cable Street and his father in Normandy.' He took a sip of whisky. 'At the age of sixteen he talked his way onto an Atlantic liner heading for New York as a sous chef. He did not make the return voyage. We assume he spent the next ten years in the States but we don't know what he was doing.' He poured himself another dram. 'When we catch up with him again in England, he'd reinvented himself as Reginald Fox Barton, the highly sophisticated scion of a wealthy Boston family. Good-looking, with plenty of money — apparently. He became a popular man about town, invited into all the best households — dinner parties in Belgravia, weekends at various country piles. You can imagine the sort of thing.'

'So how did he end up in Brixton?' asked Kim.

M. smiled dryly. 'Our friend Roland is a con man, a very accomplished one. His main modus operandi was to present himself as an expert in fifteenth- and sixteenth-century Italian paintings. Where he learned that I have no idea, but it seems he was convincing enough to persuade a lot of people.' M. sat back in his chair. Kim could tell he was warming to his subject. 'He would wait until he came across a fairly obscure painting in a forgotten corner of a country mansion. He would suggest to the owner that it might be a little-known masterpiece and offer to take it to a dealer he knew for a second opinion. He would come back and inform the owner that, sadly, he was mistaken and it was only a copy but that the dealer thought there was a market for it at the right price. He would buy the picture at a knock-down price and later present himself to another collector in a variety of different disguises, sometimes as a minor aristocrat desperate to find money to pay off family debts, or as a young man who had been left the painting by an elderly aunt who had no interest in art and just wanted to capitalize on the legacy, and so on. He would claim the picture was the genuine article, offer it at a price the collector couldn't refuse and make himself a handsome profit on the deal.' He finished his drink. 'He was doing very nicely until one owner he tried to buy from was a bit more clued up about paintings and asked for a second opinion. When told the picture was genuine, he smelled a rat and called the police.'

'And were the pictures genuine, or were they copies?'

'Most of them really were the genuine article. He knew what he was doing all right.'

'So how did he justify it?'

'His excuse was that he was merely removing a work of art from an owner who didn't appreciate it and handing it on to someone who would display it as it deserved. Unfortunately, the judge didn't see it that way. He got five years. He'd served nearly two when he suggested to the prison governor that he'd be more use to the country in the army than sat in a prison cell. He was released on that basis and someone suggested that his undoubted talents might come in useful to SOE.'

'He certainly has talents,' agreed Kim. 'He was streets ahead of the others when it came to teaching him fieldcraft. That's why I suggested to him that he might help me out with Kline. No wonder he reacted as he did when I told him my gent had visited Brixton prison.'

'How reliable is he, do you think?'

'I trust him. He loathes the Nazis and it's in his interest to prove himself. If he wasn't genuine, I don't think he'd have got through preliminary training. It's far from a soft option.'

'That's true, certainly. I'll have a look through his instructors' reports and if they're satisfactory we'll bring him. He can keep an eye on Kline while you're away.'

\* \* \*

The next two days stretched Kim's patience to the limit. The thought of returning to France left her feeling nauseous, but at the same time there was a sense of vindication. If she could go back, it would prove that the enemy had not succeeded in breaking her spirit. And if she succeeded in getting Lucien out of their clutches, it would be at least a partial revenge.

She prowled round the flat, unable to settle to read a book, or even a newspaper. Her restlessness was partly relieved by the arrival of a French seamstress who worked for F Section. She took Kim's measurements and the following day returned with two dresses and a light coat of the type any working-class girl might wear, complete with the labels of a French manufacturer. With them came a full set of underwear and nightwear, plus two pairs of ankle socks, as stockings were available in France only to the rich and well-connected.

An hour later a new visitor rang the bell. Kim checked the spy hole in the front door a saw an attractive, dark-haired woman.

'Hello, Vera! I wasn't expecting to see you,' she exclaimed, opening the door.

'And I certainly wasn't expecting to find you *here*. Are you completely out of your mind?' Vera replied, moving past her into the sitting room.

Vera Atkins was Buckmaster's secretary and trusted assistant and took a particular interest in the female agents who were sent to France.

'Do sit down,' Kim said. 'Would you like a cup of tea or coffee?'

'No, thanks. I can only stay a minute.' Vera sank into a chair and gazed at Kim. 'You can't seriously mean to go back, after what happened,' she demanded.

'There's no reason to expect it will happen again,' said Kim. 'And anyway, I shan't be there for long. I've got one mission to complete and then I'm coming home.'

Vera looked at her in silence for a moment, then she shook her head.

'Well, it's your decision. I won't ask you what you've got to do. I gather it's all very hush-hush. I've brought your new identity documents and other stuff.'

Vera extracted a slim envelope from her bag. 'This is the legend we've concocted for you.

'The rest of your story and where you will be based is something you will have to work out with Gregoire, the leader of the circuit. You'll have to square whatever it is you plan to do with him,' Vera told her as she stood up to leave. 'The *réseau* is working with the local *maquis*, so they may be able to help.'

She hugged Kim tightly. 'Good luck, Max. Take care.'

After she left Kim studied the information she had been given. This time she was to be Monique Chambord. Inside the envelope was an identity card with an address in Clamecy, a town a few miles from Corbigny, a ration card, a photograph of a man who was supposed to be her fiancé, a creased and yellowing letter from him written before he was killed in the opening battles of the war, a school photograph including a girl who might just pass as a teenage Kim and a picture of a couple who were supposed to be her parents. It was all very convincing. The background for her last mission had been as good, but it had been no help when she was caught red-handed with plastic explosive. Kim told herself that this time it would be different. She spent the rest of the day embroidering her legend, the story she would tell if anyone, either French or German, asked questions.

By the second evening Kim was back to prowling round the flat. It was a relief when she heard a key in the lock. M. let himself in, saying over his shoulder, 'Come on in. There's someone here you'll be glad to see.'

Roland followed him in and stopped dead in the doorway, staring at Kim. Then he grinned. 'They told us you'd had a nervous breakdown and been sent back to Scotland. I didn't believe it for a minute.'

Kim grinned back. 'Hello, Foxy.'

'Ah, my secret is out. Do you still trust me?' He was back in uniform and his accent had reverted to the faintly cockney inflections that seemed to go with the sergeant's stripes.

'You wouldn't be here if I didn't,' pointed out Kim.

'To business!' commanded the brigadier.

Over the next hour and another bottle of Black Label, of which M. seemed to have an unlimited supply in spite of rationing, they brought Roland up to date with the progress of the investigation.

'And so,' said Kim, 'Hast, Lyn and P.LL are all members of the British Union of Fascists, or what's left of it.'

Roland grunted bitterly. 'I guessed as much when we found out one of them had visited Brixton. Word went round when I was in there that a couple of those bastards had been brought in. Not that we had anything to do with them, of course. They were kept apart from the hoi polloi like us. Just as well. They wouldn't have lasted long otherwise.'

'I know you have no liking for the BUF,' said M. 'Was that general among the inmates?'

'Pretty well. But I had my own reasons. You won't have forgotten the Battle of Cable Street. When the police tried to force a way through for Mosley and his Blackshirts, the people living there made a human barricade to stop them. My old mum was living there then and she joined in. She was caught under the hooves of a police horse and killed.' He looked across at the brigadier with a mirthless smile. 'So you'll understand why I hate the fascists. Mind you, I don't have much time for the police either, or the people who give them their orders.'

'Understood,' conceded M. 'Let's move on.'

When it came to the revelation that Kim was proposing to be dropped back into France, Roland turned and fixed his gaze on her. 'That's about the gutsiest thing I've ever heard. You had my respect before but now . . .'

Kim dropped her eyes and shrugged. 'It's the only way forward.' But she could not deny the warm sense of pleasure his admiration gave her.

'So where do I fit in, in all this?' asked Roland. 'I can't see I'm going to learn much at Beaulieu,' he said. 'The action, whatever it is, is going to be in London, with Kline's BUF pals.'

'But how much more is to be gained by watching their comings and goings from Kline's surgery?' countered M.

'Not a lot, I should say.' Roland hesitated for only a second. 'I think I'll need to infiltrate the organization. If I can convince them I'm a sympathizer, I stand a better chance of finding out what's going on.'

'It's a risky strategy,' commented M.

'Not as risky as being dropped into France,' replied Roland, glancing at Kim. 'And that's what I signed up for, after all.'

'I'm afraid it would mean withdrawing you from the programme at Beaulieu,' said M. 'But we can find some excuse — ill health, perhaps — so you could go back with the next intake, if everything goes according to plan. But how do you propose to go about infiltrating the group?'

'I came across some pretty outspoken Nazi sympathizers in the US. There's the German American Bund, made up largely of Yanks with German heritage. I don't think it would be difficult to convince Kline's associates that I belong to that. I might even be able to persuade them that I can bring some influential Americans into the plot — whatever it is.'

M. thought for a few moments. 'It sounds plausible to me. If you can make it work, it might just give us the entry we need.' He downed the last of his whisky. 'All right. I'll arrange your withdrawal from the training scheme. Everyone will assume that you've been sent to the cooler in Scotland. Let me have a list of what documents and paperwork you need. Do you have anywhere to stay in town?'

'I kept a little bolthole in Clapham with all my clothes and other gear. But I'll need funds to make myself convincing.'

'Understood. I'll set up a bank account for you to draw on. What name shall we give it?'

Roland grinned. 'One of my alter egos was called Rufus Foxton. The flat is rented under that name. Shall we stick with that?'

'Rufus Foxton it shall be,' agreed M.

The next few minutes were occupied by a discussion of the details of what Roland would need to sustain his new identity. Then M. brought the evening to a close.

'It's late,' he said, looking at his watch. 'Are you planning to go back to Clapham tonight? There are two bedrooms here, if Kim has no objection.'

'That would be better, if it's OK with you,' he said, looking at Kim. 'I've got to get hold of the bloke I left the key with before I can move in.'

'Fine,' she agreed, suppressing a small tremor of excitement.

When M. had gone, they looked at each other. He said, 'We seem to have so many aliases between us I don't know what to call you. I've been used to Maxine or Max, but the brigadier calls you Kim.'

She responded with a lift of her shoulders. 'My name is Katherine Isobel Maxwell, hence Kim, but I'm Max in the FANY, because they regard the use of first names as unmilitary. Maxine is the name I was given when I went to France. You can take your pick.'

'Then I'd like to go for Kim,' he responded.

'And in return, what do I call you? Roland, Renaud, Foxy . . . ? I'm used to thinking of you as Roland, although it's only a cover name, but I have to admit Foxy has a certain appeal.'

'Take your pick. I'll answer to any of them.'

She yawned. 'It's been a long evening. I think I'm ready for bed.'

'Me too. Goodnight, Kim.' He leaned towards her and kissed her on the cheek. Instinctively, just as she had done in the street outside Kline's surgery, she moved her head so that her lips found his. After that, there was no need to disturb the sheets on the spare bed.

\* \* \*

Kim woke next morning to a confusion of emotions. There was pleasure in the mix, and excitement, but predominant was a sense of surprise — surprise that it had all happened so quickly, as if it had been agreed between them long before; surprise at herself for giving way to her instincts with so little hesitation. Brought up with the strict moral code of the period, she had not slept with her fiancé, Simon, before his death. They had both taken it for granted that this had to wait until they were married. Her sexual initiation had been at the hands of a Swiss ski instructor. She had enjoyed the experience up to a point but had never succeeded in shaking off the sense that she was behaving immorally. Since then, sex had been limited to kisses and some slightly embarrassed fumbling.

For the first time last night she had experienced real physical pleasure. Roland was attentive, patient and inventive — and experienced; and her body responded with an intensity she had never thought possible. It had not occurred to her to wonder if this was the beginning of a permanent relationship, or whether she should hold back until she had a ring on her finger. The likelihood of that ever happening was remote, and time was too short. They both knew that this might be the first and last time. *Seize the day!* she told herself.

She was about to get out of bed when Roland opened his eyes and reached out to grasp her arm.

'Do you have to get up?'

'Not necessarily.'

'That's good!'

Half an hour later she did get up and made tea for them both. Sitting up in bed and sipping it she said, 'There's so much I don't know about you. Can I ask you something?'

'Go ahead.'

'How does a boy from Cable Street, with I assume only a basic education, become a highly sophisticated and cultured man able to convince people that he is an expert on — what was it? — sixteenth-century Italian paintings?'

He set his cup aside and settled back on the pillows. 'Courtesy of a very rich, very beautiful lady of a certain age.'

'You were a gigolo?'

'That's one word for what I was.' He shrugged lightly. 'I was also her chef, her chauffeur — and the son she never had.'

Kim studied his face, trying to absorb this new revelation. 'Tell me how it happened.'

'I think you know I worked my passage to New York as a sous chef on board a liner. My papa was a bit of a loser in some ways but he was a damn good cook. I lived with him in Normandy for part of my boyhood and he taught me a lot. I was well able to fill my role as sous chef. I could have stayed on and worked my way up to chef but I had other ideas. I jumped ship and found a job in a Manhattan restaurant. I worked there for nearly three years and I became a very good cook — though I say it as shouldn't.' He paused and grinned at her, then went on more seriously. 'The lady I mentioned used to come to eat at the restaurant and it got to the point where she would ask which dishes I had been responsible for and choose them from the menu. Once or twice I was summoned from the kitchen to be congratulated. Then, one day, she offered me a job.'

'As a chef?' queried Kim.

He lifted his shoulders. 'That was — what shall I say? — my job description. She was a widow with a grand house on Long Island and she liked to entertain. She had a circle of wealthy, educated, sophisticated friends who all liked my cooking, and I became, I suppose you could say, a bit of a pet.' He met her eyes. 'Yes, I slept with the lady, when required, but mostly I think she enjoyed my company. She loved art, paintings in particular, and when she saw that I had an appreciation for them, albeit a very uneducated one, she started to teach me. We went to galleries and to shows and I found I had an eye for really brilliant work, even if it wasn't the most famous or highly regarded. We began to buy pictures — I mean she did, but often on my advice.' He paused and sighed. 'She was a great lady. I owe her a lot.'

'How long did that last?' enquired Kim.

'Nine — no, nearer ten years. Long enough to turn me into a very different person from the boy who jumped ship in New York.'

'So what happened?' asked Kim. 'Why did you leave?'

'Death happened. She was killed in a boating accident, and as she had no direct heirs the house and the money, and the paintings, went to a distant cousin who had no interest in art, or in *haute cuisine*. Fortunately, my benefactress had left me a legacy. Not enough to live on, but enough to allow me to pass, for a while, as a gentleman, among people who didn't know me. So I thought I'd better come home to good old Blighty and try my luck here. The rest I think you know.'

Kim gazed at him and shook her head in wonder. 'What an amazing story!'

He stretched. 'Well, it's certainly been eventful, and I was doing very nicely until it all fell apart. I wonder sometimes what I might have done if I hadn't ended up in Brixton. I'd have been found out sooner or later. I suppose I'd have had to go into the army when war broke out.' He grinned at her. 'But I'm not complaining. I've been lucky enough to get involved in something far more exciting than the average squaddie — and as a bonus, I've ended up in bed with the bravest and most attractive woman I've ever met.' He pulled her down to him and kissed her. 'Now it's your turn.'

'It's a very ordinary story compared with yours,' she said, but she told him anyway.

They spent the day alternately talking and making love, and at lunchtime he sallied out with both their ration books and raided the cupboards in the kitchen to produce the best meal she had tasted since before the beginning of the war.

In mid-afternoon the telephone rang. It was M.

'You're on for tonight. You'll be picked up by a FANY driver at seven o'clock.'

# CHAPTER 12

Kim peered down from the rear cockpit of the Whitley bomber. It was three days before the full moon and she could just make out some features of the landscape below her. Moonlight glimmered on water in what she knew must be the Canal du Nivernais. That amorphous cluster of buildings must be the town of Corbigny. Beyond that the land rose to the thickly forested hills of the Morvan. Not a light showed anywhere, and as the little plane began to circle, she strained her eyes for the signal fires that would indicate the DZ — the drop zone — where her future colleagues would be waiting to pick her up. There was nothing and she felt a sinking in her stomach. She knew that it was not always possible for the people on the ground to set the fires, or light them, perhaps because of enemy activity in the area, but without them the mission would have to be aborted and they would return to England. She had always hated parachuting, and casting herself out into the void took all her courage. Having geared herself up to face the jump, the last thing she wanted was to have to go through it all again the following night.

The pilot's voice crackled in her headphones. 'There they are! Ahead at two o'clock. I'll make one pass to check and then come in for a final run.'

She gazed ahead and saw pinpricks of light that rapidly grew and intensified as the fires took hold. Set in a pre-arranged pattern, they confirmed that this was the target.

The plane tilted as the pilot circled the area, then levelled up as he came in for the run. The dispatcher opened the doors covering a circular hole in the floor of the cabin and cold air rushed in.

'Ready?'

'Ready.' Kim took off her headset and sat down on the floor with her legs dangling down into the hole.

'Go!' A firm push between her shoulder blades sent her out into the void. For a second, she was buffeted by the slipstream, then she was free falling towards the distant fires. There was a jerk as her parachute opened and then came the few seconds of the drop that she actually enjoyed, as she hung, suspended between the stars and the dark earth, hardly aware that she was falling.

She could see the fires below clearly now. The pilot had done his job well and she saw that she was going to drop just outside the circle. A tug on the lines of her 'chute corrected the line of descent, and she could see figures moving out of the trees to receive her.

Then there was no more time.

The ground rushed up to meet her and it was just a question of remembering the drill, letting her knees bend and rolling with the impact. The jolt of the landing momentarily took her breath away, but she rallied, punching the release button on the parachute harness and hauling on the lines to bring in the unwieldy canopy. She was lying on top of it, struggling to get the billowing silk under control, when a voice above her said, '*Ca va?*'

'*Oui, ça va,*' she responded breathlessly.

A strong hand helped her to her feet. '*Eh, bien. Bienvenue en France.*'

Someone else took charge of the parachute, bundling it up and carrying it off to be buried. It seemed a shame to bury so much beautiful silk, but regulations insisted on it. In the early days, the occupying enemy had been alerted to the presence of Allied agents by the discovery that some of the locals were sporting silk shirts or blouses.

Her companion led her across the clearing to where a tall man was waiting.

'Monique?' he inquired.

'Yes. Gregoire?'

'Yes. Come with me.' He started towards the surrounding trees. Around them men were hurrying to extinguish the signal fires and cover the place where they had been with leafy branches so that they were invisible to a German reconnaissance plane. Gregoire looked over his shoulder. 'Are you all right?' he asked in French. 'I'm afraid we've got a bit of a walk ahead of us and the path is narrow and pretty rough in places. Watch your feet.'

Kim set off after him. Once under the trees it was very dark, but Gregoire forged ahead without hesitation. She followed as fast as she could, often catching her feet on rocks or tree roots.

The man who had greeted her when she landed was following behind and twice he had to catch her arm to stop her from falling, but there was no let-up in the pace set by their leader. It was a relief when they came at last to a clearing, where she was able to make out the shapes of a group of rough huts and the dim glow of a central fire. A large man holding a lantern came to meet them. He and Gregoire exchanged a few words in voices too low for her to hear.

Gregoire turned to her. 'This is Xavier. He's the leader of the *maquis* band in this area. It was his men who set the fires. Xavier, this is Monique.'

'*Salut!* And thank you.' Kim held out her hand but the big man merely nodded. He said something else to Gregoire, who shook his head and Xavier shrugged. Kim was beginning to feel uneasy. She had expected a better welcome than this.

'This way,' said Gregoire, leading her towards the far edge of the clearing, where she was relieved to see a battered Citroën parked. She hefted her pack, containing the rest of her clothes and a few personal necessities, into the back and got in beside him. He started the engine but did not put on the headlights, and they bumped down a rough track guided only by moonlight until they reached a small road. Gregoire drove in silence, and after her reception Kim felt disinclined to make small talk. At length they came to the edge of the forest and he pulled up outside a small cottage.

'This is my place,' he said. 'You'll stay here for tonight.'

He led her inside, and after checking that all the blinds were down, he lit a kerosene lamp and she was able to see him and her surroundings for the first time. He had sandy hair that fell in a fringe over very pale eyes and a face that was more fine-boned than she had expected. But it was the room that gave her the biggest surprise. It was not large and was simply furnished with a table and chairs of dark wood and one rather dilapidated easy chair with patchwork cushions. But the walls were covered in paintings, mainly watercolours with a few oils, all of rural scenes typical of that part of France. Looking around, she saw an easel folded away in a corner and a rucksack stained with paint of various colours.

'Are these yours?' she asked.

He was stooping over the range that took up one wall of the room, stoking up the fire and setting a pan of water to boil. He straightened up and glanced at the pictures.

'It's my cover. I'm a penniless artist eking out a living selling local scenes.'

Kim had a sudden vision of Roland. What would he make of these, with his eye for Italian masterpieces? She knew very little about painting, but she could tell that there was talent here.

'They're good,' she said. 'Are you a professional?'

He shrugged. 'Not exactly. You know what they say, *those who can, do; those who can't . . .*'

'You're a teacher?'

'Back there, in another life.'

For a moment Kim saw what the strain of months undercover had done to a basically sensitive spirit and her feeling of irritation at her welcome — or lack of it — evaporated.

'I'm sorry if my arrival has caused you some problems,' she said.

He shrugged. 'It's not that. Just that we've been begging for a supply drop for weeks — the *maquis* are desperate for arms and ammunition, even boots for their men. When we heard you were coming, we thought perhaps the rest of the stuff was coming with you.'

'That's why Xavier was not too pleased to meet me,' Kim said. 'I'm sorry if I'm a bit of a disappointment.'

He spooned something into two tin mugs and poured the boiling water onto it. 'And I apologise if I've seemed unwelcoming.' He set a mug on the table in front of her. 'It's a pretty disgusting brew. I think it's mainly ground acorns. But this helps.' He produced a flask from his pocket and poured a generous slug into each cup. 'It's the local *eau de vie*, rough on its own but it helps to take the edge off.'

Kim sipped. She knew better than to ask for milk or sugar. It was, as she remembered, quite bitter, but the *eau de vie* warmed her insides and eased her nerves.

Gregoire sat opposite her. 'The simple fact is, we didn't need another member of the team. I'm not sure why you've been sent to us.'

Kim nodded. 'I'll explain as much as I can but some of the details are strictly on a need-to-know basis. You'll have to bear with me on that. It concerns the young man who was sent out to you as a replacement radio operator. I know him as Lucien. I don't know what his cover name was here.'

'You mean the lad who got himself picked up by the Boche before he even completed his first transmission,' Gregoire said. His tone was dismissive.

'What do you mean, got himself picked up?'

'Well, he must have given himself away somewhere along the line, to be picked up so quickly.'

'In fact,' said Kim grimly, 'we believe he was deliberately set up.'

Gregoire's eyebrows shot up. 'What?'

'We think he had uncovered some information before he left England that certain people did not want getting out.'

'Certain people back home?' asked Gregoire.

'Yes.'

'What information?'

'I can't tell you that. We're not even sure ourselves exactly what it is,' Kim admitted. 'Suffice it to say, Baker Street is sufficiently worried about it to send me out here to find out.'

'Find out? You do realize he's in the hands of the Gestapo?'

'Of course. I'm here to get him out.'

He sat back and stared at her incredulously. 'Just like that?'

She smiled wryly. 'The difficult we do at once, the impossible . . .'

'May take a little longer,' he finished for her. 'May I ask how you intend to go about it?'

'Well, I shall need your help — Xavier's and his *maquis*, if they're willing.'

'You have mine, of course. I can't speak for Xavier. But what's the plan? Do you have one?'

Kim suppressed a yawn. It was well after midnight and she was bone tired.

Gregoire took the hint. 'Perhaps we can wait till morning. It's far too late to embark on that now. You must be exhausted. I'll show you where you can bed down for the night. Tomorrow we'll fix you up with somewhere a bit more civilized.' He pointed to a rough ladder that led up to a kind of balcony which extended over half the width of the ground floor. A curtain divided the space in two. 'I hope that's OK for one night.'

'Frankly,' she told him, 'I could sleep on a clothesline if that was all there was. This will do fine.'

'I'm afraid the jakes is out at the back,' he said. 'I'll light a lamp for you.'

Kim found her way to the privy and relieved herself, and when she returned Gregoire had set a bowl of warm water beside the sink for her to wash. He tactfully took himself off outside and she heard him light a match. She washed her hands and splashed her face and rinsed her mouth with water from a jug. Then she hauled herself up the ladder. Her pack had been deposited on a bed on one side of the curtain, so she pulled off the overall she had worn for the jump, removed her boots and crawled under the blanket. She was dimly aware of Gregoire climbing the ladder to his place on the other side but then sleep claimed her.

Kim woke next morning to find the little cottage empty, but the range had been stoked up and a pan of water was simmering on top of it. She took the opportunity to have a thorough wash and then dressed in the French clothes she had worn underneath her overalls for the parachute jump. She had just finished when she heard a car draw up outside and Gregoire came in carrying a basket, from which emanated the smell of freshly baked bread.

'Good morning,' he called. 'Did you sleep well?'

But Kim's attention was focused on the basket.

'You've been shopping.'

'Not exactly. I have an arrangement with the wife of the farmer just up the hill. I'm painting a picture of the farmhouse and its surroundings and in return she gives me a loaf from the morning's baking.' He set the bread on the table and added a small pat of butter and a beer bottle containing milk. 'And . . .' He whisked away the cloth covering the basket with the air of a magician producing a rabbit. '*Voilà*. I told her I had a visitor and look what she gave me.' Nestling in the bottom of the basket were two eggs.

'You won't get bread like this from the local *boulangerie*,' he went on, as he set a pan on the range to boil the eggs. 'The flour that's available on the ration is so adulterated you might as well eat the sweepings off the floor.'

'I remember,' said Kim.

He gave her a quick look. 'This is not your first assignment, then?'

'No, I was here last year,' she told him, but she did not elaborate and he did not inquire further.

As they sat down to eat, she said, 'You are onto a good thing there, with the farmer's wife.'

He grinned. 'I'm definitely the winner in that exchange.' But then his expression darkened. 'At the moment the farmers and the people who have a bit of land to grow things are lucky, but it isn't going to last. As every month goes by the Boche demand that they hand over more and more of their produce, for export to Germany. They are even taking the breeding stock to fulfil their quotas. The local people are ready to revolt, but the repercussions are too severe. But it's fuelling the resistance movement and bringing new recruits into the *maquis* — that and the STO.'

'That's *Service de Travail Obligatoire*, isn't it?' said Kim. 'It wasn't in force when I was here last.'

'It came in, in February,' said Gregoire. 'There are hundreds of young men who would rather go into the forests or the mountains and join a *maquis* than be shipped off for slave labour in Germany.'

'Which must be good from our point of view,' commented Kim.

'And brings us to the pressing question of the moment. What plan do you have for getting your boy out?'

'I need some more information before I can answer that,' Kim told him. 'First, do we know where he's being held?'

'The Gestapo have taken over the Hotel du Lion d'Or, the main hotel in Corbigny. From what we can discover prisoners are being held in what were the wine cellars.'

'What's the name of the man in charge?'

'Standartenführer Hoffmann.'

'A colonel?' Kim was surprised. 'The SS must think this area needs a strong presence. What's he like?'

'Exactly as you'd expect. Dyed-in-the-wool Nazi, clever and ruthless. Our boy has been in his hands for nearly a week now. Do you seriously think he hasn't cracked by now?'

Kim shook her head. 'If he had, you'd all be under arrest. Unless that isn't what they want to know.'

'You mean about this plot he's supposed to have discovered? What do *we* know about that?' he asked.

'Very little, except that it seems to go by the code name *Blitzschlag*.'

'Lightning bolt? And you think some of our people are involved?'

'I can't go into that now,' said Kim.

'Of course — "need to know" and all that.' He gave her a wry smile.

'How tight is security at the hotel?'

'Very tight. Guards on all the doors and patrolling the streets around. And the local *milice* are stopping and questioning anyone who approaches.'

'Deliveries? Laundry?'

'All carefully checked, in and out.'

'Do we have any contacts in the hotel?'

'That's the one potentially bright spot,' he said. 'The son of Madame Hulot, the woman who owns the hotel, has joined the *maquis* rather than go to Germany. He may be able to help.'

Kim thought for a moment. 'Are they still using local people as staff?'

'Oh yes. The Gestapo don't make their own beds or do their own washing up,' Gregoire said with a wry smile

'I wonder if he could persuade his mother to give me a job,' Kim suggested.

'You? What as?'

'Chamber maid, waitress, head cook and bottle washer — anything to get me inside.'

He pursed his lips. 'It would be risky.'

'It's the only way I can think of at the moment — unless you have a better idea?'

He sighed and shook his head. 'I don't — and it's not for want of trying. We haven't just sat back and washed our hands of Lucien, you know. I think we've already explored all the possible angles.'

'We?' queried Kim.

'Me and the rest of the circuit, and Xavier and his men.'

'Well, let's run with the idea of getting me inside,' Kim said. 'At least I can familiarize myself with the whole set up from there.'

'OK,' he said. 'I'll take you to meet the other two and then we'll go up into the hills to speak to Xavier.'

As they went outside Kim asked, 'How on earth have you managed to get petrol?'

'The *maquis* have a sympathizer who owns a garage in Montsauche. He lets us have the odd can from time to time. But I keep it strictly for essential travel. After today, I'm afraid you will have to make do with a bicycle, or Shanks's pony.'

The circuit code-named 'Grocer' consisted of three people: Gregoire the leader, Philippe the radio operator and a young woman who went by the name of Claudette who was the courier, the role Kim had once filled in another circuit. They went to find Philippe first. He was a small, wiry man with the weathered face of someone who had always spent much of his time out of doors. He had found a job as a gardener to the wife of the owner of the local château. Like so many women, her husband was now a POW in a German camp, and she was vehemently anti-Nazi and ready to take the risk of sheltering an Allied agent. She was also extremely devout and had close ties with the local church of St Michel. Philippe made regular visits there, carrying fresh flowers for the altar, which gave him the opportunity to climb to the top of the tower, where he had installed his radio set.

He shook hands with her but his expression remained grim. 'I'm glad to meet you, of course. But quite frankly I think you've been sent on a fool's errand. The chances of getting the poor chap out must be remote.'

'It's a long shot, I know,' she agreed. 'But it's been done before.'

He sighed deeply. 'I feel responsible in a way for what happened to him. If I hadn't been out of action he would never have been sent here.'

Kim suspected that had that not been the case Lucien would have been sent elsewhere and would have met the same fate, but she did not say so. Instead she said, 'It wasn't your fault. Don't blame yourself. What happened? Were you wounded?'

He grimaced. 'Nothing so heroic. It was food poisoning. The chaps in the *maquis* thought I'd probably eaten the wrong mushrooms.'

'Had you been picking mushrooms?'

'Not personally. Claudette gave them to me. She found them out in the forest and picked a basketful for the chaps in the *maquis* to help eke out the rations.'

'Was anyone else affected?'

'That's the funny thing. I was the only one. They reckoned I was just unlucky and got a rogue one in my portion.'

Kim cast a sideways look at Gregoire, but he just shrugged. 'Are you completely recovered?'

'Oh yes. Perfectly OK now. Just tell me how I can help.'

'If we succeed in getting him out, we shall need to arrange his exfiltration asap. All you need to do is be ready to transmit on this emergency frequency when you get my message.' She handed him a slip of paper. 'Memorize this and destroy it.'

'Of course.'

She squeezed his arm. 'I'll be in touch. Don't give up hope.'

They moved on to some riding stables where Claudette had found a job looking after the horses. She was just about to mount a bay gelding when they arrived, and Kim felt an immediate sense of recognition. It was not that she had actually met this particular young woman, but she knew the type from her schooldays and had met many more of them when she trained with the FANY — girls from comfortably-off landed gentry who had grown up with horses and cut their teeth in the hunting field. It was obvious that Claudette was in her element. The owner, an elderly widow, had relied on a couple of young men to care for the horses until they were both called up, so she had been delighted when Claudette applied for a job.

'The beauty of it is,' Claudette said, 'I have to ride out to exercise the horses, so I can go more or less anywhere. Gregoire and I have set up a dead letter drop in the woods. He can leave me messages or pick up replies when he goes off on a painting expedition, and at the same time I can keep an eye open for enemy troop movements.'

'I'll show you where it is,' Gregoire said, 'but I don't think it will be much use to you. We'll think of some other way to keep in touch.'

Leaving Claudette to her ride, they drove on up a lane leading into the hills. At a certain point Gregoire turned off along a narrow, rutted track, and Kim recognized the bumpy ride from the night before. They had not gone far before two armed men stepped out of the bushes and blocked the road.

Gregoire wound down the window and greeted them by name.

'Ah, it's you,' one of them said. 'I'll call up and let them know you're coming. You'll have triggered one of our alarms.'

He produced a walkie-talkie radio and spoke to someone, then waved them on.

'They seem to have a pretty tight security set-up,' Kim commented.

'I was able to get the radios dropped for them,' Gregoire said, 'and we set up trip wires attached to small explosive charges to give advanced warning of anyone approaching.' He grinned ruefully. 'I think we may have to abandon that idea because the charges are regularly set off by wild animals.'

At the *maquis* camp a dozen or so bearded men were lounging in the shade or sitting on logs cleaning antiquated hunting rifles. As the car drew up Xavier appeared from a tent and came to meet them. His manner was as off-hand as it had been the night before, but he unbent somewhat when Gregoire explained Kim's purpose.

'You're going into the lion's den?' he asked, looking at her with new interest from under bushy brows.

'It seems the only way,' she said.

'Louis! Come here,' Xavier shouted across the clearing. He turned back to Kim and Gregoire. 'We will see what he can do to help.'

A boy in his late teens, sporting the beginnings of a dark beard which did not quite hide the scars of youthful acne, loped over to join them and Kim explained her idea.

'Do you think your mother would take me on?' Kim asked. 'I'll make myself useful, as far as I can.'

Louis frowned uneasily. 'I don't know. You see, Maman is really only interested in one thing. She wants to keep the hotel so it is a going concern when the war is over. If that means cooperating with the Germans, that's what she will do.'

'Does she know what is going on in her cellars?' Kim asked, her tone sharpening.

The boy shrugged. 'She prefers not to.'

'What does she think of you having to come up here?' Gregoire asked.

'She thinks that is better than being taken to work in Germany,' Louis said. 'But she thinks I'm just hiding. She doesn't know we are fighting the Boche.'

'What does she expect to happen when the war is over?' Kim asked.

Again he shrugged. 'She expects the Germans will win and then they will all want to come on holiday to the Morvan.'

'And suppose the Allies win?' Kim pursued. 'I've heard that already some loyal Frenchmen and women are taking reprisals against collaborators. Has she considered what might happen to her and her hotel then?'

The boy looked increasingly uncomfortable. 'I don't know.'

'Is there any way I could meet with her to talk face to face?'

He thought for a moment. 'She goes to confession at St Michel's every Thursday.'

'That's today,' Kim said. 'What is the best way to approach her?'

Xavier cut in, 'The curé, Father Antoine, is on our side. He comes up here once a week to say Mass and take confessions. If you speak to him, I think he will introduce you.'

'Then I'll try that,' Kim said. 'Thank you.'

As they drove back towards Corbigny, Gregoire said, 'Are you sure about this? I know you can trust Father Antoine. After all, our radio set is hidden in his church tower. But you will have to reveal your real identity and your purpose here to Madame Hulot. The woman might just decide to sell you to Hoffmann.'

'The *maquis* have got her son, remember,' Kim said. 'I don't know what their reaction would be if she did that — but nor does she.'

Gregoire drove her to a small café-bar by the lock on the canal called the Bar de l'Ecluse. 'I suggest you make this your base for now. Jacques, the proprietor, is a supporter and he's proved his loyalty. He'll give you a room. I drink here most evenings, so we can keep in touch. Does that suit you?'

'Fine,' she said, 'unless I can persuade Madame Hulot to take me on. Then I presume I'll live-in at the hotel. But I should be able to get away in the evening to let you know how things are going.'

'I'm not at all happy about this arrangement,' Gregoire said with a sigh. 'I wish we could think of some other plan.'

'Well, we may have to if Madame can't be persuaded,' Kim pointed out.

* * *

Jacques was a red-faced man whose figure must once have been a testament to his wife's cooking, but was now diminished by rationing into flabby pouches of loose skin. He made them welcome and showed Kim into a small, immaculately clean room at the top of the house. She and Gregoire ate an early evening meal and then Kim borrowed a bicycle and rode up the hill to the church. She found the curé tending the vegetables in his small garden. He was an elderly man with lively blue eyes and a circle of silver hair framing his tonsure. She introduced herself with the password she had been given.

'Gregoire says the storm has passed over.'

The blue eyes took her in unblinkingly for a moment, then the priest's face relaxed into a smile and he replied with the agreed response, 'But we should not forget our umbrellas.' He added, 'Any friend of Gregoire's is welcome here. Shall we go inside?'

He showed her into a room furnished with tables and chairs in beautifully carved walnut and upholstered with faded tapestry. She had the impression that nothing here had changed since the previous century.

Kim had learned on her previous mission that sometimes the only way forward was to take people on trust, so she got straight to the point.

'I know that the Gestapo are holding prisoners at the Hotel du Lion d'Or. I have been sent from England to find out who is there and if there is any way of getting them out. I think my best chance is if I can get the owner, Madame Hulot, to take me on as a maid. Her son tells me she comes here to confession every Thursday. Could you ask her to speak to me?'

The priest looked doubtful. 'I can certainly ask. But do you wish me to tell her who you are and why you are here? I think her fear of the Germans may outweigh any patriotic feelings she may have.'

'But not her fear of God?' Kim suggested. 'It seems to me she must be a very devout woman, since she comes to confession so regularly.'

He considered her in silence for a moment. Then he said, 'I cannot reveal the secrets of the confessional, of course. But I will ask Madame Hulot if she is willing to speak with you. If she refuses . . .'

'I understand,' Kim said. 'In that case I will not trouble you any further.'

'It is almost time. I must prepare myself,' he said. 'If you will wait here . . . ?'

Half an hour later, the curé looked into the room where she was sitting and said, 'Come through to the church. Madame has agreed to talk to you.'

A portly figure stood up to greet her as she entered the church.

*You haven't suffered too much from rationing*, Kim thought. Aloud she said, 'Good evening, Madame. Thank you for agreeing to talk to me.'

The woman glanced around the church uneasily, as if suspecting there might be someone hidden behind the columns. Father Antoine had withdrawn into the sacristy, and apart from themselves the place was empty.

'I'll hear what you have to say,' Madame began, 'but don't expect me to help you. I've got too much at stake to take risks.'

*Not as much as I have*, Kim thought. Aloud she said, 'Shall we sit down?'

The narrow pews forced them to twist their bodies sideways to face each other, an awkward position for someone of Madame Hulot's build.

'I think you know there are prisoners being held in the cellars under your hotel.'

The woman shrugged. 'What of it? If they break the law, they have to take what's coming to them.'

'If they had broken the law, surely they would be in police cells? The local gendarmerie still controls such things, doesn't it? These are men who have taken a stand against the brutality of the Nazi regime. Patriots who have stood up for their country.'

'More fools them! The Germans are in charge now. There's nothing any of us can do to change that.'

'But there is,' Kim said. 'The Allies are making headway. The Germans are falling back in Italy. They have been defeated by the Russians at Stalingrad. Have you considered what might happen to you and to your hotel when the Allies are victorious? Ordinary patriotic Frenchmen and women are not going to deal kindly with collaborators.'

For the first time the woman opposite her looked uncertain of herself. Kim pressed her advantage. 'Do you not think it could be useful to be able to show that you actually were working with us, in that eventuality?'

'And how would I do that?'

'I need to find out who is being held in your cellars and how they are being treated. Give me a job. I'll do whatever you like — clean, wash dishes, serve in the restaurant.'

'Why? Who are you? Who are you working for?'

'You don't need to know that. I've worked out a cover story for you. I'll be the daughter of a distant cousin, left destitute after the death of my husband. You have taken me in as an act of charity.'

'Suppose you are right, and the Allies win. How will they know I have been working for them?'

'If I am able to succeed in the mission I have been given, then I can make sure that the relevant authorities know about it. It might get you out of a lot of trouble.'

It was an empty boast, but Kim felt no compunction about using it.

'I shall need something in writing.'

Kim raised an eyebrow. 'You surely do not want anything that would incriminate you if suspicions were raised and your rooms were to be searched. You will have to trust me on this. But I can promise you that Xavier and the *maquis* will know where your loyalties are. They can vouch for you if you decide to help us.'

She could see that Madame Hulot was struggling with conflicting impulses. Kim tried another tack. 'Have you any idea what goes on in your cellars? As a devout Christian woman, how can you ignore the suffering of those poor men?'

'What am I supposed to do about it?'

'Do as I ask. Let me come and work in the hotel.'

'And what good will that do?'

'I can't go into details. There are . . . powers at work here that you do not need to know about. Just be assured that you will be doing the right thing in the eyes of God. I think Father Antoine will tell you the same thing.'

For a moment the woman sat silent, twisting her hands in her lap. Then she gave Kim a look that combined defiance and appeal. 'Very well. But you'll work for your keep. I'm not feeding you for nothing.'

'I'll do whatever you ask,' Kim agreed. 'But there is just one thing I'd like to make clear. If you should ever consider betraying me to the Germans, you should remember that your son is with the *maquis*. They don't take kindly to traitors.'

This time the look on Madame Hulot's face told her she had won.

'Now, let's think about this long-lost cousin and the story we are going to tell.'

## CHAPTER 13

Kim found Gregoire waiting for her back at the bar and gave him an abbreviated version of the conversation. 'So I start tomorrow. Where that gets us, I have no idea, but at least I'll be able to find out exactly what we are dealing with. I'll come here whenever I can to keep you updated.'

'OK,' he said, frowning. 'But for God's sake be careful. You can't trust that woman to keep her mouth shut.'

'That reminds me,' Kim said seriously. 'There's something else I'd like to talk over. It's been nagging at me all day. Where was Lucien when he was picked up? I assume it wasn't in the church tower, or you wouldn't still be using it.'

'No.' Gregoire swallowed the last of his beer. 'I decided it would be less of a security risk if we put him somewhere different. He was in a barn up in the hills. It belonged to a farm but the farmer has been dead for some years and the place is now more or less derelict. Claudette found it on one of her rides. The house is pretty much a ruin, but the barn is still in fairly good nick and reception is excellent at that height.'

'So how did the Boche know exactly where to position their detector van to pick up his first transmission?' Kim asked.

Gregoire lifted his hands in a gesture of helplessness.

Kim pressed on. 'We know somebody back home wanted him out of the way. He had found out something but they didn't know how much, and they couldn't risk taking him prisoner in England and perhaps having to resort to torture themselves, because that would have sparked off a whole series of enquiries that might have drawn attention to what they were doing. The simplest way to solve the problem was to dispatch him out here and let their friends in the Gestapo do the job for them.'

'OK. So far, so straightforward,' Gregoire agreed.

'But why send him here? Was it pure coincidence that your circuit needed a replacement radio operator at that precise moment? Was it really an accident that Philippe was the only person to eat those poisonous mushrooms? Was it really the mushrooms that poisoned him? And then, how did the Germans know where Lucien was going to be based?'

Gregoire was frowning. 'Now you put it like that, I see it looks very sinister. I must admit I hadn't really thought it through. Truth is, my mind has been on setting up a really spectacular operation for Xavier and his lot, and Lucien's capture seemed like a bit of a sideshow. But now you've got me worried.'

'What's the spectacular operation?' Kim asked.

'If you don't mind, I'll keep that to myself for the moment.'

Kim nodded. 'Quite right. I shouldn't ask. But it does look as though you've got a traitor somewhere in the organization.'

'I agree. The question is, who?'

'Who else knew where Lucien was going to set up his radio?'

'Xavier knew. He and his men keep a close watch on movements in their area so he needed to know that Lucien was one of ours.'

'A close watch that failed to spot the presence of a German detector van.'

'You're not suggesting Xavier is working for the Boche?'

'I'm not suggesting anything. I'm just asking the question.'

Gregoire's frown deepened. 'I don't believe Xavier's a traitor. If he was, he could have sold out the whole circuit weeks ago.'

'One of his men, then?'

'That's possible — but again, why leave the rest of us free?'

'We can be almost certain that whoever is behind this was targeting Lucien specifically, but I agree it does make one wonder why they didn't make a clean sweep of it.' Kim yawned and looked at her watch. It was nearly ten. Almost time for the curfew. 'Sorry. I'm going to have to get my head down. I can't think straight any longer.'

'You do that,' Gregoire said. 'It's up to me to try and work out who the traitor might be and why he acted as he did. You've got your own fish to fry.'

'I need to ask you a favour. Can you drive me to Clamecy first thing in the morning? I need to arrive by train when I take up my position at the hotel.'

\* \* \*

Next morning Kim descended from the train and mingled with the other passengers. She asked one of them the way to the Hotel du Lion d'Or and trudged towards it, carrying her small suitcase. A hundred yards from her destination she was stopped by a young man wearing the blue uniform of the *milice*, the paramilitary organization whose members were French citizens but Nazi sympathizers. Kim felt a chill in her stomach at the sight of him. The *milice* were more dreaded by the Resistance than the occupying Germans. They were fanatical in seeking out anyone who opposed the regime by word or deed and their local knowledge made them harder to hoodwink.

'Papers!' he demanded.

Kim produced the fake ID card.

'You are from Clamecy? What are you doing here in Corbigny?'

She had agreed with Madame Hulot that her new character should appear rather slow-witted and so more easily overlooked as a possible threat to the occupiers. She blinked up at the *milicien*.

'Please, monsieur, I'm looking for the Hotel du Lion d'Or. I've got a job there.'

'What sort of job?'

'I . . . I'm not sure. I'm just going to help Madame Hulot.'

He looked her up and down. Her face was bare of make-up and she had pulled her hair back into a knot at the back of her head — a look she knew did her no favours. Her figure was hidden by a shabby cardigan and her legs were bare except for ankle socks and ended in the boots she had brought with her for tramping forest paths. She could see him deciding that she was a pathetic object, unworthy of further attention.

He stepped back and jerked his head over his shoulder. 'It's there. Right in front of your eyes.'

'Thank you, monsieur,' she murmured and scurried past him.

Madame Hulot met her at the back door of the hotel.

'Here you are! I thought you'd be here earlier than this. Come through. I'll introduce you to Michel, my chef.'

It was soon obvious to Kim that her new employer was determined to play out the charade to its full extent, and make as much use of her extra, unpaid scullery maid as she could. Kim was introduced as the orphan child of distant cousins, as agreed.

'Not very bright, I'm afraid,' she heard Madame murmur to the chef. 'You'll have to give her detailed instructions for the simplest things.'

Kim was immediately set to work peeling potatoes and then scrubbing pots, and as the morning progressed she began to think bitterly that at this rate she would learn precisely nothing of any use. She had a small break though as lunchtime approached. The hotel, she had learned, had a reputation in peacetime for the quality of its food, and Michel was preparing the sort of lunch he would have produced in the days before rationing.

'*Oh la!*' Kim exclaimed. 'So much food! Is someone important coming to lunch?'

'Important enough for us, girl,' he replied. 'This is for the colonel and his aides. He likes his grub, does the colonel — and his French wines.'

'But what about the rationing?' she asked ingenuously.

'Doesn't apply to them, does it?' came the answer.

He set aside half of one of yesterday's baguettes and a jug of water.

Kim picked up the bread and enquired innocently, 'Is this for birds? Shall I throw it out?'

'I wouldn't do that, unless you want someone to go very hungry. That's for him downstairs.'

'Him downstairs?'

'In the cellar. The prisoner, *idiot!*'

'Oh. Are there prisoners down there? How many?'

'Just the one. Poor bastard! I can't see him lasting much longer.'

Kim almost gave herself away as she was swept by a wave of pity and anger. That miserable piece of bread brought back so many terrible memories. Then she saw an opportunity. 'Couldn't we give him something better — when no one's looking?'

Michel put down the ladle he was using to stir the coq au vin and turned to face her. 'Don't even think of going near him, unless you want to end up down there with him. You just mind your own business, girl, like I do. The colonel's in charge. Nothing we can do about it. Here, take these glasses through to the dining room.'

On her return Kim said, 'The colonel will want wine with his meal. Shall I go down to the cellar and fetch something?'

'I wouldn't trust you to fetch a bottle of mineral water!' Michel said. 'And even if I could, I couldn't send you. I don't have the key. The colonel has the only one and he's not likely to give it to you.'

The kitchen door opened and a man in corporal's uniform came in. He was a big brute with a bruiser's face and hands like hams. Kim shuddered at the sight of him. She knew the type only too well. The sort of man Hoffmann would use to apply his less sophisticated forms of persuasion, the sort of work he would not sully his own hands with. The corporal took up the bread and water and left without a word.

The kitchen clock struck twelve.

'Right,' said Michel. 'The colonel will be ready any minute. Take this bread through to the dining room.'

The Lion d'Or was an old hotel and had seen better days. The main rooms were decorated with yellowing prints of country scenes, but on the other side of the baize door, where only staff were permitted, there was no attempt to disguise cracked plaster and chipped tiles. Guests entered from the front door into a gloomy hall, and the dining room led off it to one side and the lounge to the other. There was a staircase leading to the upper floors for them, and another, narrower one for staff went up from the passage leading from the baize door to the back door of the hotel. The door to the cellar was at the end of that passage. Passing through the hallway Kim had her first sight of Hoffmann as he came in from a door leading to the back of the house — a small man, with the cocky, self-aggrandizing walk of a little man determined to assert his authority. With his ash-blonde hair and blue eyes he was the paragon of Aryan breeding. As he passed Kim shrank back against the wall and bobbed a small curtsy. To her alarm, he stopped.

'Well, well. What have we here? A new member of staff?'

Madame appeared from the dining room just in time to explain. 'This is Monique, colonel, the daughter of a distant cousin of mine. She's come to help out.'

'Indeed?' He put his fingers under Kim's chin and forced her to look up at him. It was not hard for her to fake a look of abject terror. 'Well, just make sure you behave yourself and do as you're told — or I might have to reprimand you, and you wouldn't like that, would you?'

'Please, please, monsieur! I'll do my best. I always do!'

He laughed softly. 'Of course. I was only joking with you. I'm sure you're a good girl.'

He turned away and went into the dining room, but Kim had had a chance to study his face. It was a hard face with a straight nose and high cheekbones, and his blue eyes were cold as ice, but there was a softness about the mouth and chin that told a different story. This was a man who liked his pleasures. The thought of what those pleasures might be made her blood run cold.

By mid-afternoon she had made another discovery. Not only did Hoffmann like French cooking, he also enjoyed the French institution of *le midi*, the sacred two hours in the middle of the day which allowed for the consumption and digestion of a large meal. Kim was given the job of waiting on him, and she saw that he sat over his wine and cheese at the end of the meal for twenty minutes or more and then went out into the hotel garden and sat in the shade smoking until two o'clock. His aides, understandably, regarded those two hours as their own and sat in the lounge smoking and drinking beer.

*Two hours when the coast is clear. If only I had the key to the cellar!*

That evening in the Bar de l'Ecluse she asked Gregoire if he knew a locksmith who could be trusted, or a metal worker with the skill to reproduce a key. He promised to make enquiries but he was clearly distracted and there was a glint of excitement in his eyes.

'I can't stay long. We're finally going to get the supply drop I've been asking for. If the chaps back home come through with the stuff we need, we may be on for that big operation I mentioned.'

'That's good,' Kim said, inwardly cursing the fact that his attention was elsewhere just when she needed his help. She would have felt less annoyed if she had any idea what this 'big operation' was going to be, but she knew it was no good asking.

Nonetheless, she decided to put her own plan into practice. Lucien was still alive, that much she had established. But how much longer could he survive? And how long would it be before Hoffmann decided that he had wrung all the information out of him that he was going to get and he might as well dispose of him?

In the kitchen the next day, Michel unwrapped the beef the butcher had just delivered and sniffed it doubtfully.

'Is something wrong with the meat?' she asked, in her usual ingenuous manner.

'Smells a bit off,' Michel said. 'But I'll make boeuf bourguignon. He won't notice anything wrong when I've seasoned it well and put some herbs in.'

'Suppose it makes him ill?'

'Serves him right, gorging himself while other people are starving.' Michel straightened up and reached for a knife. 'He'll be all right. It's not that bad.'

It was one of the perks of working in the kitchen that Michel always made enough for him and Pierre, the sous chef, to have a good meal as well, and sometimes that was extended to Kim. But she noticed that on that day they both avoided the stew and opted for cheese instead. Hoffmann, however, as Michel had predicted, noticed nothing amiss and ate his meal with his usual relish.

As soon as she had served the last course and seen Hoffmann settle back in his chair with a fresh glass of Beaujolais Villages, Kim slipped up the back stairs and made her way to the room he occupied on the first floor. She had been given the job of making his bed and cleaning the room, as well as her tasks in the kitchen, and so had been given a pass key to open the door. In her pocket she had a bar of soap, ready to take an impression of the key, if she could find it. She stood for a moment looking round the room. Where would he keep the key to the cellar? He might, of course, have it in his pocket, but she had seen the keys to other parts of the hotel and they were heavy, old-fashioned things which would have bulged out the pockets of his immaculate uniform. She guessed that instead he would have shut it away somewhere in his room until he needed it.

She checked the wardrobe and under the bed for a strong box of some sort and found nothing. Then she turned to the chest of drawers. The top one opened easily and proved to contain a pair of gold cufflinks and a silver cigarette case, among other personal items. She imagined Hoffmann flaunting them at formal mess dinners. The next drawer down was locked. Kim picked a hairpin out of her hair and set to work.

She had just begun when the door behind her opened and Hoffmann came in.

Kim whirled round to face him, holding her hands clenched behind her back.

'You! What are you doing in here?' he demanded.

'Please, sir, I just came to see if your towels needed changing.'

'Oh yes? They were changed this morning. You did it yourself.'

'Oh, I forgot. I couldn't remember if I had done it or not.'

'So what were you doing by the bureau? That's not where you put towels. What have you got in your hand?'

'Nothing, sir.'

'Liar! Show me your hands. Both of them!'

Kim took her hands from behind her back and held them out. In her palm lay the gold cufflinks.

'So, that's it! You're a light-fingered little whore. You thought you could get away with pilfering my valuables, did you?'

'Please, sir, I'm sorry! It's not for me, it's for my boyfriend back in Clamecy.' She was improvising wildly. 'It's his birthday soon and I can't afford to buy him a present.' She knew she was getting in deeper and deeper and the story would never stand up under interrogation, but it was the best she could think of under the circumstances.

Hoffmann came over and stood very close to her. 'Do you know what happens to girls who steal?'

'Yes, sir.'

'They have to be punished, don't they?'

'Yes, sir.'

'Do you want me to tell Madame that she has brought a thief to work in her hotel?'

'Oh no, sir! Please don't do that. I'll get the sack and I've nowhere else to go.'

'Well, if you don't want me to tell Madame I shall have to punish you myself, won't I?'

Kim gulped with genuine terror. 'How?' she whispered.

'I shall have to think about that. But if I do this, if I don't give you away to your employer, or to the police, you will owe me a debt, won't you?'

'I . . . I . . .'

'Come on. Which shall it be? The sack and prison, or doing something for me to repay your debt?'

'I . . . I'll do whatever you ask me.'

'Good. Not now. Come here to me this evening, when the others are going to bed, and then we'll see. If you do exactly as I tell you, I might forget all about your attempted theft. Do you understand?'

'Yes, sir.'

Kim saw a sudden spasm cross the austere features and an image flashed across her memory of Michel sniffing the beef. It passed in a second and Hoffmann resumed his threatening tone.

'And don't think you can get away with it. If you are not here at ten thirty, I shall come looking for you, and there will be nowhere to hide. Understood?'

'Yes, sir.'

'Very well. Put those back where you found them and go about your duties.'

Kim replaced the cufflinks and as she turned, she saw a second spasm distort the colonel's face. His eyes turned to the commode in the corner of the room. Like many buildings of its age, the Lion d'Or had no indoor sanitation. There was a privy in the yard, but guests were provided with a commode for their convenience, and she knew that the colonel used his because it was her job to empty it. In the midst of her fear, the thought came to her that it was going to be a more unpleasant process than ever tomorrow.

'Ten thirty, don't forget.' The words were ground out between gritted teeth. 'I shall look for you if you're not here. Now get out. Now!'

'Yes, sir. Very good, sir.'

The door closed behind her and she leaned against the wall, trying to suppress a wave of nausea. From inside she heard Hoffmann groaning and retching. *So, that beef really was off!*

Slowly her panic subsided until she was able to think. She straightened up and made her way to the cramped, dark attic room Madame Hulot had allotted her. There she sank down on the bed and put her head in her hands.

*Damn Michel and his rotten beef. That must have been what brought Hoffmann up to his room instead of taking his usual siesta in the garden.*

It was lucky that he had come when he did. A few seconds later and she would have had the drawer open and he might have caught her with the key in her hand. There would have been no way to disguise her real intention in that case. She thanked her lucky stars that she had instinctively grabbed the cufflinks to divert his suspicions.

But that still left the prospect of whatever 'punishment' he had in mind. The nausea returned as she contemplated that. She could barely imagine what it might entail, but she was certain that Hoffmann was a sadist who enjoyed inflicting pain and she had no doubt that his sexual predilections would run on similar lines. Her first instinct was to run. To hide herself somewhere until she could make contact with

Gregoire and ask him to drive her up into the hills. She would be safe from Hoffmann with Xavier and his *maquis*. She knew the German did not have the firepower at his command to take on such a well-entrenched group. But what then? What use could she be to Lucien if she was confined to the *maquis* camp? Her mission would have failed.

She couldn't let that happen.

There was only one way forward.

She must submit to whatever pain and humiliation Hoffmann had in store for her. He could not, she reasoned, do her any permanent damage or wound her in a way that would be obvious to Madame Hulot. That way she could stay in the hotel and look for another chance to get hold of the key. Until she could manage that, there was no way to get Lucien out of that cellar.

Her thoughts were interrupted by the sound of Madame Hulot's voice calling for her from downstairs. She pulled herself to her feet and went to take up her duties.

CHAPTER 14

In a shabby public house, one of the few buildings still standing between Cable Street and the Commercial Road in London's East End, a tall man with reddish hair, wearing sergeant's uniform, made his way to a table where two others were sitting. Both were in their early thirties, one a runt of a man with a narrow, pockmarked face, the other broad and beefy with a broken nose. Both were wearing the rough clothes of a labourer. The man looked down at them with a smile.

'Well, it's like old times! You two still skiving off just like when we were all at school.'

The two men looked up at him and the larger of the two assumed a belligerent expression.

'What you talking about? Who the hell are you?'

'Oh, come on! I know it's a long time but . . .'

The small man let out a gasp as recognition dawned. 'Blimey! It isn't, is it? Foxy Leroux!'

The newcomer grinned. 'Wotcher, Piggy! How you doing?' The accent was pure cockney.

'What . . . ?' The big man looked from one to the other.

'Come on, Beano! Don't you recognize him? It's Foxy, what went missing way back.' He turned his gaze to the man standing above him. 'We heard you stowed away on a ship for America, must be getting on for twenty years ago.'

'You heard right, except I didn't stow away. I went as a kitchen hand,' Foxy told him. 'But I came back, remember?'

'Yeah, 'course you did. I remember now.' Piggy nodded sentimentally. 'You was here for your old mum's funeral.'

'That's right, I was. Now, what are you drinking? I'll get a round in.'

When they were all settled with fresh pints of bitter, the large man asked, 'Where've you been since then? I haven't seen you around.'

'Oh, here and there, round and about. Ducking and diving. You know the form. Last couple of years I've been serving His Majesty.' Foxy plucked the khaki sleeve of his uniform and looked at them. 'I see you've both managed to stay out of it.'

'Got flat feet, haven't I?' said Beano.

'And I've got a weak chest. MO had one listen with his stethy-thing and said, "You're more suitable for the knackers yard than the British Army."'

The man they called Foxy took a long draught of his beer. 'Thinking back to the last time I was round here, for my old mum's funeral, like you said. Have you had any more trouble from that fascist mob what caused the riot?'

'Mosley's lot? Nah, they're all doing time now, ain't they?' said Piggy.

'Not all of them,' said Beano. He lowered his voice. 'There's still a few around who reckon him and his Blackshirts had it right.'

'Round here?' asked Foxy.

'There's a bloke what drinks at the Pig and Whistle who's always carrying on about how we ought to have signed a deal with Hitler when we had the chance. Reckons we'd have been better off siding with the Germans than fighting alongside them lily-livered Frogs.'

'Really, even after everything that's happened?' queried Foxy.

135

'He's got a point, though,' said Piggy. 'There's hundreds of people who'd still be alive, and thousands would still have a roof over their heads if we'd have done that before the Blitz.'

'That bloke who says that, does he have a name?' asked Foxy casually.

'Frank something . . . Hopkins, Hopcock, something like that.'

The conversation veered off into memories of school-days and catching up on mutual acquaintances until Foxy declared that he must be on his way because his forty-eight-hour leave would be up at midnight and he didn't want to be posted AWOL. He finished his beer, said goodbye to his old friends and left.

Next evening, dressed in civilian clothes, Foxy approached a man sitting alone in the saloon bar of the Pig and Whistle pub.

'Mr Hopkins?'

The man looked up. He had a thin face with a sharp nose and narrow eyes. Foxy was reminded of a ferret. 'Who wants to know — and it's Hopkirk, not Hopkins.'

'Sorry. The friend who told me about you wasn't sure of your name. Do you mind if I join you? What can I get you?' The voice had lost its cockney edge.

'I'll have a half of mild and bitter and a whisky chaser, if you're buying.'

'Right. Won't be a minute.'

When he returned with the drinks Hopkirk said, 'Didn't catch your name.'

'It's Fox, Ronald Fox.'

The narrow eyes regarded him suspiciously. 'What can I do for you, Mr Fox?'

'It's a bit tricky . . . not something I can come straight out with. This friend I mentioned told me he'd heard you expressing certain views . . .'

'Views about what?'

'About the war. You don't think we should be fighting it.'

Hopkirk's look sharpened. 'What are you, some kind of government informer?'

'No.' Foxy shook his head reassuringly. 'I was afraid you might think that. Would it help if I told you I was in Brixton with John Beckett?'

'Oh yes?' Suspicion was being replaced by curiosity. 'What were you in for?'

'Nothing serious. A con that went wrong. But I got talking to John and what he said made a lot of sense to me.'

'Makes sense to a lot of people. That's why they put him in jug.'

Foxy took a mouthful of beer. 'So, let me get this straight. You think we'd have been better off signing a peace treaty with Hitler back in 1940?'

'Stands to reason, doesn't it? Look what he's done for Germany. He's made it a country people are proud to stand up for.' Hopkirk leaned forward, jabbing his finger on the table to emphasize his words. 'What we need here is a strong leader like him, someone to get the economy on the right lines and get rid of the Jews who have taken over our newspapers and our cinema and undermined our industry with their sweatshops. If we'd allied ourselves with Hitler, we could have divided Europe between us, instead of wasting our money and our energy, and the lives of our soldiers, in a war we can't win. Never mind the French and the Poles and all that lot. We'd be the Master Race, like Hitler's made the Germans.' He sat back with the air of one who has made an unassailable case.

'Well, you make a very persuasive argument,' his companion said. 'But where's this strong leader to come from? Most of the men at the top of the movement are in prison, like John and Barry Domville, aren't they?'

'Sure, they are. But there are others — people too high up in society for the police to touch. And then there's . . .' He broke off, seemingly aware that he might have said too much. 'Well, he's not even in the country yet, but he's waiting in the wings, waiting for the summons. You'll see. The day is going to come when the ordinary people will see they've been conned. Democracy has had its day. It's time for a new regime.'

Foxy leaned closer. 'And if I wanted to offer my services? Where would I find these people?'

'What makes you think they'd want to talk to you?'

'I've got friends, contacts that might be useful. I've lived in the United States. I know people over there who think the same as you. They could be useful.'

Hopkirk considered him for a moment. Then he said, 'Some of them like to dine at Rules, or the Savoy Grill. You need to find Lord Russell or Lord Hastings or Lord Lyndham. Or there's a bloke called St John Philby — he reckons to be an expert on the Arabs. Any of those could introduce you to the men who run the show. But don't blame me if they tell you to get lost.'

\* \* \*

Kim was in the kitchen, listlessly scrubbing carrots, when she heard the bell that signalled the approach of an ambulance. It screeched to a stop outside the hotel and she heard the front door open and Madame Hulot's voice issuing urgent instructions. Heavy boots thumped into the hallway.

The first glimmers of hope flickered in Kim's mind. Was it possible that they had come for Hoffmann? That beef must have been more off than she had realized.

She dropped her scrubbing brush and ran to the door leading into the main hall, but when she peered round it all she could see were the backs of two men disappearing towards the rear of the house.

They *must* have come for Hoffmann! Who else would be down there? She did not dare linger in the hall. Instead she ran up the back stairs. Her room had a window overlooking the street, and when she got there, she was just in time to see the men loading a blanket-wrapped figure into the ambulance, which then drove off at top speed. Seconds later Hoffmann's staff car followed it, with one of his goons at the wheel.

Kim stepped back from the window and sank onto her bed. Her legs felt weak. She was saved! At least for the time being. Hoffmann would probably recover quite quickly and return to his duties, but by then he might have forgotten what he planned to do to her . . . Suddenly she realized that this was the opportunity she had been waiting for. She took the bar of soap from her washstand and headed back down to the first floor.

Hoffmann's room stank of excrement and vomit. The stench made her gag, but keeping her breath shallow, she went quickly to the chest of drawers. The lock on the second drawer yielded without difficulty and she rummaged through a collection of personal papers and other items, but there was no key. She tried the other drawers, without success. She had already checked the obvious places, like under the bed. Now she lifted the mattress, but it revealed only cobwebs and a soiled handkerchief. She went to the wardrobe and found Hoffmann's dress uniform, but a search of the pockets produced nothing of any use. Frustrated, she stepped back and tried to think.

Then it dawned on her. Hoffmann had been in the cellar when he was taken ill. He would have had the key with him. In that case it was beyond her reach unless . . . Was it possible that in the rush to get him to hospital the door had been left unlocked?

She hurried back down the stairs, but as she reached the passage leading to the back of the house Michel appeared from the kitchen and barred her way.

'Where do you think you're going? These vegetables won't prepare themselves, you know.'

'But—' began Kim.

'Never mind "but". Get on with your work.'

'But if the colonel isn't here for dinner—'

'That's his business. I don't want him coming back and finding there's nothing to eat.'

'That beef—'

'There was nothing wrong with the beef! Now get back in the kitchen.'

Kim had no option but to do as she was told. Michel seemed determined to ignore the fact that his casual attitude to the smell of that meat had had serious consequences. In the meantime, she could think of no reason to go to the cellar door.

Her mind raced in circles as she scrubbed and peeled, until a new thought struck her. If the door had been left open and Hoffmann had taken the key with him there was no way it could be relocked, unless he handed it to one of his men, and so far, she had seen no sign of any of them. She was tortured by the thought that Lucien might realize what had happened and try to stage an escape on his own. He might already be hiding somewhere in the hotel, or even out in the street. She knew enough of Gestapo methods, however, to assume that he would not be capable of going far without help.

At last the vegetables were ready and Michel sent her to set the tables in the dining room. Kim checked he was still in the kitchen, then slipped out into the hall and tiptoed back along the passage. The door to the cellar was locked.

Somehow, in all the confusion of the emergency, someone had remembered to lock it. Kim gritted her teeth. With Hoffmann out of the way she'd had a chance, but now it seemed she was back to square one. The only consolation was the fact that she need no longer fear her appointed encounter with him.

Everything was ready for dinner to be served, but unsurprisingly the dining room remained empty. Kim asked to be excused from further duties, claiming to feel unwell, and permission was grudgingly granted. She fetched her hat and a light coat and slipped out of the back door. She needed to talk the situation over with Gregoire and she prayed that this was not the evening, of all evenings, for his big operation.

She rounded the front of the hotel and stopped dead. The staff car had just drawn up and Hoffmann was getting out, as cocky and self-confident as ever.

CHAPTER 15

Rules, the famous restaurant in London's Covent Garden, was crowded. In spite of the Blitz, in spite of rationing, it still attracted those who were drawn by its comforting Edwardian ambience and its traditional English menu. Renaud Leroux, aka Foxy, aka Roland, immaculate in dinner jacket and black tie, greeted the head waiter like an old friend and was shown to a table. He surveyed the clientele, searching for a familiar face. He had just ordered the steak and oyster pie and taken the first sip of his 1934 Clos du Pape when his eye was caught by three new arrivals. It was several days since he had last seen them, and the circumstances were very different, but he was in no doubt that two of them were men he and Kim had seen visiting Dr Kline's surgery — the men who had been listed in the appointment book as Hast and Lyn and whom M. had identified as Randolph Hastings, Duke of Evesham, and Gerald Weston, Viscount Lyndham — both known sympathizers of the British Union of Fascists.

He waited until they were settled at a table. Then he got up, taking his glass and the bottle with him, and made his way over to them.

'Rufus Foxton, at your service, gentlemen.' The accent was pure east coast, USA. He made a small bow. 'I wonder if I might have few moments of your time.'

The three men looked up suspiciously. Lyndham asked, 'Have we been introduced?'

'No, sir, we have not. But I know you gentlemen by repute, and I believe we have a great deal in common.'

'Such as?'

'I'm sure you are familiar with the German American Bund.'

'I know it was disbanded on the outbreak of war.'

'Officially, yes. But many of its members still hold the same beliefs that were articulated at the rally in Madison Square Gardens in February of 1939.'

'Are you a member?'

'Let's say I sympathize with the sentiments expressed.'

Lyndham and the others exchanged looks and for a moment Foxy thought they were going to refuse him. Then he saw Lyndham's eyes go to the very expensive bottle in his hand. He said, 'I think you had better sit down.'

\* \* \*

Kim scurried through the darkening streets to the Bar de l'Ecluse. There was no sign of Gregoire. Her heart sank, but she ordered a glass of the local wine and a few moments later he came in, looking triumphant. He bought a glass of *fine* and joined her at their usual table in a quiet corner.

'It arrived! Everything we've been asking for. Now we can really start to do some damage.' He stopped at the look on her face. 'What's wrong? What's happened?'

As briefly as possible she told him how Hoffmann had caught her and what the consequences were likely to be. He reached across the table and gripped her wrist.

'You can't go back there! Come with me. I'll drive you up to Xavier's camp. You'll be safe there.'

Kim shook her head miserably. 'I can't. What use can I be to Lucien stuck away up there? I have to go back to the hotel and . . . and take what comes. After all, what can he do to me? Nothing that would alert Madame Hulot.'

'Do you imagine she would take your side against him?' Gregoire snorted derisively. 'Don't fool yourself. You mustn't think of putting yourself through whatever nasty little games he has in mind.'

'It's nothing to what he's putting Lucien through, is it?' she murmured, adding with a sigh, 'I thought for a while I'd got out of it.'

Gregoire raised a questioning eyebrow.

'The chef served up some very dubious beef and it made Hoffmann ill,' she explained. 'That's why he came up to his room. I could tell even when he was bullying me that he was desperate to use the commode. And then, about an hour later, an ambulance arrived and someone was carried off on a stretcher. I thought it must be him, that it was real food poisoning, but just as I left to come here, he came back, looking as right as rain.'

Jacques, the proprietor, appeared at their side. '*Pardon, m'sieu, 'dame.* There is a man at the bar saying he needs to speak to someone about a private matter. He says he has been told to come here by Father Antoine.'

'A private matter?' queried Gregoire. 'Who is he?'

'He didn't give a name but he says he's a doctor at the hospital.'

'At the hospital?' Kim looked at Gregoire in wild surprise.

'Ask him to come over,' he said.

The man who joined them was middle-aged. His face was worn and tense, but there were lines at the corners of his blue eyes that suggested he had once laughed easily.

'My name is Doctor Laval,' he said. 'I am *chef de service* at the hospital. I need to speak in confidence about one of my patients.'

'What makes you think you can do so with us?' Gregoire asked.

'My first thought was to turn to our curé, Father Antoine, for advice. He told me I might find someone here who could help me.'

Gregoire and Kim exchanged looks. They knew that the priest was well aware of what they were planning and could be trusted completely.

'Please, sit down,' said Gregoire. 'You can call me Gregoire, and this is Monique. So, tell us what your problem is and we will do our best to assist, if we can.'

'A young man was brought into the hospital this afternoon by a German officer. He was suffering from cyanide poisoning . . .'

'Cyanide!' Kim met Gregoire's eyes. They both knew what this implied. 'He's dead, then,' she said flatly.

'No, no,' interjected Laval quickly. 'The cyanide had been only partly ingested. The German officer said they had made him vomit, but he insisted that we should pump the young man's stomach. He seems to have swallowed some form of capsule.'

'So, can you treat him?' asked Kim.

'We have given him activated charcoal to neutralize the effects and put him on a drip.' He spread his hands. 'I think he will survive, with care.'

'And he is still in the hospital.'

'At the moment, yes. The officer wanted to take him away as soon as we had completed the stomach pumping, but I told him that if he did that the boy would certainly die. The thing is . . .' Laval stopped uncertainly. 'When I examined him, I found evidence that he has been treated most inhumanely.'

'You mean tortured?' Gregoire said.

'I think so, yes.'

The two agents exchanged looks again. Kim felt a flutter of hope in the pit of her stomach.

Gregoire said, 'How long can you keep him in the hospital?'

The doctor lifted his shoulders. 'A day, maybe two. Normally I would say longer, but if the German officer insists . . .'

'You said he was on life support,' Kim put in. 'So presumably that would mean he couldn't be moved.'

'That is so, but he cannot stay like that for long. Soon he will regain consciousness . . .'

A plan was forming in Kim's mind, even as she spoke.

'Could you keep him sedated, in a state where he would be incapable of responding to questions, for a day or two?' she asked. 'It is important that the German officer believes there would be nothing to gain from removing him . . .'

The doctor's eyes brightened. 'I think I begin to understand. But it could not be longer than that. My colleagues would begin to wonder why it was necessary. But are you thinking there may be a way to remove him, to get him out of the Germans' hands?'

'It will not be easy,' said Gregoire. 'But if you can stall the German officer for a couple of days, we will try to find a way.'

The doctor bit his lip uneasily. 'You appreciate, not all my colleagues think as I do. Many of them say that it is our job as doctors to treat the sick, whatever their nationality, and not to involve ourselves in politics, or military matters.'

'Surely,' Kim said, 'no patriotic Frenchman can believe that we should simply bow down to a foreign occupier. And no humanitarian can accept the sort of treatment this poor young man has endured.'

The doctor shrugged. 'Many of them are afraid of the consequences if they oppose the regime. They cover it up with platitudes, but that is the fact.'

'Then we must thank God for a few like yourself who are prepared to take action,' Gregoire said. 'We are agreed, then? You will keep the young man in your care under sedation for as long as possible and you will resist any attempt by the Germans to take him away. You can communicate with us through Father Antoine, if that becomes necessary.'

'Just a moment.' Kim had been thinking rapidly. 'Could you give me a job, in your hospital?'

'As a nurse, you mean?'

'No. I don't have the skills required to pass as a nurse. I would be unmasked as soon as anyone asked me to change a dressing. A cleaner, perhaps?'

'It is true, we are always short of cleaners.' There was new hope in the doctor's eyes. 'I'm sure that could be arranged. You have papers, of course?'

'Of course.'

'Come to the hospital in the morning and ask at the reception desk if there is a job for you. It shouldn't be a problem.'

'Then that's a start.' Kim spoke decisively. 'I shall be on the spot to help with whatever rescue plan we devise. Where is he? Which ward?'

'He is in a private room, number three,' said Laval. 'It's in a corridor just off the main medical ward. But he is under guard. A German soldier is on duty all the time.'

'Inside the room?' asked Kim.

'No. I told him he must remain outside.'

'That's good.'

Laval got up. 'Then I can leave matters in your hands?'

'Yes.' Gregoire rose also. 'You will never, of course, speak to anyone about this conversation or reveal anything that might lead to us being identified. I'm sure I do not need to emphasize the point.'

'And if you see me in the hospital,' added Kim, 'you must not give any indication that you recognize me.'

'Of course, you may trust me on this.' Laval held out his hand. 'I shall pray for the success of your plan.'

When the doctor had left Kim and Gregoire looked at each other. 'Cyanide,' she said softly.

'What I don't understand is, if he had come to the point where he was prepared to do that, why didn't he bite the thing instead of swallowing it?' responded Gregoire.

They were both well aware of the properties of the small yellow capsules each agent was given before he or she left on a mission. Bitten, death would be painful but almost instantaneous. If swallowed, it would take some hours for the capsule to dissolve, though in the end the result would be the same.

'Perhaps he just couldn't face it,' suggested Kim. She paused, a thought occurring to her. 'I'm surprised he still had it. The Gestapo are well aware of the possibility and they usually carry out a thorough search.'

'Presumably Hoffmann recognized the symptoms in time to get him to hospital. But why bother? Why not just let him die and move on?'

'Because then Lucien would have won,' guessed Kim. 'Hoffmann hadn't got the information he was looking for, and he's a man who can't bear to admit defeat.'

'Perhaps. Anyway, whatever the reasons behind it, we now have a chance to get Lucien out. We need to work out how.'

Kim suddenly looked up at the clock above the bar. 'It's gone ten o'clock. Hoffmann said if I didn't show up at ten thirty, he'd send men to look for me.'

'There's no need for you to go back to the hotel now,' said Gregoire. 'Things have changed.'

'They have indeed, thank God! But it's like I said, he can't bear to be beaten. If I'm not there at precisely 10.30, I wouldn't put it past him to set up roadblocks on all the roads out of town and start a house-to-house search.'

'It that case, we had better move.' Gregoire got up and threw down some coins from his pocket to pay for their drinks. 'Come on, I'll drive you up to Xavier's camp. We can talk on the way.'

They were almost past the last houses on the road that led up into the hills when Kim jerked forward in her seat, feeling her stomach clench. Ahead of them a temporary barrier had been erected across the road, manned by a small group of German soldiers.

'They can't be looking for you yet,' said Gregoire.

'Unless Hoffmann's guessed I'm not going to show up and taken measures in advance.'

'We'll just have to brazen it out. Got your papers?'

'Yes, of course.'

Gregoire stopped the car at the barrier and wound down the window. 'Good evening, sergeant. Who are you looking for this time? Poachers? Black marketeers?'

'Papers,' was the only response.

They both handed over their documents and the sergeant scrutinized them by the light of a torch. Then he shone it into the car, looking first at Gregoire, then at Kim.

'Where are you going at this time of night?'

'Home,' said Gregoire. 'You can see from the address on my papers, I live just up the hill.'

'Huh,' grunted the sergeant. 'And you, mademoiselle? According to this, you live in Clamecy.'

'I'm working at the hotel in town, the Lion d'Or,' Kim told him.

'So what are you doing heading this way?'

Gregoire gave a remarkably genuine-sounding chuckle. 'Oh, come on, sergeant! You know how these things happen. It's taken me three whole evenings to persuade this lovely girl to come back to my place for the night. Don't be a killjoy.'

The sergeant looked from his face to Kim's for a long moment. Then he stepped back and waved them on.

Neither of them spoke until they had put three bends in the road between them and the barrier. Then Kim said, 'I've just thought. I left a bag of stuff at your cottage. I shall need some of the things in it for tomorrow.'

'OK. We can call in and pick them up. It's on the way.'

The cottage, when they reached it, seemed a haven of safety. The stove was banked down but still warm, and in the flickering light of a candle Gregoire's pictures on the wall almost seemed to come to life. Kim looked around the room where she had slept on her first night with some regret. It was late and it had been a roller-coaster of a day. The thought of curling up on the bed was very appealing.

'Why don't we stay here for the night?' she suggested. 'It'll be closer for me to get back to the hospital tomorrow.'

Gregoire shook his head. 'That German sergeant took a good look at you. If Hoffmann sends out an alert when he realizes you're not going to keep the appointment he may remember this address and put two and two together. We can't risk it.'

'No,' agreed Kim wearily. 'You're right. Let's go.'

The headlights, masked to comply with blackout regulations, gave only a narrow slit of light as they wound round the bends in the narrow road, but Gregoire drove with the confidence of one who had followed that route many times. After a while, they came out of the trees and the road opened onto wide views of the valley they had left. Gregoire stopped the car and pointed.

'Look!'

Way below them they saw lights moving through the trees — cars heading upwards. Then the lead vehicle stopped.

'Isn't that where your cottage is?' asked Kim, with a chill at her heart.

'What did I tell you?' he responded.

'Your cover's blown,' she said.

'Not necessarily,' he said. 'I might be able to bluff it out, say that you picked me up in the bar and talked me into taking you home with me.'

'So how would you explain the fact that we're not there now, tucked up in bed together?'

'Good point.' Gregoire sighed. 'I suppose I'll have to abandon the cottage. But that may not be such a bad thing, as it happens. I really need to base myself up here with Xavier and his lot, now things are hotting up.'

'But your paintings . . .' said Kim.

'Yes, I'll be sorry to lose some of those, but I'd never have been able to take them with me, would I? My easel and paints are in the car, so at least I've still got them.' He started the car and drove on.

At the beginning of the track leading to the camp they were stopped, as before, by two *maquis* sentries. It was reassuring to know that Xavier was running a tight ship where security was concerned. He was waiting for them when they drove into the clearing, where the last embers of the campfire were still smouldering. Gregoire explained their unexpected arrival as briefly as possible, and Xavier offered Kim a hand like the paw of a grizzly bear.

'You are welcome to stay as long as you need.'

She thanked him, but told him she would be gone again in the morning.

She was offered food and drink, and when she declined them, she was shown a small tent, where a sleeping bag was laid out. She wondered briefly whose bed she was taking, but any sense of guilt was rapidly extinguished by sleep.

* * *

Kim woke to the smell of fresh bread and crawled to open the tent flap. A small man was raking leaf-wrapped packages out from the embers of the fire. The bread she had smelled was inside.

'I'm a baker by trade. Jules.' The man held out his hand. 'This is thanks to a local farmer who supplies the *maquis* with flour.'

Over a breakfast of bitter ersatz coffee and fresh bread she and Gregoire went over their plans.

'Are you sure you want to do this?' he asked again. 'If Hoffmann comes in person to try and interrogate Lucien, he might recognize you.'

'He won't,' said Kim. 'I can promise you that. And once I'm in there I should be able to make contact with Lucien once he regains consciousness and prepare him for what we intend to do.'

'And what exactly do you have in mind?'

'According to Laval most of the hospital staff are collaborators, or at any rate unwilling to risk any conflict with the Germans. So if we try to remove Lucien without authority, they might be obstructive.' She chewed her lip. 'What we really need is German uniforms.'

He smiled grimly. 'As it happens, I can help there. Some of the *maquis* ambushed a German patrol that was getting a bit too close for comfort. As a result, we have a sergeant's uniform and a couple of *Obergefreite* — corporals.'

She met his eyes. 'What happened to the men?'

He shrugged and looked away. 'The *maquis* don't have any facilities for keeping prisoners.'

Kim nodded and said no more. This was war, after all, just as much as on the front line.

'Next question,' she pursued. 'Do we have anyone who speaks good German?'

'Me,' he said. 'My mother is German — a Jewess. My father met her on a walking holiday in Bavaria. Her family opposed the marriage but they went ahead anyway. Now she doesn't know what has happened to her parents, or any of her relatives.'

'Dear God!' muttered Kim. 'That's tragic.'

'Not as tragic as it would have been for her if she hadn't met my father. Anyway, she wanted me to be able to speak her native language, so I grew up speaking English to him and German to her. French came later when I went to study in Paris. I should be able to put on a convincing performance.'

'Brilliant! Next question: Is there any chance of getting hold of an ambulance?'

'That's going to be more difficult,' Gregoire admitted. 'But these chaps here have a lot of local contacts and the people of the Morvan have no reason to like the Boche. They might be able to persuade the ambulance drivers for the hospital in Montsauche to lend theirs to us.'

'If we can fix that,' said Kim, 'I think we can get him out. The timing is going to be crucial. You have to get there as soon as Laval is ready to discharge him but before Hoffmann's men arrive.'

'How are we going to communicate? We can't meet at the bar any longer.'

'Dead letter drop?' she suggested. 'Claudette could pick up a message and bring it to you.'

'Where?'

'Where would you suggest?'

'In St Michel's,' he said. 'Third row of pews from the back, on the left-hand side. Leave a message at the back of the first missal. I'll tell her to make regular checks.'

'That will be fine as a day-to-day expedient,' Kim agreed. 'Claudette can leave messages for me to let me know if you've been able to arrange the ambulance. But we shall have to have a more immediate form of contact when it comes to picking the right moment for you to arrive.'

'Good point,' he said. 'We need a visual signal of some kind.'

Kim thought hard. 'You can see the roof of the hospital from the church. I noticed it when I went to visit Father Antoine. I'll have to find a way of displaying a sign of some sort. We'll have to leave it until I can make a recce. When I work it out, I'll leave a message for Claudette to pick up. She'll need to make pretty frequent visits. As you say, the timing is going to be crucial.'

'Agreed,' he said. 'So, is it time we got moving?'

'Give me five minutes,' she responded.

Kim retrieved her bag from the tent and found a place a short distance from the camp where she was concealed by the trees. A few minutes later the men of the *maquis* — who were being instructed on how to clean and load the new rifles they had been sent — looked up and were surprised by the apparition of a woman in a plain blue dress, whose blonde hair was visible from the edges of a tightly tied headscarf and whose eyes were partially hidden by heavy-rimmed glasses. Even Gregoire looked slightly alarmed when she appeared in front of him. Then his face relaxed into a grin.

'I see now why you said Hoffmann wouldn't recognize you. Ready?'

'Yes, let's go.'

## CHAPTER 16

Half an hour later Kim presented herself at the reception desk of the hospital.

'Good morning. I've been told that you are looking for cleaners?'

The woman behind the desk scarcely looked up from her paperwork. 'Cleaners? Yes. You need to speak to the housekeeping manager. Go down that corridor. You'll find him in the basement.'

By mid-morning, armed with a broom and a bucket containing various cloths and bottles, Kim was sweeping the floor of the main medical ward. As she had expected, no one took much notice of a woman performing such menial work, and she was able to make her way slowly to the corridor leading off the ward. As she began to sweep it, she saw a German soldier leaning against the wall outside one of the rooms. Not surprisingly, he looked bored. She swept industriously, her eyes lowered, until she reached his feet.

'*Pardon, m'sieu,*' she mumbled and he reluctantly shifted his position so she could clean where he stood.

Kim finished the floor of the corridor and opened the door to the side room next to the one where Lucien was. It was empty and she made a point of clattering her bucket and banging about with her broom inside. Then she headed back to the door of Room 3.

'*Nein!*' The guard thrust an arm across the door. 'No entry,' he added in German.

Kim blinked at him uncomprehendingly and moved to touch the door handle.

'*Nein!*' he repeated.

Kim indicated her cleaning equipment. 'The room must be cleaned,' she said in French. 'Otherwise, *pouffe!*' She sagged her head dramatically to one side to suggest the death of the occupant.

He clearly did not understand French, but her mime was sufficient to convey her meaning. She could see him weighing up the consequences of disobeying orders or allowing a valuable prisoner to die on his watch. In the end he apparently concluded that any harm she might do if allowed in was outweighed by the risk to his prisoner if she was kept out.

He jerked his head to the door. '*In Ordnung. Aber schnell!*'

Kim carried her bucket and mop into the room and closed the door softly behind her. The man on the bed was lying very still. An oxygen mask covered most of his face and he had a drip in his arm. She clattered her equipment as if she was cleaning energetically but he did not stir. She worked her way over to the bed. In spite of the mask, the evidence of repeated beatings was clear to see in his bruised and swollen eyes. His hands were bandaged and she thought she knew why. What damage was concealed under the sheet she could only guess, but the mere thought of it set off a visceral terror that she had to fight to overcome.

She knelt down by the bed as if reaching to clean underneath it. Bringing her lips close to the young prisoner's ear she whispered in English, 'Lucien? If you can hear me, don't try to speak. Just blink twice.'

For a few seconds there was no response, then the bruised lids lifted and closed, lifted again and closed.

Kim felt a surge of relief. 'My name is Kim,' she whispered. 'We are going to get you out, but you must be patient for another day or two. Above all, you must not give any sign that you can hear or respond to questions. You must keep still and quiet. Do you understand?'

Once again, the heavy lids lifted and fell twice. Kim laid her hand on his arm and pressed it gently. '*Courage, mon brave!*'

She mopped the rest of the floor and left the room.

'*Merci, m'sieu,*' she mumbled, and the guard responded with a grunt and turned to watch a pretty nurse at the other end of the corridor.

Kim's next objective was to find some way of signalling to Gregoire when the moment came.

She carried her bucket and mop up the stairs. The hospital had three floors. On the ground floor there was an emergency department and the administrative offices. The wards and the operating theatre were on the first floor, but along the top corridor she found a series of doors that must lead to smaller rooms.

She opened the first one she came to and peered in, ready to present her cleaning equipment if anyone queried her presence. The room was empty but it was clearly a bedroom. A nurse's cape hung on the back of the door and there was a hairbrush and other toiletries on the small dressing table.

*These must be nurses' accommodations.*

Kim worked her way along the passage, glancing into each room. About halfway down, she found one that appeared to be unoccupied. She crossed quickly to the window and peered out. Across the sun-drenched rooftops, she could see the church tower. She felt a surge of relief.

It occurred to her for the first time that she did not have anywhere to sleep that night. She wondered if she might be able to kill two birds with one stone.

She went back to the manager who had given her the job.

'Forgive me, m'sieur. I notice that there is an empty room on the top corridor. Is there any chance I could stay there?'

He frowned. 'Stay? Where are you living at the moment?'

'You saw my papers. My home is in Clamecy — well, it was but . . .' Kim sniffed back tears. 'I had to leave. There was a man — he said he loved me, but he hurt me. I had to get away. I'm so grateful to you for giving me a job, but I don't know where I'm going to sleep tonight.' She gazed up at him appealingly.

He seemed to hesitate, but then his expression softened. 'Well, it's highly irregular but the room isn't being used at the moment. You can stay there for the time being, but you'll have to make permanent arrangements once you are settled. Will that do?'

Kim clasped her hands. 'Oh, thank you! Thank you! I'll look for somewhere else. It will only be for a night or two, I promise.'

She immediately moved the few possessions she had brought with her into the room.

That evening, when her working day was over, Kim walked up to the church. In her pocket was an already encoded note, which would read when decoded, *Contact made*. That was all she could say for the present.

She slipped into the church. The weather was warm and the walk up the hill had made her sweat. The interior of the church was delightfully cool and there was a smell of incense and old books. She slipped into the third pew on the left and sat for a moment with her head bowed. She had ceased to believe in any organized religion years ago, and in any case, this would not have been her church, but she still found the atmosphere comforting. She took a missal from the rack on the back of the pew in front of her and slipped her note inside the back cover. She had harboured a slight hope that there might already be a message from Gregoire hidden inside, but there had been little time for him to arrange anything, so she was not surprised that there wasn't one.

As she reached the road leading back down to the town, she heard hoof beats behind her and turned back to see Claudette ride into the churchyard. She tethered her mount to the bough of a tree and went into the church. Kim waited, leaning on the gate into the churchyard, knowing Claudette would have to remain inside long enough to light a candle or offer a prayer to give credence to her visit. A few minutes later she came out and rode away. Soon, Kim knew, the note would be deposited in the dead letter box she had arranged with Gregoire, for him to pick up. She glanced around her. The churchyard was deserted so she went back and checked inside the missal, but there was still no message from Gregoire. Nevertheless, she walked back to the hospital feeling optimistic. The systems they had set up were working. If Gregoire could do his part there was a chance that, against all the odds, they might succeed.

She woke the next morning with the same feeling, and after breakfast in the staff canteen she collected her mop and bucket and set off for the medical ward. She set about her duties conscientiously. Whatever her ulterior motives, they were important for the well-being of the patients and they kept her cover intact. She had worked her way almost to the corridor leading to the private rooms when she heard raised voices and the door to Room 3 opened.

'Colonel, I must insist!' It was Dr Laval's voice. 'The young man is still in a deep coma. If you remove him now, he may never recover.'

'And how much longer is this going to go on?' She could hear the frustration in Hoffmann's tone.

'A day, two days. I cannot give you a definite—'

'I'll give you until tomorrow, midday,' Hoffmann interrupted. 'If his condition has not changed by then I am taking him away, whatever you say. Understood?'

'Very well,' said Laval, 'if you insist. But I cannot answer for the consequences.'

'That is my responsibility, not yours. Tomorrow midday. I shall be back then.'

Kim ducked her head and scrubbed at a mark on the floor as the colonel stalked past, but she could tell out if the corner of her eye that he had not even noticed her presence. Her mood of optimism evaporated. Unless Gregoire could come up with an ambulance before tomorrow midday their plans would come to nothing.

She waited until Laval had left the ward, then pushed her bucket along the corridor. She cleaned the first room and moved on. She was glad to see that the same man was on guard outside Lucien's room and he accepted her presence as a matter of routine. Inside, she went to kneel by the bed as before.

'Lucien? It's me, Kim.' His eyes opened more rapidly than before and he seemed to take her in for the first time. She whispered, 'You're doing brilliantly. Just keep up the pretence that you can't hear what's being said. We're working to get you out.'

His lips moved, framing the word *tomorrow*.

'I know,' she said. 'I heard what Hoffmann said. We'll find a way, before he comes for you.'

He looked at her and the expression of trust in his eyes almost reduced her to tears. She pressed his arm. 'I'll be back, when I can. Stay strong.'

In her lunch hour Kim headed back up to the church, carrying a message telling Gregoire how urgent their mission had become. To her delight, there was a message from him already there at the back of the missal. The code they used was so familiar to her that it took only minutes to decipher it.

*Ambulance arranged. I'll be painting in the churchyard all day tomorrow. What's the signal?*

She wrote, *White sheet from central top-floor window. Seen from tower. Must be before midday.*

Later, she found her way to Dr Laval's office.

He looked up, irritated, as she came in with her bucket. 'Not now! You can clean later. I'm busy.'

Kim removed her heavy glasses. 'It's Monique, Dr Laval. We met at the Bar de l'Ecluse.'

He stared at her. '*Mon dieu!* I would never have recognized—'

She cut him short. 'Tomorrow morning an ambulance and some German soldiers will come to collect your patient—'

'I know!' he exclaimed petulantly. 'Hoffmann is insisting. I can't stall him any longer.'

'No! You don't understand.' Kim moved closer to the desk and lowered her voice. 'These will not be Hoffmann's men. I need you to be ready to discharge the patient into their care. Will you do that?'

He gazed at her in amazement. 'Of course. I will not ask how you are going to accomplish the feat. What time?'

'It must be before midday.'

He nodded. 'I usually do my ward round at about ten. I will examine the young man then and sign the discharge papers. After that, I will try to find reasons to be in the vicinity, in case there should be any queries.'

'Excellent!' Kim smiled at him. 'I begin to believe that, due to your courage in contacting us, we may yet save this poor boy's life.'

'God willing!' He returned her smile.

Before her shift ended Kim found reasons to clean the medical ward again. A different guard was on duty but he was busy trying to attract the attention of one of the prettier nurses and took no notice when Kim carried her bucket into Lucien's room. She remembered Roland saying that people simply did not notice waiters or domestic servants. Inside, she knelt as usual by the bed, her mop in her hand.

'Tomorrow, men in German uniform will come for you. They will not be Hoffmann's men. Do not resist. Remain silent. All will be well.'

She touched his hand and to her relief he blinked twice. Sure that she had done all that she could do for the time being, she collected her bucket and left the room.

That night Kim slept badly. She tossed and turned on the narrow bed, going over in her mind all the things that might go wrong with their plan. Suppose Hoffmann got impatient and sent his men earlier than agreed. Would Laval be able to get rid of them until her own people arrived? Suppose the ambulance refused to start or broke down. Would Gregoire be able to see her signal? Was it possible to reach the top of the church tower? The door might be locked, though Father Antoine would have a key — but what if he was out on a pastoral visit and did not return in time . . . Try as she might to shut her thoughts down and relax it was all but impossible.

At last the distant church bells struck five and she got up. The churning in her stomach stopped her eating anything for breakfast. Well before ten she was busy cleaning the medical ward. She was tempted to go into Lucien's room but there was a different guard there who looked as if he was taking his duties seriously. He interrogated the nurse who came to carry out routine checks before letting her pass. Kim decided not to risk arousing his suspicions by insisting on being allowed in.

At ten o'clock Laval arrived in the ward. He exchanged a few words with the sister in charge and then went into Lucien's room. A few minutes later he came out and Kim heard him say to the sister, 'This patient is being discharged today. Soldiers will come for him soon.'

'Discharged?' Kim heard the distress in the sister's voice. 'Can't we keep him a bit longer?'

'Impossible, I'm afraid,' said Laval curtly. 'Please see that the process is completed as smoothly as possible.'

Kim raced upstairs to her room and dragged a sheet off the bed. She opened the window and draped the sheet over the sill. To anyone else it would look as if she was simply airing it. Looking up, she was glad to confirm that she could see the church tower clearly. She wondered if Gregoire was already there, watching for her signal. She could only pray he was.

Then, to her relief, a light winked from the tower, sunlight reflected from a mirror. The dots and dashes of the Morse code were second nature to her and she read ROGER, the universal signal meaning message received and understood.

The minutes passed and Kim's tension increased. She had already worked her way to the end of the corridor and cleaned everything twice, and she was afraid that soon someone would notice and send her away. As the clock ticked round, she strained her ears for the sound of boots on the tiled floors, but when at last it came her stomach turned over. Was it Gregoire? Or was it Hoffmann, arriving early?

Three uniformed soldiers entered the ward, followed by two men dressed as ambulance men. Kim dared not stare too obviously, but one thing was certain — none of them was Hoffmann.

'You have a patient for us to collect?' The voice was Gregoire's but the German-accented French was perfect for the character he had assumed.

'Yes. This way.' Kim could hear the barely concealed anger and contempt in the sister's voice and wished she could let her into the secret.

'What is this?' the guard demanded in German. 'Who are you?'

'We have been sent by Colonel Hoffmann to collect the prisoner,' Gregoire replied in the same language.

'The colonel told me he would be coming in person.'

'He has been unavoidably detained. He sent me instead. Now, get out of my way. That's an order.'

'My orders were to hand the prisoner over to him and no one else. I cannot let you pass.'

'Do you want me to tell my men to detain you and hand you over to the military police for refusing to obey an order from a senior officer?'

'I already have my orders . . .'

Voices were getting louder and Kim was afraid it would raise the alarm in the main ward. She glanced at the clock. It was ten minutes to noon.

Without further thought she stepped up behind the guard and brought the edge of her hand down sharply on the side of his neck. It was a technique she had been taught in her training at the SOE school in Arisaig. The guard slumped, unconscious, into Gregoire's arms.

'Good work,' he hissed.

Between him and the two *maquis* he had brought with him, they half carried, half dragged the unconscious

German into Room 3. The two ambulance men followed. Kim remained outside, continuing to mop the already pristine floor. Looking back towards the main ward she was relieved to see that none of the nurses appeared to have noticed the fracas in the corridor.

A few moments later Gregoire and the others came out, the two ambulance men carrying Lucien on a stretcher.

Kim watched them walk through the ward and then hastily picked up her bucket and followed them into the main reception area. A rather shabby ambulance was waiting outside and she held her breath while the stretcher was loaded into it. Even now Hoffmann could arrive with his men or the guard might regain consciousness and try to intervene. It was not until the ambulance had driven out of the gates and turned the corner that she began to breathe again.

They were not home and clear yet, she reminded herself. When Hoffmann did arrive and discovered that his prisoner had been spirited away there would be hell to pay. Kim was half tempted to stay and enjoy the spectacle of his fury, but she had tasks of her own to carry out.

She went back to her room and retrieved the sheet. Then she removed her blonde wig and changed her dress and packed her few belongings into her bag.

If anyone noticed the dark-haired young woman leaving the hospital, no one queried her. She wondered briefly if anyone would ever connect the cleaner who appeared and disappeared so mysteriously with the missing patient, but she thought it unlikely.

At the church she found a new message.

*Go to Father Antoine. He will bring you to a place where we can meet.*

That was a relief. She had been wondering how she was going to get back to the *maquis* camp by herself.

She found the priest, as before, tending the vegetables in his garden. He greeted her warmly.

'I hope everything has gone according to plan? I have been praying for our success.'

For the first time Kim allowed herself a grin of triumph. 'Thank you for your prayers, Father. So far, I believe, they have been answered.'

'So, Gregoire has asked me to drive you to a rendezvous. Are you ready to go?'

'Yes, but there is one thing I must do. I need to give a message to Philippe.'

'We can call at the château on the way.'

'That would be perfect.'

As they drove Kim watched the road for any sign of unusual activity. It was after midday and she quite expected to see roadblocks being set up, but so far everything was normal.

Philippe was in the garden, cutting stems of gladioli.

'Monique!' he said. 'I've been wondering if you were still with us. It's good to see you. How are your plans getting on?'

'Very well.' Again she found herself grinning. 'I want you to transmit this message as soon as possible on the emergency frequency.' She had encoded the message the previous night, in the hope that everything went according to plan. It read, *Mission accomplished. Urgent exfiltration required*, and gave the coordinates of the dropping zone.

Philippe took it. 'I was just going up to the church with these, so I'll send it straight away.'

She thanked him and said goodbye, with the passing thought that this would probably be the last time they would meet.

CHAPTER 17

Gregoire was waiting at the appointed spot. Father Antoine wished them Godspeed and left with their fervent expressions of thanks, and Kim got into the car.

'Did everything go all right?' she asked. 'You got to the camp OK?'

'Yes, no problem. I've left Lucien in the care of our medic. The poor kid's still very weak.'

'No doubt about that,' said Kim. 'But provided Baker Street can organize a flight we should have him in an English hospital very soon. I've given Philippe a message to send, but I'm not clear how we will get the answer.'

'No problem,' said Gregoire. 'He and Claudette have got a system in place. If there's something urgent, he gets Father Antoine to fly the banner for the appropriate saint's day from the church tower. Fortunately, there seems to be one for every day of the year.' He turned the car into the forest track leading to the camp. 'Claudette will see it when she takes her regular ride and she will go down to the château. There's a bridle path running right alongside the boundary, and what could be more natural than for her to pause and pass the time of day with the gardener. He will probably give her something — a flower for her buttonhole or a carrot for the horse — and with it will be the answer to your message.' He paused to navigate one of the deeper potholes. 'She will then deliver it to the letter box we've set up, and I will check two or three times a day until we get it. Philippe will have sent yours by now, so provided Baker Street pull their fingers out we might have an answer by tomorrow morning — tomorrow evening, latest.'

'The moon is just past full and the weather seems to be set fair, so conditions are good for a landing, provided there's an aircraft available,' Kim said eagerly. 'It's possible the pickup could happen as early as tomorrow night.'

As they approached the camp a new thought struck her. 'Tell me something. How did you get hold of the ambulance?'

'Ah, that turned out to be easier than expected. I underestimated the amount of support there is in the local area for the *maquis*. Not long ago the Boche demanded that every farmer should hand over most of his cattle to be transported to Germany. They loaded the beasts into trucks, but Xavier and his men ambushed the convoy and released the cattle. It took some time for each farmer to identify and round up his own animals, but the locals have never forgotten the debt they owe. So when he went down to the local hospital and explained why we needed an ambulance, the two drivers not only offered the vehicle but insisted on coming with us.'

'So those two I saw were the genuine article, not *maquis* dressed up?'

'Absolutely. They said they didn't trust anyone else to do the job properly.' Gregoire laughed. 'But I'm sorry we cut it so fine. At the last moment they had an emergency call-out to a woman in labour and it took an extra half hour to deal with it.'

Another question occurred to her. 'How did they know it was time to go?'

'Same way I responded to your signal. I had watchers posted on three strategic hilltops. Good job it was a sunny day!'

The road wound up into the hills and before long they drove into the camp where the *maquis* had already erected a hut to serve as a temporary hospital and dressing station, and a local doctor, Dr Gerard, had agreed to make regular visits. Lucien had been taken there. When Gerard heard Gregoire and Kim outside he came out to join them. He was past middle age, but like most of his profession he had been forced to take on a massively increased workload as younger men were called up and were killed or taken prisoner. In spite of that, he had not hesitated to take on the dangerous job of ministering to sick and wounded *maquis*. His face normally showed the signs of strain, but now his expression was grim.

'*Mon dieu!* I knew these Germans were ruthless, but I would never have believed any human being could behave with such savagery. It's a miracle that boy is still alive. But I have made him as comfortable as possible.'

'What did they do to him?' asked Gregoire, but Kim had no wish to listen to a recital of the same brutality she herself had once suffered.

'Can I speak to him?' she asked.

'Yes. He is conscious. But don't tire him.'

She went into the hut. As it happened Lucien was the only patient at that moment. He was lying on a makeshift bed, propped up on several sacks stuffed with bracken. Kim crouched down beside him.

'Lucien, I told you we were going to get you out, didn't I?'

He frowned at her. 'I'm sorry . . . I don't know . . .'

'Oh, of course. I'm sorry. I'd forgotten I look different now. Think of me with fair hair and a bucket.'

'You! You were the cleaner?'

'Yes, that's right. Except that that was just a cover, to get to you.'

'Oh, now I understand!' His voice was weak and husky but there were the beginnings of a tremulous joy in it. 'But you put yourself in so much danger just for me.'

'Not nearly as much as you were in,' she said. 'The important thing is, you're free and soon a plane will come and pick us up. You'll be back home before you know it.'

He shook his head with a look of wonder. 'It's hard to believe.'

'But it's true.' Kim squeezed his fingers gently. 'You'll see.'

Gregoire came in and pulled a stool across to sit on the other side of the bed. 'How are you feeling?'

'A hell of a lot better than I did when I woke up this morning,' said Lucien. 'But I don't know how to say thank you for all the risks you took.'

'There's no need,' Gregoire assured him. 'But I should like to ask you one thing. When you finally came to the point that you couldn't take any more and decided to finish it, why didn't you bite the capsule instead of swallowing it.'

Lucien looked momentarily confused. 'Oh, that was an accident. I never intended to . . . The capsule was hidden inside a false tooth. That's how the men who searched me missed it. One of Hoffmann's thugs punched me on the jaw and broke the tooth. I'd swallowed the thing before I could stop myself. If Hoffmann hadn't realized what I'd done and rushed me off to the hospital I'd have been a goner.'

Kim sat back on her haunches. 'That is incredible! If that hadn't happened, I don't think we'd ever have got you out of that cellar, so by that thug punching you, he actually brought about the conditions for your release!'

Gregoire chuckled and Lucien managed a brief laugh. 'God works in mysterious ways,' said Gregoire.

'I'm sure Father Antoine would agree,' said Kim.

The doctor came in. 'I think this young man needs to rest now. I've given him a sedative. You can talk to him again when he wakes.'

Later in the afternoon Kim saw Gregoire in urgent conversation with Xavier. Both men looked as if they were discussing something urgent and potentially problematic.

'We've run into a possible difficulty. You remember that big operation I've been talking about?' asked Gregoire when he came to join her.

'Of course.'

'Xavier has just had information that it has to be tomorrow night.'

'But it's possible that the plane to pick me and Lucien up could come tomorrow night,' said Kim in alarm. 'We shall need Xavier's men to set the signal fires. Couldn't your operation wait another day?'

'Unfortunately not,' said Gregoire, shaking his head. 'Let me explain. The Boche are using the Canal du Nivernais to ship bulk goods like coal from the north. They need it to keep the power stations operating and the military machine running. Our plan is to blow up one of the locks just below Corbigny. Xavier's men have been watching traffic on the canal, and they have just brought the information that a convoy of coal barges is heading south and by tomorrow evening it will be waiting for the lock to be opened next morning. If we can blow the lock, that will not only disrupt traffic until it's repaired but we have a good chance of destroying some of the barges, or at least driving them aground as the water floods out. The lock-keeper has already been alerted and told to get his family out of the way for one night. It's too late to start changing the plans now.'

'But what about my flight?' asked Kim. 'It's probably too late to change that too.'

'It's quite likely that it won't happen until the following night,' Gregoire pointed out. 'It's a very tight schedule to get it organized for tomorrow. But if it does come, I'll arrange with Xavier to leave some of his men with you. The fires can be prepared during the day and it will only need six or eight men to light them when the moment comes and help you get Lucien on board.' He looked at her apologetically. 'It's not ideal, I know, and I would wish to be with you to see you safely away. But there's no way round it, I'm afraid.'

There was nothing more to be said, but for the rest of the day Kim wandered round the camp, feeling oddly deflated. After the tensions of the last few days it was strange not to have anything to occupy her mind. As the sun began to drop behind the trees she took a bowl of soup, specially prepared by the camp cook, into the hut. She found Lucien awake and struggling to sit up. She rearranged the sacks of bracken to support him and spooned some of the soup into his mouth.

'Oh, that's good!' he murmured. 'I can't remember when I last tasted proper food.'

She waited until he had finished the soup and some well-watered wine and then said, 'Do you feel able to talk? There are some questions I'd like to ask.'

He nodded. 'I'll tell you whatever I can.'

'Just a minute, then. I'll call Gregoire.'

When they were seated either side of the bed Kim said, 'OK. First question: What is *Blitzschlag*?'

Lucien closed his eyes and she saw a look of despair on his face. 'If I knew that, I'd have told Hoffmann days ago and spared myself . . . a lot of pain.'

'You don't know what *Blitzschlag* means?' asked Gregoire, in a tone of disbelief.

'But that was the one word you transmitted before the Boche arrested you,' said Kim.

'I know, I know.' Lucien shook his head as if to clear it. 'It means "lightning strike", but that's all I can tell you.'

'So where did you hear it?' asked Kim. 'Who said it to you? Or was it written somewhere?'

'It's what Hoffmann kept asking me, over and over again. *What is Blitzschlag? Who told you about it? Who have you told?*'

'OK,' said Kim gently. 'I know this is hard, but remember you're safe from him now. No one is going to hurt you. But we do need to find out what is so important to the Germans about that one word.'

Lucien hitched himself higher on his pillows and swallowed a gulp of wine.

'OK. I'll start at the beginning. I'd been at Beaulieu for several weeks, done all the tests, jumped through all the hoops, but I still wasn't being sent to France and I didn't know why. I suspected it was something Dr Kline had written

169

in my records. I never felt we got on all that well. One night, a couple of weeks ago, it was very hot and I couldn't sleep so I decided to have a wander round the grounds.

'I was looking back at the house and I saw the windows to all the offices, and I suddenly got this mad idea of breaking into Kline's and searching his filing cabinet for my file to see what he'd written about me. It was well after midnight so I was pretty sure there wouldn't be anyone about.' He shrugged faintly.

'Well, we're taught how to burgle our way into places, aren't we? And the windows in Palace House aren't very secure. If you remember, all the windows are very deep, they go down almost to ground level, so once I had it open it was easy to just step over the sill. Of course, there were full-length curtains inside and they were closed because of the blackout. I was just about to pull them aside and go into the room when I hear the door open. I froze, as you can imagine. I could hear two voices. One was Kline's. I couldn't identify the other one. But the thing is, they were speaking German.' Lucien looked at Kim as if to check that she found this as significant as he did. 'I know Kline is Austrian so German is his native language, but I didn't know anyone else on the staff who spoke it. Of course, there probably are. Most of them are good linguists, and maybe someone just wanted to keep in practice, but why in the middle of the night?'

'Why indeed?' asked Kim encouragingly.

'Anyway, there was nothing I could do but wait. I was afraid if I moved I'd give myself away. I don't speak German but there was something about their tone of voice, particularly Kline's, that struck me as — well, suspicious. They were talking very quietly but with a sort of urgency. It sounded as though Kline was giving instructions and several times I heard this one word, *Blitzschlag*. I had no idea what it meant but it stuck in my mind. After a few minutes I heard them say goodnight — that much German I did understand — and the door opened and closed. I thought they had both gone but I'd lost the nerve to go hunting in his filing cabinet, so I climbed back out of the window. I'd just got outside when the curtains were jerked back and I found myself face to face with Kline.'

'Good Lord! What did you do?' asked Gregoire.

'I said the first thing that came into my head. I said I was walking in the garden and I noticed his window was open and I thought it must have been left open by mistake so I was trying to close it.'

'That was quick thinking,' said Kim. 'Did he buy it?'

'I thought at first he hadn't, but then he just asked what I was doing out in the garden at that time of night and I told him I couldn't sleep. He said I'd got no business wandering about at that time of night and told me to get back to bed. So I thought I'd got away with it.'

His voice was becoming increasingly husky and he was obviously tiring, but Kim felt she could not leave the story at that point. She poured some more wine and water and handed it to him. 'But you hadn't?'

'No, obviously not. All the next day I couldn't get it out of my head. I went to the library and looked up *Blitzschlag* and I kept wondering if I should tell someone what I'd heard, maybe mention it to Raoul, my conducting officer. But then I thought I'd have to admit what I was up to and I might be chucked off the course and sent to the cooler, so I said nothing. Then I got a message saying that Kline wanted to see me. You can imagine, I was in a dead funk when I went into his office. But he didn't ask me about the night before. He was quite pleasant, almost affable.'

'Did he say why he'd sent for you?'

'Yes. He said it was just a routine check-up on my psych assessment.'

'And what did you talk about?'

Lucien frowned. 'He started by asking me what I thought about the war — did I think it was worth all the sacrifices we were making. Then he asked me what I would like the result of our sacrifices to be, what sort of society I was sacrificing myself for. I thought they were pretty rum questions to be asking in the circumstances. But then he said I seemed tense and he told me to sit back and relax. And this is the really weird part, after that I don't remember anything. I've got no recollection of the rest of the conversation. It's as if I slept through it.'

'And what happened after that?'

'Raoul suggested I should spend the night with Lily. I didn't really want to. That sort of thing, paying for sex, doesn't appeal to me. I mean, I know I didn't have to pay her, but it's her job, isn't it? Vetting agents to see if they talk in their sleep and that sort of thing.'

'But you went?'

'Raoul said it would be good for me, help me to relax. Actually, it wasn't as . . . as difficult as I expected. She's all right, Lily. She's a very kind person.'

Kim shot Gregoire a glance, warning him to say nothing about the murder yet. 'Lily said you were talking in your sleep, mumbling about storms and lightning.'

'Was I? I'm not surprised. I was dreaming about them all night.'

'Tell me something,' said Kim, 'have you ever been up in a plane in the middle of a storm?'

'No. Why? I'd never flown at all until I did my parachute training at Ringwood.'

Kim paused. This opened up a line of suspicion she had no wish to pursue. At length she said, 'Have you ever had a bad experience in a storm?'

'Once, when I was a kid, I was walking with my parents in the Brecon Beacons and we got caught in a storm. Lightning struck a tree a short way ahead of us. That was pretty scary, I suppose. But I hadn't thought about it for years. I've told you. I couldn't get this *Blitzschlag* business out of my head. I'm sure that's what was disturbing my sleep.'

'So you weren't worried about the flight out to where you were going to be dropped?' asked Kim.

'Not about the flight, no. But—' and now Lucien frowned again — 'it all seemed a bit rushed. I'd been kicking my heels for days and asking when I was going to be sent out, and all of a sudden I was told, "You're off at once. There's a circuit that's desperate for a pianist." It was as though they couldn't wait to get rid of me.

'Before I knew it, I was dropping here and being met by Gregoire, and it all seemed great at first, but then I'd no sooner set up and started my first transmission when I heard the Huns drive in. I knew they couldn't have picked me up that quickly so I felt sure it was because of what I'd heard that night. There was no time to send out a proper message, so I just sent *Blitzschlag* and hoped it might start some alarm bells ringing back home.'

'And it did,' Kim told him, 'which I why I was sent out to try to get you away from the Gestapo and find out what this is all about.'

'But I can't help you,' Lucien said wearily. 'I've cudgelled my brains to recall what Kline said to me, but it's no good. It's gone. Sorry.'

'You have nothing to apologize for,' she told him. 'All through this you've acted with great presence of mind and enormous courage. You deserve a medal. Maybe when all this is over you will get one. For the time being, you've done your bit. It's up to us now to follow the lead you've given us.'

His face and his voice were showing the strain he was under and Kim laid a hand on his arm. 'Try to rest. Is there anything you need before you settle down for the night?'

Lucien's eyes went from her to Gregoire. 'I need a piss,' he said uncomfortably.

Gregoire stood up. 'It's OK. I'll help you with that.'

Kim took her cue and wished Lucien goodnight. The *maquis* were congregating for the evening meal, but she took her plate and found a seat on a fallen log a little away from the circle round the fire. Gregoire joined her after a few minutes.

'Are you thinking what I'm thinking?' he asked.

'That Dr Kline hypnotized Lucien? Yes, that seems to be the only explanation.'

'But with what object?'

'Hoping to recruit him? To turn him and make him act as a double agent?'

'That's a possibility, I suppose. But he clearly didn't succeed.'

'I don't know much about hypnotism, but I've read somewhere that some people are much more suggestible than others. Some can't be hypnotized at all. It just doesn't work. Obviously, Lucien doesn't fall into that category, but for some reason he resisted whatever ideas Kline was trying to put into his head. Then, when it was reported to Kline that he'd been babbling about *Blitzschlag* to Lily, Kline realized that they were both security risks and had to be silenced.'

'So he murdered Lily — or had her murdered, in which case the question is, by whom?'

'Yes, indeed,' said Kim, feeling a weight settle around her heart.

'But he couldn't risk having Lucien bumped off at the same time, because that would have triggered too many uncomfortable inquiries. So he did the next best thing. He got Lucien dispatched out here asap, before he had a chance to talk to anybody, and arranged for him to be picked up as soon as he arrived.'

'That must be right,' agreed Kim, 'but why hand him over to Hoffmann? The simplest thing would have been for him to be shot while—' she indicated inverted commas with her fingers — '"trying to escape".'

'Hoffmann kept asking him what *Blitzschlag* was, where he'd heard it, who he'd told about it,' Gregoire reminded her. 'Presumably Kline wanted to know how much he remembered and whether he'd passed the information on.'

'Or . . .' said Kim, thinking aloud, 'possibly this whole operation is something dreamed up by a maverick cadre behind the backs of the top brass. Maybe they've got wind of it, and they're just as eager to find out what it means as we are.'

'That puts a whole new complexion on things,' said Gregoire.

'And there's another thing,' added Kim. 'Those questions he asked Lucien about his attitude to the war. He asked me the same things when we were first introduced. I had a feeling then that he was sounding me out. At the time I concluded he was trying to make sure I wasn't a security risk after . . . after what happened to me last time. But maybe I was wrong.' Kim paused, searching for the best way to express this new consideration. 'Maybe he was trying to see if I might be double agent material. If that is what he's doing at Beaulieu, trying to subvert our recruits, who else has he targeted? Who else has he hypnotized? He might have been more successful with them.'

'That is a very disturbing thought,' said Gregoire.

'And one we shall need to follow up when I've got Lucien home.' She yawned suddenly. 'It's been a helluva day. I can't think straight any longer. I'm going to bed.'

## CHAPTER 18

Lucien woke the next morning noticeably stronger and was able to get up with Gregoire's help. He wanted to know more about why Kim had been sent to get him out of the hands of the Gestapo, and she had to explain the circumstances that had motivated M. to send for her. When she told him about Lily's killing, he was shocked and distressed.

'It was because of me! If I hadn't blabbed about storms, Kline would have had no reason to kill her.'

'You mustn't blame yourself,' Kim told him. 'In fact, Lily's murder may turn out to be vital to the whole security of the country. It's alerted people like M. to the fact that there's a plot of some sort that could have far-reaching consequences.'

Leaving Lucien to rest, Kim went outside. The camp was seething with suppressed excitement in anticipation of the operation planned for that night. Small groups were taking turns at target practice with the new rifles. Anonymous packages were being loaded into a lorry that looked suspiciously as if it had once been French Army property. Xavier bustled here and there, giving orders.

Gregoire set off with his easel and paints to check the post box he had set up with Claudette, but he returned empty-handed. However, he came back from a second expedition just after midday looking excited.

'Baker Street haven't hung about. Your flight's coming tonight.'

'Tonight! So that does conflict with your operation on the lock.'

'Yes, I was afraid it might. But don't worry. I've spoken to Xavier and he has promised to detail some of his men to look after you and Lucien. We'd better go and sort things out with him now.'

The ten men selected were not pleased to be missing the excitement of the long-planned operation, but they all knew how much Lucien had suffered and there was a great deal of sympathy for him, so one way or another they reconciled themselves to the change of duties. Kim went with them to prepare the signal fires. She had very little recollection of the location in which she had been dropped, except that it had involved stumbling down a steep path in the dark following Gregoire. Now, having followed it in reverse, she found that it led to a small plateau surrounded by trees, just big enough to allow a small aircraft to land and take off. A rudimentary runway had been created by clearing some scrub and levelling off the worst of the bumps, but she found herself wondering if even the daring pilots of 161 Squadron would be prepared to attempt a landing. She did not voice her doubts, however, and the men got to work building the signal fires. There was no shortage of dry timber, and the job was soon completed.

By the time they had finished the sun was setting. Back at the camp the evening meal was ready and was being eaten in an atmosphere of barely suppressed impatience. As soon as it was finished Xavier gave an order and the men began to climb into the back of the lorry. Gregoire and three others would follow in a Peugeot, liberated from the possession of a known Nazi sympathizer.

Kim held out her hand. '*Bonne chance, mon ami!*'

'*A toi aussi,*' he responded. 'Or, as they say here, *merde alors!*'

'I wish I was going to be here to see the results.'

He grinned. 'If everything goes according to plan, you should hear a massive explosion just before you take off. You might even see the effects once you're airborne.' He hesitated, then went on, 'I'm sorry you got a rather chilly reception when you arrived. It's been a pleasure working with you — and a privilege.'

'For me, too,' she said. On an impulse she leaned up and kissed him on the cheek. 'Until we meet again.'

'I'll look forward to it.'

He turned away and climbed into the car. There was a cheer from the men in the truck, echoed by their comrades left behind with Kim, and the small convoy moved off.

Kim turned to her little group. 'Time we were moving too.'

Lucien was still far too weak to attempt the long climb up to the plateau, but two of the bigger men had devised a kind of sling that could be attached to the shoulders of one of them like a haversack. They helped Lucien into it and heaved him up so that his head was close to the man's shoulders and his feet protruded on either side of his waist. The second man steadied him from behind, taking some of the weight as the path grew steeper. In this way they reached the plateau with time to spare before the expected arrival of the Lysander. The two bearers set Lucien down on the grass and the others went off to their appointed places, ready to light the fires at a signal from Kim.

The minutes dragged past. Kim scanned the sky. The conditions were perfect, a moon just past the full and not a cloud to be seen. Provided the plane was not intercepted, and provided it was able to land in that confined space, all should be well. In a couple of hours they would be back in England. For a moment she found her thoughts turning to Roland. How would he feel about their relationship, after this break? How did she feel about it herself?

She looked at her watch. It was almost time.

Lucien was lying back against the folded sling. Abruptly, he sat up. 'The king!'

Kim stared at him. This was no time for him to start experiencing hallucinations. 'What?'

'It's just come back to me. Something about the king . . .'

At that instant Kim's ears detected the sound she had been listening for, the distant thrumming of a Lysander's Bristol Mercury engines.

'Wait!' she whispered urgently. 'Tell me when we're on the plane.'

She got to her feet, took a powerful torch from her pocket and flashed a signal to the men beside the fires. Within seconds three bright tongues of flame licked skywards. The sound of the engines faded, then returned louder. She scanned the sky. From behind the screen of trees the plane appeared, its silhouette clearly outlined against the stars. Kim pointed her torch skywards and flashed a Morse recognition signal. An answering light blinked from the cockpit.

The two men looking after Lucien were on their feet, supporting him.

'He's not landing!' exclaimed Lucien.

'Don't worry,' she reassured him. 'He'll circle round and come in for a second run.'

High above the engines faded, then swelled again as the plane turned. Kim glimpsed it for a moment, then it disappeared below the treeline. A few breathless seconds later it reappeared, so low that its wheels seemed almost to brush the topmost branches. It dropped sharply, levelled up and touched down, swaying and bouncing on the uneven ground. Kim held her breath. Would the pilot be able to stop before he hit the trees at the far end? She heard the engine note change as it came to a standstill, and three men appeared from among the trees and grabbed the wings to help turn the plane by 180 degrees so that it could taxi back to the point where it had touched down. There, other men jumped forward to turn it once more into the wind, ready for take-off. The propellers were still turning, and already Lucien's helpers were half carrying him towards the plane. Kim followed. Her heart was singing. She'd done it! She had promised to get Lucien home and she was going to succeed.

The hail of bullets came from nowhere and she saw Lucien and his helpers go down. Something struck her thigh like the kick of a horse and sent her stumbling to the ground. Bullets whined around her and she could hear them thudding into the ground on either side of her. She forced herself to lie still, knowing that her only chance of survival was to play dead. She prayed Lucien and the other men had come to the same conclusion. There was more firing now, and she recognized the sound of the Lee Enfield rifles.

The *maquis* were firing back.

Through the crack of rifles she heard the engines of the plane revving up and she raised her head long enough to see it accelerating away to take off.

'No! No!' she screamed, but whether in a vain attempt to stop the plane or a cry of despair at the cruelty of fate, she did not know. Her rational self understood perfectly well that a plane was too great a prize to be allowed to fall into enemy hands.

The firefight continued for what felt like half a lifetime, though it was probably only seconds, and then she heard another sound.

The ground she was lying on shook in response to a distant but massive explosion. There was a sudden silence, then a single shot and the scream of a wounded man. It was followed by shouts of alarm and the sound of breaking branches and undergrowth being trampled underfoot.

Then a French voice rang out. '*Ils s'enfuient!* They are running away!'

More trampling followed, but there was no more shooting. Kim lifted her head cautiously and tried to get up. Pain flared along her leg and she could feel the warm stickiness of blood soaking into her overalls. She dropped to her stomach and dragged herself forwards, towards the three still figures lying on the ground a few yards ahead of her.

She saw at once that there was no chance any of them were alive. Their bodies were riddled with bullets. She checked for a pulse in each of them, but there was no flicker of life. Lucien had fallen face down. She managed to turn him over and gazed down at his face. There was still a faint trace of a smile on his lips.

He had thought he was almost home.

Kim lowered her head to his shoulder and gave way to helpless sobs.

'Oh, my dear! I'm so sorry! I'm so sorry!'

Footsteps close by brought her head up and silenced her sobs. Was this to be the end for her too?

A man's voice said, in French, 'You are alive! Praise God!'

She looked up. It was Jules.

'But they are dead!' she choked. 'All dead.'

He stooped to check and nodded. 'Yes, all dead. But you. Where are you wounded?'

'My leg,' she mumbled.

He pulled off the scarf he was wearing and bound it tightly around her thigh. 'That's the best I can do until we can get you back to camp. It should stop the bleeding.'

She rolled over and sat up.

'What happened?' she asked. 'Where did the shots come from?'

'They must have found their way up here after we set the fires. They were hiding in the undergrowth. But they've gone now. I think that explosion scared them off.'

'All of them?'

'We killed one and the rest won't get far. Our men are after them and they know these woods better than the Boche.'

'Any of our men hurt?'

'One or two flesh wounds. Nothing serious, I think. Can you stand if I help you?'

'Yes, I think so.' She hauled herself to her feet with his assistance but her left leg refused to bear her weight.

'Get on my back,' Jules instructed her. 'I'll carry you down.'

'But these three!' she protested. 'We can't leave them here.'

'There's no way we can carry them. We can send men up for them when the rest of the group come back.'

She had to accept that he was right and allowed him to hoist her onto his back. On the way down they were joined by two more of the group, who reported that they had lost track of the Germans but that some of the others were still on their trail.

As they reached the camp, they heard the sound of the vehicles returning, and by the time Jules set her down, the men were climbing out of the lorry. The Peugeot drew up and Gregoire got out. Kim was shaken to see that his face was streaked with blood, seeping from a bandage round his head. Several of the men, she now saw, also wore makeshift bandages or slings. She limped towards them, with Jules's help, and Gregoire stopped short at the sight of her.

'*Mon dieu!* What happened? Why are you still here?'

'What happened to you?' she asked.

'We were ambushed. They were waiting for us.'

'So were we.'

They looked at each other in silence for a moment, stunned by the implications. Then Gregoire said, 'You need medical attention. Jules, get her into the hut. The doctor should be there already.'

Sure enough, Dr Gerard, forewarned that he might be needed, was already tending to the wounded. All around, other wounded men were being brought in, and Gregoire looked around as Jules set Kim down on one of the beds.

'Can these men wait? We need to give Monique some privacy.'

'Don't be stupid!' said Kim. 'Do you really think it worries me if a man sees me in my underwear? Doctor, look after any of the others that are more seriously injured first.'

'I think your need is as great as any,' the doctor assured her. 'Now, let's have a look at this leg.'

His examination showed what Kim had guessed, that it was only a flesh wound, but the bullet had passed right through the fleshy part of her thigh and a good deal of stitching was required. He offered her an injection of morphia but she refused, knowing it was in short supply and would certainly be needed for someone else, if not that night then at a later date.

So he did the stitching under local anaesthetic and gave her a couple of painkillers.

Physically and emotionally exhausted, Kim fell into a restless doze that deepened into a sleep that lasted until the sun was well up the next morning.

## CHAPTER 19

Kim woke to find Gregoire sitting by the bed with a mug of water. After she had slaked her thirst, he said, 'So, tell me what happened.'

Piecing together her fragmented recollections, she told him the story, and found herself weeping again. 'I promised to get him home, Gregoire. We were so nearly there. Another thirty seconds and we'd have been in the plane. And now he's dead! After all he suffered.'

Gregoire put a hand on her arm. 'Don't distress yourself. There was nothing you could have done. And, actually, in the final analysis, it might have been better for Lucien's life to end this way.'

'What do you mean?' She stared at him in amazement.

'I didn't tell you what Gerard said after he examined him. The fact is, after what Hoffmann did to him, he would probably never have been able to have normal sexual relations. Never been able to father children, anyway.'

Kim looked at him in horror. 'Oh God! That swine! May he rot in hell!'

'Hell's too good for him,' said Gregoire.

After a moment she asked, 'So, what happened to you last night? I heard the explosion. I think it might have saved me. Hoffmann's men ran off as soon as they heard it. I think they decided they'd done what they came for and had better get back to find out what was going on. Besides, they hadn't reckoned on Xavier's men being so well armed. But you say you were ambushed too?'

'Yes. We arrived at the dam and I was ready with two other chaps I'd trained to set the explosives, when suddenly what looked like half the German army rose up out of the maize field on the other side of the canal and opened fire. I had to leave Xavier and his men to return fire, and the two other men and I managed to get into the shelter of the lock-keeper's cottage and then let ourselves down into the dam to set the explosives against the gate. The lock was empty, so the upper gate was holding back the water in the canal. I was using a time pencil. I'd planned to give us a good fifteen minutes to get away before it blew, but I saw that if we did that the Boche would have time to get someone in there to dismantle it, so I had to gamble. The ground was higher on our side of the canal, and I reckoned that once it blew, we would have time to get out of the way of the flood water, but the maize field where the Boche were positioned was quite flat and more low-lying. So I sent the other two back up out of the lock and set the fuse for two minutes. I just made it up to the top of the gates and onto the towpath before it went up.'

He paused and ran a hand over his face with a fleeting expression of triumph.

'I have to say the results were quite satisfactory. The water flooded in and soon filled the lock and overflowed. Two of the coal barges broke loose from their moorings and one ended up on top of the lower lock gates. I think the other one sank. The rest went aground. We had to climb up the bank pretty damn quick to escape the flood, but the Boche in the maize field must have got very wet indeed.' He chuckled humourlessly.

'I know the Boche will have it repaired in a matter of days, but it still uses time and resources they could employ elsewhere. It's only a pinprick, but it's one of many happening all over the country, so they can never feel they have the place under their complete control.'

'It's exactly what Churchill wanted when he set up SOE,' Kim said. 'Well done.'

Gregoire stood up. 'We've still got a serious issue to discuss, but let's leave it until after breakfast. What can I do to help?'

'If you could get me as far as the latrines . . .'

'Of course. I'm sorry we don't have any other women in the camp . . .'

'Don't worry,' she said. 'I'll manage.'

Later, when they had eaten, Gregoire took Kim to where his car was parked and helped her in, so that they could talk without being overheard.

'So,' he said, 'we have a traitor in the camp somewhere. The question is, who?'

'Think about it,' said Kim sombrely. 'Who knew about both these operations?'

'With regard to the attack on the dam, it could have been anyone. One of Xavier's men, the lock-keeper or one of his family . . . But your flight? It must be one of the men we had helping you.'

'Not possible,' Kim said. 'None of them knew anything about it until yesterday afternoon and after that they were with me the whole time. There is no way one of them could have made contact with Hoffmann or his people. And there wouldn't have been enough time to set up an ambush like that.'

'A leak back at base, then?' suggested Gregoire. 'Someone at Baker Street or one of the radio operators at Grendon?'

Kim shook her head. 'Think!' she repeated. 'Who were the only two people apart from ourselves who knew the time *and* date of the flight and the location of the landing ground?'

He looked at her and she saw the implications of what she had said dawn in his eyes. 'Philippe and Claudette.'

'And who gave Philippe the mushrooms that made him ill, so that you needed a replacement radio operator at short notice?'

'Claudette — but I can't believe . . .' He shook his head.

'I know. It's hard. She seemed the sort of girl I'd trust with my life'. She stopped as a new thought came to her. 'Did she go through Beaulieu?'

'Yes, of course. We all did.'

'But when?'

Gregoire frowned, thinking. 'She came to join us about six months ago, back in the spring. Our original pianist was picked up by the Boche . . .' He gazed at Kim, aghast.

'Kline arrived at Beaulieu last January. You and I both passed through there long before he arrived, so we never came across him, but we know — we think we know — what he did to Lucien. And I raised the question then about who else he might have worked on in the same way . . .'

Gregoire nodded slowly. 'So, the chances are he tried the same thing on Claudette, but with more success?'

'It's a possible explanation.'

'And how many others . . . ?' He threw up his hands in a gesture of despair. 'If you're right, Baker Street need to recall anyone who passed through his hands in the last six or seven months.'

'Yes,' she said unhappily. 'And not just agents who are in the field now. I can think of at least one person who is now helping to train new recruits.'

'Who?'

She hesitated. 'Did you ever meet Raoul?'

'No. I don't think so.'

'I trained with him. We were good buddies, so when I was seconded to Beaulieu I was really glad to find him already working there. He'd had the best part of a year in the field and been recalled for a rest. But I know he lied to me about something. He told me the cause of Lucien's nightmare was an experience he had flying through a storm before the war.

But Lucien said he'd never been up in a plane before he started parachute training.'

'That sounds suspicious,' said Gregoire. 'But it could be a misunderstanding.'

'There's more. You remember the mock interrogations we were all put through.'

He shuddered. 'How could I forget?'

'Kline had me put through another one.'

'But you were there as an instructor!' He stared at her.

'Believe me, I told them. Not that they listened. And one of the men conducting the interrogation was Raoul. I thought at the time he was just obeying orders, but there was nothing half-hearted about the way he roughed me up.'

'But why? What was the object?'

'Kline thought I was asking too many questions. It was all designed to break me down and have me sent back to the cooler.' She ran a hand through her hair. 'It bloody nearly succeeded too.'

'Dear God!' He looked at her with shocked compassion. 'After what you had already been through.'

'That was the whole point,' she said grimly. 'But the sad fact seems to be, Raoul is now working for him.'

'But what can he possibly expect to gain?' Gregoire asked.

'Oh, this business has ramifications far beyond anything that has happened out here.' She looked at him apologetically. 'I can't talk about that, but the more I learn the more worried I am.'

'So, how do we proceed?' he asked. 'With Claudette, I mean.'

'We need to set a trap. I think we can trust Philippe, don't you?'

'Well, I can't imagine why he would nearly poison himself with those mushrooms — and he doesn't actually know where the landing ground is. The pilot bringing him out got the location wrong and dropped him five miles away, on the other side of the canal. He had to make his way here on foot.'

'That seems to rule him out.'

'What do you suggest we do?' asked Gregoire.

A kernel of an idea had begun to formulate in Kim's mind. 'I suggest we get Philippe to pass a fake message to Claudette, giving another date and time for an exfiltration. Then we lie in wait. If the Boche turn up again, we know she must have told them.'

'Can we be sure they will turn up again? If the object was to silence Lucien, they've achieved it.'

'Good point. So Claudette must be told that he survived, wounded but still alive, and that's why they're sending another flight to pick him up.'

'OK,' he said. 'But will Hoffmann believe that Baker Street is willing to risk another landing, after what happened last night?'

'Ah.' She frowned. 'You're right. So we need another plausible scenario. What other possibilities are there?'

'There are only two other routes out of the country that I can think of. One is to go south, over the Pyrenees into Spain, which is obviously impossible for a wounded man. The other is over the border into Switzerland, which would not be easy either.'

'That doesn't matter, since we're not going to attempt it,' Kim pointed out. 'We just have to convince Hoffmann that we're going to try. Do you have a map?'

Gregoire produced one, and after studying it for a moment Kim said, 'Imagine there is an agent in Besançon who knows a route over the border. If we convince Hoffmann that we have a rendezvous arranged somewhere in that area, we would need to go via Arnay-le-Duc. There are only two possible roads from here, so he would need to block them both and search any vehicles going that way. If that happens, we have our proof.'

Gregoire thought it over for a moment. 'It should work. We just need to write a message for Claudette to pick up from Philippe. But what about you? You need a genuine way home.'

She made a rueful grimace. 'I don't think 161 Squadron would be too keen to try another landing, after what happened. But perhaps if we can convince them that we've found the source of the leak and stopped it, they might give it a go.' She stretched her arms. 'For now, let's concentrate on setting the trap. If it works, I'll get in touch and see what can be done.'

She dug a pencil and pad out of a pocket in her overalls and wrote, *From HQ to Grocer. Rendezvous with Agent Cobbler at* . . . She chose a random set of coordinates from the map that identified an area somewhere between Besançon and the Swiss border: *at 17.30, 27 August. Exfiltration will be organized from there.*

Soon after that Gregoire set off with his paints and his easel to St Michel's church, and Father Antoine took a message to Philippe asking him to meet him there. In the quiet of the nave Gregoire explained to the radio operator that they suspected a traitor somewhere among their colleagues, without mentioning anyone by name, and handed him the message.

'I want you to write this out as if you have just received it from London and decoded it. Then pass it on in the usual way.'

Father Antoine obliged by raising the banner of the appropriate saint's day and Philippe returned to the château to await Claudette's arrival. He handed her a copy of the words Gregoire had given him and a few hours later Gregoire collected the same message from the secret letter box in the forest. The trap was set.

'Now we need to convince Hoffmann that we are trying to get away from the Morvan,' said Kim. 'To get to Besançon in time we'd have to leave by mid-morning, but my bet is he'll have the roadblocks in place soon after dawn.'

Gregoire grinned. 'I think we need a little help from our farmer friends.'

* * *

The day specified in the fake message was two days hence, so Kim spent the next forty-eight hours trying to rest her injured leg and fidgeting with impatience. Early on the morning of the twenty-seventh a farmer's lorry loaded with young heifers set off along one of the roads leading from the nearest village to Arnay-le-Duc, and another towing a trailer full of sheep set off along the other. They were followed at intervals by a tractor pulling a load of manure, three young men on bicycles, the ambulance from Montsauche and a Daimler belonging to an elderly lady of impeccably aristocratic pedigree.

As Kim anticipated, the roadblocks were in place. Xavier had set watchers on both roads and they returned chortling with delight at the scenes they had witnessed. Young German soldiers who had obviously grown up far from the sight of a cow were forced to enter the lorry and poke about with their bayonets in the straw laid on the floor. Then they had to do the same with the trailer full of manure. The sheep escaped and headed back along the road towards their familiar pastures, causing a complete traffic jam and preventing Hoffmann from reaching either roadblock. The three young men were stopped and forced to remove their shirts, to prove that one of them was not in fact female, and the aristocratic lady gave the sergeant in charge of the platoon who stopped her a tongue lashing that he would remember for the rest of his life. The roadblocks remained in place, to the frustration of all concerned, until well into the afternoon.

Kim and Gregoire permitted themselves a grim smile at the images conjured up for them, but in truth it was no laughing matter. 'Well,' said Kim, 'we have our proof. Only Claudette could have alerted Hoffmann.'

'Indeed,' agreed Gregoire. 'So now we have to arrest her. We'll take a couple of Xavier's men and go up to the stables.'

'Just a minute,' cautioned Kim. 'She may not be there. She could be out riding. If we turn up in force at the stables looking for her and don't find her it might warn her off.'

'So what do you suggest?'

'How often does she check the letter box?'

'Twice a day, at least.'

'She's bound to expect a message from you to be handed on to Philippe, either explaining that we've been arrested, or that we got through and are on our way to the rendezvous. If we keep watch on the letter box, we should be able to take her by surprise.'

'That means waiting until tomorrow.'

'I know. But she has no reason to think we suspect her. Just keep to the usual routine.'

'OK. And what do we do with her when we've got her?'

'I need to get her back to London for questioning. I think I'll use Philippe's radio to send a message of my own. We'll have to hope 161 Squadron are prepared to give it another try.'

Next morning, at Gregoire's request, Xavier sent two of his men to keep watch at the stables in case Claudette escaped them. Then he and Kim set off for the letter box, accompanied by three more of Xavier's men, with Kim sitting on Gregoire's bike because she was still unable to walk without limping painfully.

Before leaving she had borrowed a length of rope from the *maquis*'s store and now carried it looped over her shoulder. The letter box was situated at the junction of two tracks. One led back the way they had come and went on in the opposite direction towards the town and the stables, the direction from which they expected Claudette to arrive. The other went off deeper into the forest.

'Where does that go?' Kim asked.

'Right up into the hills,' one of the men told her. 'It's only used for logging.'

Kim considered. If their quarry tried to make a break for freedom, there would be no point in heading towards the camp, or back to the stables. In Claudette's place, she knew which route she would take. Leaving the others to conceal themselves in the undergrowth she limped a little way down the other track. She found a tree growing close to one side and tied one end of her rope to it. Then she fed the rest of the rope back across the path, concealing it in the deep carpet of fallen leaves. Satisfied, she settled down to wait, hidden behind a bush of holly.

The letter box was, in fact, a crack in the trunk of an oak tree. Gregoire had brought a folded piece of paper, such as he would normally use for a message, and he tucked it into the cleft as usual, so that Claudette would have to dismount in order to collect it.

After a wait long enough for Kim to begin to get cramp in her legs they heard the sound of hoof beats approaching at a canter and Claudette appeared, mounted on a chestnut gelding who snorted his disapproval when she pulled him to a stop. Kim saw Gregoire begin to rise from his hiding place, but Claudette, instead of dismounting, merely leaned down from the saddle and fished the paper from its hiding place.

Before she could ride on, Gregoire stepped forward and greeted her as casually as possible. '*Bonjour, Claudette. Ça va?*'

'What do you want?' she demanded.

'Just a chat. Will you get down?'

At that point the three men they had brought with them stepped out of the trees. It was sufficient to confirm the girl's instinctive suspicion. She wrenched the gelding's head round and dug her heels into his sides, sending him thundering down the track where Kim was waiting. Kim held back until the last second, then tugged on the rope. It rose from the concealing leaf litter inches ahead of the trampling hooves, catching the gelding's feet and sending him plunging head over heels. Claudette was thrown clear. Within seconds she was on her feet, but this time Kim was armed.

She levelled her pistol at the other girl. 'Don't try to run. I can't tell you how much pleasure it would give me to have an excuse to shoot you.'

Gregoire had reached them and Claudette swung round to face him. 'What is this mad woman on about? She could have killed me.'

'It would have been no more than justice, considering the lives you have sacrificed,' he told her.

'What are you talking about? I haven't sacrificed anyone.'

'You have betrayed our plans to the enemy, which amounts to the same thing. Now put your hands behind your back.'

As he tied her hands she spat out, 'You fools! Don't you understand you're fighting on the wrong side? Do you want to see England bombed back into the stone age, when there's peace to be had for the asking?' Then she seemed to realize she had said too much and clamped her mouth shut.

Kim turned to where the horse was now quietly grazing the grass at the side of the track. She hobbled over and collected the reins.

'Sorry about that, old chap,' she said running her hands over the horse's forelegs. 'But needs must . . .' She looked round at Gregoire, who had handed his captive into the care of two of the men. 'Give me a leg up, would you? I'd rather ride this than your bike.'

'Can you ride?' he asked doubtfully.

'My dear chap, I went to the same sort of school as Madame over there. Of course I can ride.'

On the way back Claudette met all further questions with a grim silence.

'Never mind,' Kim said. 'When I get you back to England there are people there who will persuade you to talk.' It was an empty threat, but she saw the other woman blanch.

The problem of how to deal with a captive, particularly a female one, in a fairly primitive camp full of *maquis* was not easily solved, and Kim realized that the sooner she could make arrangements to get them both back to England the better. There was also the horse to be returned to its owner, but this presented a solution to one of her difficulties — the need for mobility. Dismissing Gregoire's misgivings, she mounted up and rode back along the forest track until she reached the château. Philippe heard the hoof beats and came to the fence.

'Monique? What has happened to Claudette?'

'Unavoidably detained,' Kim told him. 'Listen, I need to use your radio to contact base. Can I meet you at the church?'

He was there almost as soon as she was and helped her to climb the steep stairs to the top of the tower. She waited while he deployed the aerial around the belfry and set up the radio, then handed him the message she had ready encoded. *Leak stopped, no further danger of ambush. Urgently need exfiltration for two people. Please advise.*

'Signal in the usual way when you get a reply,' she told Philippe. 'I'll collect the message myself.'

She rode on to the stables and told the owner that the horse had been found wandering loose, having thrown its rider, who was now being cared for by Dr Gerard in Montsauche.

*That should pre-empt any search for the time being,* she thought.

How Claudette's ultimate disappearance would be explained she left to Gregoire. Father Antoine had readily agreed to collect her from the stables and drive her to a pre-arranged rendezvous with Gregoire, and by lunchtime she was back at the camp.

Claudette had been put into one of the rough huts that had been thrown up around the compound. One of the *maquis* was a blacksmith by trade and he had forged a cuff which was locked around her ankle and attached to a piece of chain, which was in turn fastened to a log. It was a rough-and-ready arrangement, but the best that could be devised. As the only other woman, it fell to Kim to keep an eye on her and tend to her needs, including taking her to the latrines that had been dug a short distance from the camp. This she did with a pistol in her hand.

The banner went up on the church tower before noon the next day, and to Kim's relief the message told her that another landing would be attempted the following evening.

The hours passed slowly. Any attempt at conversation, even on mundane subjects, was met with obstinate silence, and after a few attempts, Kim left Claudette mostly on her own.

Kim's leg was healing but she still limped, so it fell to Gregoire to organize the building of the signal fires.

When at last the time came for them to make their way up to the landing ground Claudette was unchained but roped by the wrist to Jules, who had volunteered to take charge again of the men detailed to assist the landing, while Gregoire lent a strong arm to help Kim on the steep ascent. Settling down to wait, Kim could not banish from her mind the memory of the last attempt.

*This time will be different,* she told herself.

To Claudette she said, 'You do understand that because of you, a young man who had suffered terribly at the hands of the man you work for, and who thought he was at last going home to safety, was killed? Don't you have any regrets?'

Claudette simply shrugged her shoulders and remained silent.

The weather was less settled than on the previous night, with a blustery wind driving clouds across the moon. Kim watched the sky and prayed that conditions would not get worse. Another failed attempt would be the last. If that happened, she and her prisoner would be stuck in France for the foreseeable future, unless another way of getting them home could be found. She began to contemplate the imagined route to Switzerland as a genuine possibility.

Her thoughts were interrupted by Gregoire. 'Listen!'

Over the whistling of the wind in the trees came the thrumming of aero engines. Kim got to her feet, her pulse racing. Gregoire gave the signal and the fires leaped into life. As before the pilot overflew, watching for the recognition signal. As she saw the response flashing from the cockpit, Kim found herself saying out loud, 'Oh, you wonderful man! Yes! We're here! Come and get us!'

The plane circled, disappeared behind the trees, reappeared and touched down. Gregoire held out his hand to Kim.

'*Bonne chance, ma chère.*'

She embraced him. '*Merde alors!* And thank you for everything. Take care of yourself!'

'I'll try,' he said, and she thought suddenly how he must envy her, heading back to the safety of England.

The plane had been turned around to face into the wind and a ladder was being lowered from the cockpit. Jules handed the end of Claudette's rope to Kim.

'Come on,' she said. 'You don't deserve it, but you're going home.'

## CHAPTER 20

When they landed at RAF Tempsford Kim was not unduly surprised to find M. waiting for them on the tarmac. Surprise and dismay, however, were written plainly on his face as she and her prisoner alighted from the aircraft.

'Who is this? What has happened to Lucien?'

Kim was suddenly overcome by an immense weariness. She had forgotten that although the colonel would have been informed about the abortive rescue attempt, there was no way he could know about its dire consequences.

'Lucien is dead,' she said, tonelessly. 'And this woman is a traitor who must be arrested.'

M. looked at her and asked no further questions. Claudette was taken away by two military policemen and Kim found herself in the back of a large car, being driven to London. On the journey she told him the story of Lucien's rescue, the firefight at the landing strip and the ruse by which they had established Claudette's guilt.

'I don't understand,' M. said. 'How did it come about that a woman like that was persuaded to become a double agent?'

Kim drew a long breath. 'It's complicated . . .'

He took pity on her. 'It'll keep till tomorrow. You need a good night's rest.'

Dawn was breaking by the time the car drew up outside the London flat. As they entered the hall the door to the sitting room opened and Roland stood in the doorway, his shirt half unbuttoned and his hair tousled as if he had fallen asleep in his chair.

'Kim! You're safe! Thank God!'

Then his arms were round her, and she buried her face in his shoulder and breathed in the suddenly familiar smell of him and knew that she was truly home.

M. waited a tactful moment, then said, 'Kim needs a long rest. Take care of her, Foxy. I'll be back this evening.'

Roland had not gone to bed that night either, so they both slept through the day in each other's arms, waking in time to eat a curious meal, half breakfast, half supper, before M. arrived.

He looked Kim up and down. 'Well, you look a bit less like death warmed up than you did last night. But you're limping. Why?'

'It's nothing. I took a bullet in the thigh when we were ambushed. It's healing.'

'I shall send our doctor to check it out, nonetheless,' he said. 'Now, we have a great deal to talk about, if you feel up to it.'

Kim insisted that she was fine and they adjourned to the sitting room, where M. poured them all a generous slug of whisky.

'So,' he said, 'your little trip to France has opened up what I believe Foxy's American friends would call a "can of worms" which requires urgent investigation. That, on its own, is very valuable. But unfortunately you failed, through no fault of your own, in your primary mission. We still do not have Lucien so we can't ask him what he knows about *Blitzschlag.*'

'I don't think we would have learned more even if I had managed to get him back,' Kim said. 'I questioned him myself while we were waiting for the flight to be arranged, and the simple fact is he didn't know much more than we do.'

'Didn't know?' repeated M. incredulously.

Kim relayed her conversation with Lucien and the tentative conclusion she had come to.

'Hypnotized?' said M. 'You really believe that?'

'It's the only explanation I can think of,' Kim said. 'But there's more to it. I believe that was how Claudette was turned. She also passed through Beaulieu after Kline started work there.'

'Good God!' exclaimed M. 'If you're right we could have half a dozen or more double agents out there in France.'

'And here too,' said Kim, and related her suspicions about Raoul.

M. ran his hand through his hair and was silent for a moment. 'OK. That is one investigation I shall have to put in train urgently. But let's concentrate on one thing at a time. The *Blitzschlag* affair. Foxy has succeeded in infiltrating the group that seem to be the prime movers — on this side of the channel, at least. Bring us up to date, if you will, Foxy.'

Kim looked from one man to the other. To her, the man who was now her lover was inescapably Roland, although that was no more than a cover name for the purposes of SOE, but it amused her to see how easily M. had accepted the nickname Foxy.

The man in question stretched out his long legs and sat back in his chair.

'Right.' He returned Kim's gaze. 'We're talking about the three men we watched going into Kline's consulting rooms, plus a few others equally eminent in their own walks of life. I've managed to convince them that I'm a member of the German American Bund, or Brotherhood, a group of Nazi sympathizers who are violently opposed to America's involvement in the war in Europe. They believe I have useful contacts in the upper echelons of the administration who would be willing to back any scheme that gave Hitler victory and allowed American troops to be withdrawn. They meet in a house in Flood Walk in Chelsea, and I've been allowed to sit in on some of their meetings. It's clear that they're plotting something big, though what it is I haven't yet been able to discover. They talk about a "big event", something that's going to create chaos in the administration and alarm in the general public. When that happens, they expect Oswald Mosley to be freed from internment and to assume some form of authority. It seems there's been some form of contact between him and Hitler, with the possibility of a peace treaty.'

Kim sat up sharply. 'That reminds me. When we first arrested Claudette, she called us fools for preferring to allow the country to be bombed into submission when there was peace to be had for the asking.'

'Did she now!' commented M. 'If Kline has brainwashed her into believing that, it fits with what Foxy has discovered.'

'There's something else,' Roland went on. 'They keep talking about someone "waiting in the wings", but I can't make out who they mean. Maybe Hess or another of Hitler's pals, ready to come over and sign the treaty?'

'It's possible,' agreed M. 'Is there anything else you can tell us?'

'Nothing of any significance,' said Roland. 'But there is one little thing that's been puzzling me.'

'What's that?'

'At the end of each meeting everyone is given a glass of wine and a glass of water and they drink the "loyal toast" — you know, to the king. But when they do it, they pass their wine glasses across the glass of water.'

It was M.'s turn to sit up. 'That's an old Jacobite habit. After James II had gone into exile and been replaced by William and Mary, and later Anne, there was an element in society that wanted the Stuart dynasty, in the shape of James's son, James Francis, the erstwhile Prince of Wales, to be restored to the throne. When these people were obliged to drink the loyal toast, they did it exactly as you describe. The implication was that they were drinking to "the king over the water" — in other words James, who was in France.'

'I don't get the significance,' said Roland.

'The significance is that we too currently have a king in exile, a man many people believe should have been allowed to continue his reign alongside his American bride.'

'The Duke of Windsor!' exclaimed Kim.

'Of course! I should have spotted it,' said Roland. 'They've got a photograph on the wall in the hallway of a young man standing next to Hitler. They treat it like a sort of shrine, with vases of flowers and candles. I couldn't think who he was but now I understand.'

'Are these people really plotting to bring him back?' asked Kim.

'It makes sense, I've heard them talking about the present king. They say he's not a well man, that he could die quite young, and the prospect of Princess Elizabeth becoming queen gets them really riled up. I heard Lyndham say he'd rather go into exile than have to kneel and pledge fealty to "a silly girl" — that's what he called her.'

'Well, that fits with what I know of people who belong to the English Array,' said M. 'They are misogynists to a man. They long for the old days when the king had sovereign power and they, the aristocracy, ruled the country and were answerable only to him. The idea of a female ruler is anathema to them.'

'Have they forgotten the first Elizabeth?' wondered Kim.

'I think they regard her as an exception, a kind of honorary man.'

'As she did herself, didn't she?' Roland said. 'You know, "I have the heart and stomach of a king . . ."'

M. looked mildly surprised. 'Quite. So the duke is the man waiting in the wings, not one of Hitler's toadies.'

'Wasn't he quite friendly with Hitler before he abdicated?' asked Kim. 'I seem to remember reading something about that.'

'Oh yes. He and the duchess visited Hitler at Berchtesgaden in thirty-seven. He definitely has Nazi sympathies.'

'Which make him the ideal figurehead for a pro-Nazi regime in this country,' said Roland.

M. shook his head wearily. 'This business is getting to the stage where I shall have to hand over to the big guns, but not until we have something more definite to go on. When do you meet these people again, Foxy?'

'Day after tomorrow.'

'Well, we must wait until then and hope that someone will let slip what this big event is supposed to be.' M. turned to Kim. 'Now, what about you? You need to rest up.'

'Oh, not Scotland, *please*!' she begged.

He smiled. 'Very well, since you have such an aversion to my country. How about a quiet week in the country, or by the sea?'

'I'd much rather stay here,' she said.

M. looked from her to Roland and gave in. 'Very well. You must look after her, Foxy. Make her rest that leg.'

'I will,' Roland promised with a smile.

'I'll be back in three days' time to hear what more you've been able to find out. Until then, lie low, both of you. England needs you.'

\* \* \*

For Kim the next two days felt like a honeymoon. She and Roland made love and talked and made love again, and ate delicious meals that he conjured up from the unpromising ingredients available on the ration. On the evening of the second day she watched him dress in an impeccably tailored suit, enlivened with a slightly too colourful silk tie, in preparation for his next meeting with the conspirators.

Looking into his face before he left, she said, 'Are you sure these people don't suspect you?'

'As sure as I can be,' he answered. 'They've never given me any sign of it.' He kissed her. 'Don't worry. I'll be back by eleven.'

In spite of his assurances she spent the evening unable to relax, until she heard his key in the lock. One look at his face told her that something important had occurred.

'You've learned something?'

He nodded. 'Do you mind if I save it till the brigadier gets here, so I don't have to say it all twice?'

M. arrived very soon afterwards, looking worried.

'What's wrong, sir?' asked Kim.

'It's probably nothing to do with our present business, but I've just come from a security briefing. Air reconnaissance reports suggest a build-up of German forces along the Channel coast.'

'They can't be thinking of launching an invasion at this point, surely?' she said. 'With the Italians caving in and the Russians advancing from the east, they've got their hands full.'

'Quite,' agreed M. 'But the reports seem pretty consistent. Maybe they think the threat will make us recall some of our troops from Italy.'

'It could be connected to our business,' said Roland. 'It would fit with what I've heard tonight.'

'Let's sit down,' said M. 'Then you can explain.'

When they were settled in the sitting room with the now routine glasses of whisky, he said, 'Well? What news?'

'The talk tonight was all about what's supposed to happen when the big moment comes. It's—' Roland paused and took a mouthful of his drink — 'it's quite a plan! First, as I said, there's supposed to be an event of some sort that will spread panic in the general populace.'

'Such as the rumour of a fresh invasion?' suggested M.

'That's what I meant about the possible connection,' Roland said. 'Whatever it is, a mob of Mosley's Blackshirts is supposed to gather in Parliament Square. At the same time, Lord Lyndham and Lord Hastings will present themselves at Holloway with a forged letter from the home secretary ordering the governor to hand Mosley and his wife into their custody. They will whisk him straight to Westminster, where the House will be packed with all the MPs who opposed the war back in thirty-nine. The mob will invade the building, shouting, "Mosley for Prime Minister". He will seize the mace and insist on speaking, and his supporters will shout down any opposition.'

'Good God!' M. looked shocked.

'There's more,' Roland said. 'At this point in the meeting, Lyndham produced a piece of paper, which he said was a preliminary draft of the speech they expect Mosley to give. I can't repeat it all from memory, and for obvious reasons I couldn't make notes, but I remember the way it begins. "Ladies and gentlemen," he will say, "I am here to offer you an end to this terrible war. I have here a letter from Herr Hitler offering an honourable peace, to come into being from the moment certain conditions are met."'

'What conditions?' asked M.

'The restoration of Edward VIII to the throne, with Mosley as Prime Minister. He'll then go on to draw a picture of a future where Britain and Germany will be the dominant forces in the Western world, Germany controlling most of Europe while Britain dominates the majority of trade through the Empire.'

'And what are the Americans supposed to think of that scenario?'

'America will then be free to concentrate on defeating Japan and becoming the major power in the Pacific region. Or that's the way they see it.'

'I can see that, for a lot of people, that would look like a very attractive possibility,' said M. grimly.

'How can Edward be restored to the throne?' asked Kim. 'What is King George supposed to say to that?'

'That's another part of the plan,' Roland said. 'There's a Group Captain Louis Greig, a supporter of Mosley, who is also a gentleman-in-waiting to King George. He has apparently got influence with several highly placed court officials.

'When the balloon goes up, his job is to convince Their Majesties that for their own safety they should decamp to Balmoral with the two princesses. Once there, the feeling is that George can be persuaded that, for the good of the nation, he should abdicate in favour of his brother. They reckon he'll be quite glad to be relieved of the position. Edward will be waiting for the summons and they will have a plane standing by to fetch him.

'Oh, and one more thing,' Roland added. 'Another group, backed up by some of the Blackshirts, will force their way into Broadcasting House and force one of the newsreaders to make an announcement telling everyone that the war is over and declaring three days' bank holiday in celebration.'

M. let out his breath through pursed lips, in a sound somewhere between a sigh and a whistle. 'As you say, it's quite a plan!'

'There's something they don't seem to have thought of,' said Kim. 'We already have a prime minister, a very popular one. Mr Churchill's not going to sit back and let this happen.'

'The prime minister is currently in America, conferring with President Roosevelt,' said M. 'Which gives us a hint of the timescale. This would have to happen before he gets back.'

'Which is when?' she asked.

'I believe the scheduled date is the ninth of September.'

'That's less than a week away!'

'Quite. If only we knew what this major event was going to be, and when it's supposed to happen!'

'That's the one thing I wasn't able to discover,' said Roland. 'Sorry.'

'My dear chap, don't apologize! The information you've already given us is gold dust.'

'Could it be an invasion?' asked Kim. 'Or is that just an added threat? Sign the deal with Hitler, or we attack?'

'I think that's more probable,' said M. 'I can't see the Germans being realistically in a position to mount a full-scale invasion in less than a week. When's the next meeting scheduled for, Foxy?'

Roland rubbed a hand through his hair. 'That's the worrying thing. I don't know. I got a feeling that they don't want me around for that one.'

'Hmm. That makes things even more difficult. Is there any chance of getting listening devices into the building?'

'They have the room swept for bugs before every meeting.'

'Anything in writing?'

Roland shook his head. 'Not that I've seen. Their security is pretty tight.'

The three talked around the problem without finding any further likely approaches, until M. stood up and stretched his arms.

'There's no point in going on any longer. We all need to get some sleep. I'll come back tomorrow morning, when I've had a chance to digest what you've told me.'

\* \* \*

M. was back while they were still eating breakfast.

'I think there's another approach we could try. Foxy, how do you feel about trying to infiltrate the people who are organizing this mob? It seems to be an important part of the plan. They must know when it's all going to happen.'

'Great idea!' Roland looked more cheerful. 'And I think I know where to start. Lyndham mentioned a bloke called Young who will take charge of that side of things. He operates from a pub called the Star in Hackney Downs.'

'Good,' M. said. 'I'll leave you to follow that up.'

'Who owns the house in Flood Walk?' asked Kim.

'Chap by the name of Justin Verney,' Roland told her. 'Why?'

'Does he employ any domestic staff? If he has a cook, or a cleaner, maybe we could ensure that they became unavailable for a day or two, so he would need to turn to an agency for a substitute.'

'Meaning you?' asked M.

'It would give me a chance to have a nose round, see if I can pick up any hints.'

'It won't work, I'm afraid,' said Roland. 'The only staff is one elderly lady who comes in every morning. She's been with Verney since the year dot. I can't see him letting a stranger into the house.'

'If we knew when the next meeting was going to be, maybe I could burgle my way in and eavesdrop.'

'Too dangerous!' protested Roland.

'If it comes to it, we may have to take that option,' said M.

'Then I'll do it!' he said.

'Don't be stupid. I've got a lot more experience of this sort of thing than you have,' retorted Kim.

'Children! Children!' said M. placatingly. 'There's no point in squabbling over it. If it comes to it, I shall make the decision. But you have given me an idea, Kim. The men we're talking about are all members of the House of Lords. We know already that quite a few peers are sympathetic to Mosley's philosophy. I have no doubt that Lyndham and Hastings will be canvassing for support for this coup. And the most likely place for that to happen is in the bar or the restaurant. It might be very useful to have eyes and ears on what's going on there.'

'You're thinking I might get a job working there?' said Kim. 'But under what pretext?'

M. pursed his lips. 'I think I can get someone to suggest to the manager that there's a threat to national security — possibly give him the idea that the IRA are planning to plant a bomb . . . Leave all that to me. Assuming of course that you are willing to undertake the task.'

Kim grinned. 'Why am I starting to feel that there's something about me that fits the role of serving wench, or a Mrs Mop? Yes, of course. Anything rather than sit here biting my nails.'

'Good. I'll see what I can arrange. Meanwhile, Foxy, see if you can get any useful information from these Blackshirts, if you can contact them.'

\* \* \*

Hackney Downs was one of the more pleasant areas of East London, with broad streets lined with mainly Victorian houses. Compared with nearby areas it had not suffered as much damage from enemy bombers. The Star occupied a large building on a corner, and at lunchtime the public bar was busy with working men, while in the saloon bar respectably dressed businessmen and a few ladies were enjoying a drink and a sandwich. Roland bought himself a pint of bitter in the public bar and looked around him. Most of the men were middle-aged, but there were a few younger ones in uniform — men on leave, presumably. There was also a small group of men in civvies who looked young enough to have been in the forces. Roland leaned on the bar and attracted the attention of a barmaid with bleached-blonde hair growing out to reveal mousy brown roots.

''Scuse me, gorgeous. I'm looking for a man called Billy Young.'

She nodded across the room to a table by the window where a narrow-faced man with a chin darkened by five o'clock shadow was talking to two others. 'That's him over there.'

Roland carried his beer across to the table she indicated. 'Excuse me, gents. I wonder if I could have a word.'

Young looked at him noncommittally. 'Depends on who you are and what you want.'

'Name's Fox, Ronald Fox. Some people call me Foxy.'

'Do they now?' Young raised his eyebrows. 'And what can I do for you, Mr Fox?'

'Bloke at the Pig and Whistle in Whitechapel told me you might have use for a man who wishes he'd had the sense to put on a black shirt before they were banned.'

Young leaned back in his seat. 'What makes you think that?'

Roland pulled up a chair and sat down. ''Cos I've been thinking for a long time that we're fighting this bloody war on the wrong side. We should have listened to Oswald Mosley years ago. I've been looking to join up with other blokes who think the same way.'

Young regarded him through narrowed eyes. 'How do I know you're not a government nark?'

'Would it help if I told you I've just got out of Brixton? I was in there along with Barry Domville and John Beckett. Talking to them made me see the light.'

'What was you in for?'

'I was called up, wasn't I? Army reckoned I was spreading seditious ideas among the troops, so they kicked me out and sent me to Brixton, under Defence Regulation 18b. I convinced the governor I'd changed my ways and wanted to join up again and he let me out.'

'Are you going to join up?' Young enquired.

'Me? Fight against the men we should be calling brothers? What do you think?'

Young looked round at his companions and raised his eyebrows. A couple of them nodded.

'And you're prepared to help the cause?'

'Just tell me what I can do.'

'Come to this address at seven o'clock tonight, and we'll see about it.'

Roland stood the group a round of drinks and then made his excuses and left. Half an hour later he was back at the flat.

When Kim heard about the appointment, she looked at him in horrified amazement. 'Are you out of your mind? You could end up with a knife in your back.'

'I can handle myself. We've both been through the same training at Arisaig. All that unarmed combat has to come in useful sometime.'

'If you get a chance to use it.'

'Look, you know what they say? You can't con a conner. I've been doing this sort of thing most of my life. Trust me!'

Kim saw that it was impossible to dissuade him and gave up the attempt. He cooked them a quick supper of Spam fritters and then it was time for him to leave again, if he was to reach Hackney Downs at the appointed time. He kissed her goodbye and she held him close for a moment.

'Good luck, my darling. Be careful.'

'Trust me,' he said again, and was gone.

It was dark by the time he arrived. The address he had been given turned out to be a lock-up under the railway arches near the station. In the pitch darkness of the blackout he had to almost feel his way to the door.

'You turned up, then.' The voice came out of the darkness a few yards to his right. 'You're taking a fucking risk!'

'Why? Can't I trust you?'

'Question is, can we trust you?'

'I'm here, aren't I? Why are we standing around in the dark?'

There was a pause, then he heard a key rattle in a lock and a door opened with a groan of rusty hinges.

'Inside!' he was ordered.

Roland stepped forward, prepared to hear the door being closed behind him, ready to swing round and throw his weight against it before it could be shut; but instead a dim electric light bulb came on and Young and three other men followed him inside.

'Get the bloody door shut before we have the ARP after us for showing a light,' Young ordered.

Looking around Roland was astonished to see a printing press and a stack of paper. Young crossed to a table and picked up a leaflet from a pile.

'Take a look,' he said.

The leaflet bore the insignia of the BUF and the slogan *TAKE BACK OUR COUNTRY*. Underneath that were the words: *The Germans are not our enemies. The real enemies of our country are the Jews and the Communists who are conspiring to control commerce and the press. Join the BUF and keep England for the English!*

'Blimey!' said Roland. 'That's telling them straight!'

There was a tap on the door and a murmured exchange of passwords and three young women were admitted. They were all, as far as Roland could tell in the dim light, attractive girls. All three were wearing nondescript raincoats, but when they shed them, they revealed smart black shirts and trousers, tucked into shiny black boots.

Young introduced them by their first names only, adding, 'This is Foxy. New recruit. You'll need to show him the ropes.'

'Pleasure, I'm sure!' The girl introduced as Gloria fluttered her eyelashes at him.

'Right!' Young went on. 'There's fifty each to be posted before it gets light. You know the places. Noticeboards, walls, bus stops, anywhere people are bound to see them. Just watch out for the rozzers and the air raid wardens. Got your torches? Remember, only use them when you have to and keep your fingers over them to cut down the light. OK?'

He handed Roland a sheaf of leaflets. 'Just don't get caught with them or you'll end up back in Brixton.'

'I didn't bring a torch,' he said.

'Never mind. You can share mine,' whispered Gloria. 'Billy said to show you the ropes. You stick with me.'

Aware of the jealous glares of the other two girls boring into his back, Roland let her lead him out into the night.

## CHAPTER 21

Kim spent the evening torturing herself with the thought of what might be happening to Roland. At eleven she forced herself to go to bed, but she couldn't sleep.

She recalled how she had been warned during her training of the dangers of becoming too attached to her fellow agents. It could compromise your ability to act rationally in an emergency. She was beginning to understand the strength of the argument — not that there was an emergency right now, but her anxiety was making it hard to think clearly. Without adequate sleep she would be less able to deal with whatever the day might bring. Around midnight she convinced herself that falling in love with Roland had been a *very* bad idea.

That did not, however, prevent her from jumping out of bed and throwing her arms round him when he came into the room shortly after 1 a.m.

She recoiled immediately. 'You stink of cheap perfume! What the hell have you been doing?'

He ran his hand over his hair with the rueful grin she was coming to know so well. 'Oh, one has to make sacrifices for the good of the cause.'

'Sacrifices? What sacrifices?'

'Allowing myself to succumb to the charms of a young lady by the name of Gloria.'

'You've been making love to a woman who smells like that!'

He spread his hands, palms outward, in a gesture of pacification. 'It was a kiss, that's all. Nothing more, I swear.'

'And in what way was this necessary for the good of the cause?'

'I had to establish my credentials, didn't I? You remember "adding verisimilitude to an otherwise bald and unconvincing narrative"? I didn't want them to think I had divided loyalties.'

She stood back and looked at him. 'All right. I'll accept the excuse, this time. But for Pete's sake go and have a shower before you come to bed.'

Over breakfast next morning he told her about his night's adventures and showed her a copy of the leaflet. 'It's sickening stiff and I hated myself for sticking them up all over Hackney Downs. But needs must . . .'

Kim examined the leaflet and looked up abruptly. 'You're right, it is sickening. But look! The symbol of the BUF! It's a lightning bolt!'

He took the paper from her. At the top of it was a red square enclosing a white circle filled in with blue. Slashed across the blue was a jagged white line. 'You're right! I hadn't seen it in the light until now. So, now it makes sense! *Blitzschlag*!'

'Yes,' she responded. 'It's the symbol I saw drawn in blood on the headboard of Lily's bed. If we ever needed it, here's the proof that this whole business is being orchestrated by the BUF.'

M. arrived shortly afterwards and listened to Roland's report.

'Good. You seem to have found yourself a good position to pick up any hints of when this coup is planned to take place.' He took a sip of the coffee Kim had poured for him and turned his attention to her. 'Now, Kim. I've arranged things with the manager of the restaurant in the House of Lords. Someone will be along shortly to escort you there and introduce you. Once you're in situ there are a couple of names you should look out for. One is Esmond Harmsworth, Second Viscount Rothermere.'

'Doesn't he own the *Daily Mail*?' Kim put in.

'Among other publications, yes. His father, Harold, was an unashamed admirer of Hitler and vehemently opposed to the idea of fighting him, and made that clear when he ran the paper. The son is not as strident, but his sympathies are distinctly right wing and he has come out in opposition to the resettlement of Jewish refugees in this country. These men we are watching are bound to need the support of an influential newspaper for the planned coup, and the *Daily Mail* is the obvious choice. Lyndham and Hastings will want to give him some advanced warning, so watch out for any contact between them. The other one to watch is David Mitford, Baron Redesdale. He's a curmudgeonly old bugger and a supporter of appeasement before the war. Since the outbreak of war he's made a point of broadcasting his patriotism and his hatred of the Hun, but his eldest daughter is Diana, Lady Mosley, and another daughter, Unity, was rumoured to be in love with Hitler and tried to shoot herself when we declared war. The family attended the Nuremberg rally and were entertained by Hitler at Berchtesgaden in 1938. I suspect that the BUF's brand of patriotism would appeal to him, so the plotters might try to recruit his support. There's no guarantee that either of them will be there today or in the next few days, but Lyndham and his cronies will want to pack in as many supporters as possible for Mosley's big speech, so they will probably be networking among all the peers in attendance. Just watch out for any promising contacts. Understood?

'Very good, sir.' Kim felt a tremor of excitement at the prospect of action. She'd had enough of sitting around in the flat waiting for other people.

Later that morning Kim was escorted by a plain-clothes police officer, whose name and rank she was never told, to the staff entrance to the Upper Chamber and introduced to the manager in charge of the Peers' Dining Room. She was given the uniform black dress and white cap and apron and shown where to change, then handed over to the head waiter. He seemed slightly bemused to discover that he had, in fact, been short-staffed for some time without being aware of it, but after a brief interrogation to establish that she had some experience — questions she had anticipated and answered from the legend she had created for herself in the hours since M. had suggested the plan — he gave her a brief tour of the long, gloomy dining room with its panelled ceiling and heavy gold-framed portraits of past members and passed her on to a waitress who introduced herself as Julie. Julie was plump and cheerful, with a roguish twinkle in her eye. Kim confessed to her that she was a little nervous of serving such eminent gentlemen, but Julie reassured her that most of them were lovely old gents.

'Just watch out for your bottom being pinched when you're in the middle of serving the soup.'

Kim's experience of waiting at table began and ended with her stint in the Lion d'Or, but growing up as a diplomat's daughter she had attended enough formal dinners to understand the intricacies of silver service, and she managed to get through lunch without pouring mock turtle soup over a prominent, pinstripe-clad belly or dropping a hot potato down the neck of a minister of the Crown.

She recognized Viscount Lyndham and Lord Hastings from her surveillance of Dr Kline's consulting rooms and tried without success to eavesdrop on their conversations with other peers, but by the end of her duties she felt she had gained little useful information.

She got back to the flat as Roland was preparing to go out. There was no point in telling him to be careful, so she contented herself with saying, 'Don't come back tonight stinking of that awful scent! There are limits to the sacrifices we can be expected to make.'

He laughed and kissed her. 'I'll do my best.'

* * *

Roland found the lock-up already crowded with people. He slipped inside and found a position at the back of the group. As before, Young took charge.

'Before you go out leafleting, we need to have a council of war, so grab yourselves a seat and pay attention.'

Once everyone had all found somewhere to perch, Young looked around at them, holding the gaze of first one then another. Roland recognized grimly that this man was a fanatic.

'You all know a big day is coming, and it won't be long now. When we get the word, each of you will have an important job to do. As you know, we have been asked to assemble in Trafalgar Square, preparatory to marching on Westminster. We are to travel in ones and twos, some leaving early, others coming along later, so that the police don't get the idea that a demonstration is happening until it's too late. And we shall not be alone. Groups will be coming from Poplar, Stepney, Bethnal Green and Walthamstow and there will be more from south of the river. I'm going to give each of you a phone number. When you get the word from me, you are to call that number. All you need to say is "Heil, Mosley" and the person at the other end will know it's time to move. Don't go jumping the gun. Wait until I tell you. But it is vital that everyone gets the message. Understood?'

There was a murmur of assent. Young produced a notebook from his inside breast pocket and began to copy out numbers onto a sheet of paper. When he had finished, he tore the sheet into strips and handed one strip to each person present. Roland looked at the number he had been given. It began BAT, which he knew was Battersea. Young put the notebook in his pocket.

Roland watched him through the corner of his eye. If he could come into possession of these numbers, it would be invaluable in tracking down leading members of Mosley's Blackshirts once the coup had been thwarted.

Roland recalled the lesson he had been given at Beaulieu in how to pick pockets. It was a risky strategy. If he was caught there would be no way of convincing Young that his motives were innocent and he would probably end up in the Thames with his throat cut. But the possible gain was worth it.

One of the young women was brewing cocoa on a Primus stove. Roland took the mug that was offered him. Young was stooping over a table, counting out leaflets into bundles of fifty. Roland wandered over.

'Need a hand?'

As he spoke, his foot caught on the table leg and lurched into Young, spilling hot cocoa down the front of his jacket.

'Look what you're fucking doing!' Young yelled at him.

'Oh Christ! I'm sorry. Here, let me wipe it for you.' He had a handkerchief ready and began energetically mopping the front of the jacket, apologizing as he did it. By the time Young shrugged him off with an irritable 'That'll do! Get off me!' the notebook had been transferred from his pocket to Roland's.

The problem now was to copy the numbers without being seen, and before Young missed the book. To act too fast might look suspicious. Roland forced himself to finish what was left of his cocoa. The others were putting on outdoor coats, ready to sally out for another night of leaflet posting.

'Blimey, that cocoa's gone straight through me!' he exclaimed. 'I'll have to have a slash.'

In a dark corner under one of the adjacent railway arches he pulled out the notebook and flicked on the small torch he had brought with him, masking the light with his hand. He hastily copied the numbers onto a sheet of paper, which he then screwed up and added to a collection of old bus tickets and sweet wrappers in his trouser pocket.

All that remained now was to get the book back into Young's pocket without being detected.

To Roland's relief, when he went back inside, Young's jacket, still slightly damp, was hanging on the back of a chair. While he was busy handing out leaflets, Roland slipped the book back into his pocket.

Gloria sidled up to him. 'I was wondering where you'd got to. Are you ready?'

He looked at her. Had she noticed anything? But her expression conveyed nothing more than a flirtatious invitation. He contrived to look slightly embarrassed. 'Look, I think I ought to manage for myself tonight. I don't want Billy to think I need a babysitter. I mean, last night was good, but I've seen some of the looks the other girls gave you. I don't want to cause a quarrel. We need to stick together — as a team, I mean.'

He thought for a minute she was going to argue, but she just shrugged her shoulders and turned away. 'Suit yourself. I was only offering.'

He went through the motions of posting up his share of the leaflets, in case he was being watched, and headed home with a sense of triumph. It had been a really productive evening.

Arriving back at the flat he was greeted by Kim with a suspicious sniff. 'Oh! No nasty scent tonight? That's an improvement.'

\* \* \*

The Peers' Dining Room was crowded next morning. Julie noticed it and remarked, 'What's brought them all out of their comfy boltholes? Must be an important debate or something.'

'Who's that red-faced gent over there?' Kim asked her.

'Him? That's Lord Redesdale. You want to watch out for him. He's got a terrible temper on him. One false move and he'll bawl you out so the whole room can hear.'

'Thanks for the warning,' said Kim.

M. had given her photographs of both Lord Redesdale and Esmond Harmsworth, and she was delighted to see the second man come into the dining room shortly afterwards. Lyndham and Hastings were both already there, sitting separately and chatting affably to their neighbours. Kim watched them as well as she was able while doing her job. At one point she nearly bumped into another noble gentleman when she was carrying a tureen of soup and was curtly told to look where she was going.

Neither Redesdale nor Harmsworth had chosen to sit at one of the tables she had been allocated to serve, so it was hard to get close to them. Her opportunity soon came.

'You, girl! What do you think you're playing at? This soup is stone cold.' Redesdale's voice rang out across the dining room. 'It's inedible.'

'Yes, sir. Sorry, sir,' apologized Julie hastily. She hurried back into the kitchen and returned with a steaming bowl.

He was still complaining as Kim passed behind him.

'If I wanted cold soup, I'd move to bloody Spain.'

Back in the kitchen to collect the main dishes, Kim sidled sympathetically up to Julie. 'What an awful man. I heard him having a go at you. Would you like me to serve him this course?'

'Be my guest,' said Julie hotly. 'I'm so cross, I feel like chucking it over him.'

Kim took him his plate of calf's liver and then took her time serving his vegetables.

'Get a bloody move on,' he growled. 'I want to eat this for lunch, not dinner.'

'Sorry, my lord.'

She was about to move away when she saw Lyndham coming towards them. Kim bent to pick up an imaginary pea from the carpet and heard him mutter, 'Need to talk. Gents. Ten minutes.'

Looking around the room, she saw Hastings approach Esmond Harmsworth and exchange a few words. Kim's pulse quickened. This could be exactly what M. had predicted. Lyndham wanted to give his friends prior warning of what they were planning. She needed to hear what was said. She carried her empty dishes back to the kitchen and slipped out into the corridor.

If only Roland was here. Someone needed to be in the gents when this meeting took place, but what possible excuse could she give for being there?

There was one possibility. She made her way towards the gentleman's cloakroom. Not far from it there was a small cupboard where cleaning materials were kept.

With a feeling of déjà vu, she armed herself with a mop and bucket and went to the door. She took a deep breath and pushed it open, ready to retreat with an apology if the room was occupied.

Miraculously, it was empty. She went into one of the cubicles and locked the door. Her watch told her that the ten minutes were almost up. She heard the door open and Lyndham's voice.

'Enjoy your lunch, old man?'

The reply was an unintelligible grunt, followed by the sound of someone using the urinal.

The door opened again and she heard Redesdale enquire grumpily, 'What's all this about?'

'Hang on!' A warning tone, in Lyndham's voice.

More splashing as one of them relieved himself, then the unidentified man said, 'Got to get off. I'm supposed to be in a meeting.' And the door opened and closed again.

'Now, what's so urgent you have to drag me away from my lunch?' grumbled Redesdale.

'All in good time,' responded Lyndham, adding, 'Ah, here they are,' as the door opened once more.

'Who's this?' asked Redesdale.

'A guest of mine.' A new voice — Hastings's, presumably. 'Don't worry. He's safe. I can vouch for him.'

'So, does this mean we're going ahead?' said Redesdale.

Hastings spoke again. 'Are you quite sure this chap is up to the job?'

'Certain.' Lyndham told him. 'He's a superb marksman. He's won medals.'

The door opened and closed again. 'Well, I'm here.' That must be Harmsworth. 'What have you got for me?'

'I just want to suggest you hold the front page on Thursday the ninth. You'll have the scoop of the century for the later editions.'

'The ninth? So is that—?'

'Wait!' Another voice cut in — not that of any of the noble gentlemen she had seen earlier, but a voice that sent a chill through her stomach. 'Are we sure we're not being overheard? Check the cubicles.'

Doors banged open. Then hers was rattled. 'Who's in there?' A pause, then, 'Come on out, whoever you are.'

'Maybe the door's stuck,' someone suggested.

'Soon fix that!' Lyndham's voice.

When the door burst open, yielding to his shoulder charge, Kim was on her knees, scrubbing the toilet bowl.

'What the hell are you doing there?'

'Sorry! Sorry, my lord.' She kept her head down and roughened her voice. 'It ain't my fault. Someone made a bit of a mess and I was asked to clean it up.'

'Just a minute!' It was the stranger again. 'She's lying. Get her out here so we can see her.'

Strong hands grasped her arms and she was dragged out of the cubicle. She rose slowly to her feet and found herself looking into the hypnotic gaze of Leopold Kline.

# CHAPTER 22

When M. arrived at the flat to hear the reports of his two agents, he found Roland pacing the floor, his face tense with anxiety.

'Kim isn't back. She should have been here an hour ago.'

'I'm sure there's a good reason why she's been held up,' said M. 'But if she doesn't show up before I leave, I'll get one of my contacts in the police to make some inquiries at Westminster. Now, what have you got for me?'

Roland forced himself to sit down and relay what he had learned the night before.

'So the organization is more widespread than we realized,' commented M. soberly. 'We really thought it had largely fizzled out after Mosley's arrest, but not so, it seems. No hint of when you will make this phone call, I suppose?'

'No, I'm afraid not, except that it will be any day now.'

'I keep racking my brains about potential targets. I've already alerted Special Branch to make regular searches of the Houses of Parliament, in case the fascists are planning to take a leaf out of Guy Fawkes's book, and I've dropped hints with the royal protection squaddies to be extra vigilant. Though from what you told me, it isn't the royal family they're aiming for. But at least we should be able to nip this plan to assemble a mob of supporters in the bud, thanks to your efforts.' M. ran a weary hand across his face. 'I don't suppose there's a chance of getting hold of those telephone numbers?'

Roland felt in his pocket and retrieved the screwed-up paper, producing it with the air of a conjuror completing a trick. 'You mean these?'

M. raised an eyebrow in astonishment as he took the paper. 'How did you manage to get these?'

'I seem to have added pick-pocketing to my criminal skills. But then, I had a good tutor.' Roland looked at his watch. 'Where the hell is she?'

M. got up. 'I'll get some people out looking for her. Don't worry too much. She may be following up a lead, or waiting for Lyndham and his pals to make a move of some sort. After all, not much harm can have come to her in the hallowed confines of the Palace of Westminster. Meanwhile, I need you to keep your appointment with Young and his Blackshirts.'

'But—!' protested Roland.

'No! You must go. Tonight might be the night the word goes out to use those phone numbers. We can't afford to miss that.'

* * *

How she had been transported from Westminster to where she was now — wherever that was — Kim had only the vaguest idea. She had a confused recollection of a hand over her mouth and the sharp jab of a hypodermic needle, and of being half led, half carried down a flight of stairs, with Kline's voice saying reassuringly, 'A sudden collapse, a seizure perhaps. Don't worry, I'm a doctor. I'll see she's taken care of.' After that there was a blank until she came round to find herself tied to a chair in what appeared to be someone's kitchen.

Kline was sitting opposite her, with Lyndham standing behind him. Hastings and a man she did not recognize were huddled in a corner as if for mutual safety.

'Are you finally going to enlighten us about who this woman is?' demanded Lyndham, his voice raw with anxiety.

Kline lit a cigarette and smiled gently. 'Let's ask her, shall we? I know her as Maxine, but I'm sure she has many other names.' He leaned towards Kim. 'Tell us who you really are.'

Struggling to clear her mind of whatever drug it was they had given her, it seemed to Kim that honesty might be the best policy. 'My name is Katherine Maxwell. I am a lieutenant in the First Aid Nursing Yeomanry, and as you quite well know, Dr Kline, I am a member of an elite group of special forces. In that capacity I have been training recruits, at the Inter-Services Research Bureau at Beaulieu.' She thought she saw a flicker of uncertainty in Lyndham's eyes at this information.

'In fact, not to put too fine a point on it, you are a spy,' said Kline.

'I am a patriot, working to protect our country in a time of great danger,' countered Kim.

Kline sniffed derisively at that. 'Who ordered you to investigate the activities of these gentlemen?'

'I wasn't ordered to do that by anyone,' she lied. 'I am operating on my own initiative. I want to know who killed poor Lily Harvey.'

'So what, pray tell us, were you doing masquerading as a waitress in the dining room of the House of Lords?'

Kim met his eyes. 'Earning a little extra pocket money. The rewards for spying are derisory.'

Kline got up and she saw a spark of anger in his eyes. 'Don't try to make light of this. What we are about is not a laughing matter. Hold her!'

For the first time she realized that there was someone standing behind her. Her hair was grabbed and her head was pulled back so that she was staring at the ceiling. Kline moved over to her and with quiet deliberation stubbed out his cigarette in the hollow where her collar bones met her sternum. Kim gritted her teeth and stayed quiet. This, she knew, was just the beginning.

'For Christ's sake!' broke in Lyndham. 'Ask her what she heard and who she has told.'

'I imagine she heard you, my lord, ill-advisedly telling Lord Rothermere to hold the front page on a certain date.' Kline's tone was silky but left no doubt about the contempt he felt for his fellow conspirator. 'However, since she has been in our custody from that moment on, there is no way she can have passed on the information, unless she is carrying some form of radio device.' He addressed the man behind Kim. 'Strip her.'

The bonds that held Kim to the chair were cut and she was hauled to her feet. Her dress was ripped from neck to hem so that it fell about her feet. A knife severed the fastening of her bra and it was pulled away, leaving her naked except for a suspender belt holding up her stockings and her knickers.

'Take them off,' commanded Kline, and knowing that refusal would result in a humiliating struggle, she complied.

Standing naked, she looked around at the men. Kline's face was expressionless. Lyndham looked embarrassed, and she saw Hastings's hand on his groin. The man beside him, an effete-looking character with a long fringe that partly hid his eyes, giggled — a high-pitched sound quickly cut off. It was clear that this was something completely outside their experience.

'Search her,' ordered Kline.

Rough hands ran over her body, feeling in her armpits, under her breasts, between her legs.

'She's clean.'

'So there we are,' said Kline, looking at the others. 'She cannot possibly have passed on what she heard. All we need to do is make sure she doesn't get the opportunity.'

'Then kill the bitch!' It was Hastings. He was aroused by her nakedness, and he knew she had seen it and was embarrassed.

'Oh, come, come,' said Kline. 'Do we need to soil our hands? I'm sure Justin doesn't want blood all over his kitchen. There are other ways.' He turned to the man with the fringe. 'I take it this house has a cellar?'

Cold fear ran through Kim's nerves. Physical violence she had been prepared for, but she should have expected this. Kline knew it was the one thing that would break her when all else failed.

'Yes, it has,' the man called Justin responded doubtfully. Where had she heard that name recently?

'Does it have a delivery hatch? One that opens onto the street?'

'It did have. But I had it bricked up. I meant to use it for a wine cellar but I never got round to it.'

'So what is in it?' demanded Kline.

'Nothing at all.'

'Excellent. Show us the way, please. Bruno, bring the young lady.'

'But she's been eavesdropping.' There was something about the voice that sounded familiar, a wheedling tone like a child denied a treat. 'Don't you think she deserves to have her ears stoppered?'

'Not this time, Bruno. We haven't got time for little refinements like that. Bring her.'

'Just a minute!' cut in Lyndham. 'What exactly are you planning? We could never let her go, you know, even after . . . She has to be silenced.'

'Of course. Tell me. Have you ever visited a medieval castle and been shown the oubliette? It's a hole in the ground leading to an underground chamber from which there is no exit. A place in which to dispose of your enemies and forget them.' Kline moved to the door. 'Bring her, Bruno.'

Her arms were pulled behind her and she was shoved towards a door. She twisted sideways, breaking his hold for a moment, and caught sight of his face.

Sykes, the Beaulieu gardener.

'*You!* You killed poor Lily.'

These thoughts flashed through her mind as she was pushed out into the hallway and along a passage. One fleeting image struck her as she passed — a large, framed photograph of a young man standing beside Adolf Hitler, flanked

227

by candles and flowers, like a shrine. This was the picture Roland had described — the house in Flood Walk. So that's where she was. As they passed a half-open door, she caught the acrid smell of fresh paint.

Justin, who seemed to be on the brink of hysteria, gave another high-pitched giggle.

'Don't mind the smell of paint, chaps. The front window was blown out by a bomb blast and I've only just managed to get someone in to redecorate.'

Then a door was opened at the end of the passage, and beyond it was only darkness.

Someone touched a switch and a light came on, showing a steep flight of stairs leading downwards. Bruno jerked her to the top step and gave her a shove that sent her headfirst into blackness. By the time she had picked herself up, the light had been turned off and the door slammed shut. Bruised and shaken, she felt her way back to the steps and sat on the lowest one, running her hands over her body in an effort to assess the damage. Her left arm was hurting, but she could still flex her fingers, so at least it wasn't broken. She could feel a trickle of blood running down from her left knee, but the wound did not seem to be extensive.

She got up and groped her way to the top of the steps. The door was solid and unyielding. Turning back, she became aware that the darkness was not total. Somewhere over her head there was not exactly light, but a thinning of the gloom, and as her eyes became more accustomed, she realized that set into the roof was a panel of small, thick glass panes — the kind she had often noticed when she was walking along city streets. At the time she had wondered vaguely how much use they could possibly be when they were so covered in grime and debris, but now she regarded the little squares of glass as if they were a miracle.

Now that she could see, her incarceration was much more bearable and, after all, she reminded herself, she had the means to ensure that it was only temporary.

Kline and his cronies had searched her, but not quite thoroughly enough. She ran her hands through her hair and extracted a clip. Anyone noticing it would have assumed it was purely decorative, but in fact it was a cleverly constructed lock-pick. Her instinct was to put it to use at once, but she forced herself to be patient. Not until she was sure that everyone had left or retired to bed did she dare to proceed.

She felt her way back to the bottom step and sat down, trying to breath evenly and still her racing thoughts.

She tried to calculate the time. It had been lunchtime when she was taken. She could not tell how long she had been semi-conscious but she thought probably not more than an hour. The interrogation had not taken long, so it must still be afternoon. Peering up at the glass in the roof, she could see it was still light outside. At this time of year, darkness would not come until after eight o'clock. With the blackout there would be no street lights. She told herself that she must not make her move until it had been dark for at least three hours. How to calculate that was going to be difficult. Her watch had gone with her clothes.

In the half-light she examined her surroundings. The cellar was perhaps fifteen feet square, with brick walls encrusted with mould and a stone-flagged floor, and as Justin had said it was completely empty. Abruptly, the door was opened again, but before she could scramble to her feet something was thrown down to her and the door slammed again. She groped around and touched something soft — a blanket!

So someone up there had a conscience and felt some pity for her predicament. She wondered who. The likely candidate seemed to be the man called Justin. He struck her as a very unlikely conspirator. Did the others have some hold on him? She wrapped the blanket round herself, grateful for its warmth. The cellar was cool, rather than cold, but without any clothes on she was already beginning to feel the damp chill seeping into her bones. The thought of what Kline intended for her sent a shudder through her body. Had he meant what he said about the oubliette — the place where an enemy could be forgotten and left to die? No, surely he intended to bring her out for questioning once her spirit had been broken. That was the technique he had learned from the Gestapo.

Above, the glass panes darkened periodically as people walked over them, and she was tempted to try shouting for help, but she doubted if the sound would penetrate to the street. Besides, it might result in Kline deciding she must be silenced after all. She needed him to leave her here overnight if she was to have any chance of escaping.

As if her thoughts had summoned him, she heard noises from the top of the steps. She got to her feet, her heart pounding,

The door stayed closed but the noises persisted. After a minute, she climbed the steps and pressed her ear to the door. She could hear a muffled thumping and scraping but could not deduce what the cause might be. Once or twice she heard voices, but could not make out any words. Eventually the noises stopped. She remained for a while, straining her ears for any sound, but all was silent.

* * *

The flat was still empty when Roland returned from Hackney. He was about to pick up the phone to call M. when the Brigadier arrived.

'Not good news, I'm afraid. My contact in the police reports that a young woman apparently in a state of collapse was escorted out of the House of Lords by a man claiming to be a doctor. When pressed further, he said he thought the doctor had a German accent.'

'Kline! Kline's got her!' Roland's voice cracked on the words. 'We've got to get her out of his hands before . . . before . . . There are no limits to what that man is prepared to do. We have to find her!'

'Of course.' M.'s calmness checked Roland's rising panic. 'The question is, where is he likely to have taken her? The obvious place is his consulting rooms in Harley Street. I've obtained an emergency search warrant on the grounds that we suspect an enemy alien may be hiding out there. The police will be there as we speak and I've given them this number. Now, what news have you for me?'

'None, I'm afraid. There's still no hint of when the balloon is supposed to go up.'

M. pursed his lips. 'Tomorrow is the eighth. I was convinced this attack, or whatever it is, must be timed for before Churchill returns, but perhaps I'm wrong.'

'When does the PM get back?' asked Roland.

'HMS *Renown* is due to dock at Greenock on the morning of the ninth.'

The telephone rang and M. snatched it up. 'Nothing? You're quite sure? Yes, of course. I'm not suggesting you were anything but thorough. Sorry to have sent you on a wild goose chase. Yes, thank you. Goodbye.'

'They haven't found her,' said Roland flatly.

'No, I'm afraid not.' M.'s expression was grim

'You don't think he might have taken her back to Beaulieu?'

'It seems unlikely, but I'll get onto the CO and have him institute a search. With the security they have I wouldn't have thought he would risk taking her there, but still . . .' He reached for the phone.

While M. spoke on the phone Roland resumed his distracted pacing.

The brigadier put down the receiver. 'They'll search, but I don't hold out much hope.' He looked at his watch. 'It's too late to do any more tonight.' He put his hand on Roland's arm. 'Try to get some sleep.'

'No chance of that,' Roland replied grimly.

* * *

The hours crawled past. Kim's stomach growled with hunger and her throat was parched. She forced herself to keep moving, in an effort to keep warm.

At last the light faded and she was left in encroaching darkness. She forced herself to wait longer, counting the seconds and ticking off every minute on her fingers. After she had counted ten, she found it impossible to concentrate any longer and instead sat hunched on the step, gazing into the darkness. When that too became unbearable, she got up stiffly and crept up the steps. There was no sound from beyond the door.

Her fingers were numb with cold and she had to massage them and flex her hands to make them supple enough for the work she had to do.

She ran her fingers over the lock. It felt like a simple, basic mechanism. She pulled her lock pick out of her hair and within seconds she felt the lock yield. She stood still, listening again, but the house was silent. As she hoped, it seemed the conspirators had gone home and the owner was in bed.

Slowly, she turned the handle, careful to avoid any noise, and pulled the door open.

Instead of the exit to the hall she was confronted by a brick wall.

For a moment she thought she must somehow have become disorientated. This must be a different door, one she had not noticed when examining the cellar. This couldn't be the one she had come through.

But of course it was.

This was the only way out.

And it was blocked.

Not by some temporary barrier but by a solid wall.

She put her hands flat against it and pushed. It did not give. She felt round the edges. Every gap had been filled with mortar. She moved back as far as the step she stood on would allow and threw herself against it. The only result was a bruised shoulder.

She understood now what those noises had been. It was not hard to imagine where her captors had obtained the necessary materials. All over London there were bomb-damaged houses, skeletons where a few walls remained standing among the rubble. She assumed Chelsea had suffered along with the rest of the city. And Bruno Sykes had many skills, brick-laying among them.

Stunned, she sank down on the steps again and made herself think. It could not be more than a few hours since the wall was completed. Surely mortar took longer than that to set completely?

She stood up again and tried scraping at the mortar at the edge of one brick. Some of it came away under her fingernails. With new hope, she set to work. Her only tool was the lock pick and she had hardly succeeded in clearing one edge of the brick before it snapped in half. She persisted with the other half until that too broke off. After that, she was reduced to using her fingernails. It felt like ages, but at last she succeeded in loosening one brick. By wriggling it from side to side she was finally able to pull it out. Now, surely, all that remained was to push out enough bricks to make a hole large enough for her to crawl through.

No light showed through the gap she had made, but that was not surprising. The house would be in darkness. She shoved at the bricks on either side and felt them move, but then they seemed to meet some obstruction. She reached into the hole. Instead of passing through her hand struck a solid surface.

With a sob of frustration she rammed her fist against it. It responded with a dull thud. In desperation she punched again and again, until her knuckles were bruised. She was forced to accept that after finishing the wall her captors, to make doubly sure she would never escape, or perhaps to conceal what they had done, had then secured a solid panel of wood — possibly a door taken from one of the bombed-out houses nearby — in front of it.

The implications were devastating. If Foxy searched the house, as she felt sure he would, would he remember there had been a door to the cellar? She recalled Justin's apology for the smell of paint. There were decorators working in the house. It would be easy to paste some wallpaper they had left over the new panel, making it indistinguishable to anyone who did not know the layout of the house.

No one would ever suspect the existence of a cellar.

Kline had never intended to bring her out. She was trapped and there was no way out.

The perilous grip she had kept over her emotions crumbled away. She lifted her head and the sound she emitted was the howl of an animal in pain. Mingled with that were words, begging for help, begging for mercy; but the walls of the cellar echoed them back in mockery and eventually they subsided into sobs and finally into silence.

CHAPTER 23

Unable to rest, Roland spent the hours after M. had left roaming the streets around Westminster, stopping taxis to ask the drivers if they had picked up a doctor with a young woman in a state of collapse that afternoon. It had started raining hard so there were few people about, and the taxi drivers were disinclined to spend time searching their memories when they could be searching for a paying passenger. Then, when it was almost midnight, he had a breakthrough.

'Matter of fact,' said the cabbie, 'I do remember something like that. I was flagged down by a well-dressed gent outside the Houses of Parliament, and when I stopped this other bloke appeared, holding a girl up. I thought at first she was pissed, but it turned out she'd had some kind of seizure and the bloke with her was a doctor.'

'Can you describe him?' Roland caught hold of the man's sleeve in his excitement.

The taxi driver pulled back out of reach. 'Not very tall, big head. Had a funny accent. What's all this about? You a copper?'

'Private investigator. We think the young lady in question may have been kidnapped. Where did you take them?'

'Chelsea way, somewhere. I don't recall the address.'

'Would it have been Flood Walk?' Roland suggested eagerly.

'Yeah, that's it! Name like that I ought to remember. The way it's been raining it's probably under water by now.' The cabbie spoke with a laugh.

Roland pulled a half crown coin from his pocket and handed it over. 'Thanks, chum! You've been a great help.'

\* \* \*

Kim was roused from an uneasy doze by the sound of steady drumming above her head. She sat up, pulling the blanket tighter. The cellar was in darkness but in the world above it was raining, and raining hard. She got up and stretched. She no longer felt hungry but she was tormented by thirst. How long had she been here? It was still night-time, so it was only a matter of hours, but felt like eternity.

A sudden gleam of hope struck through her despair. Roland knew of this house. When he realized that she had been taken, he would search for her — that she knew, and this would surely be the first place he would look. But had he ever seen the door leading to the cellar? Probably he had never been further than the sitting room. Might he even notice the newly built wall, where a door had once been?

Then a new thought struck her like a blow. If Roland were to search the house — really search it — he would alert Justin and the other conspirators. They would have time to alter their plans, whatever they were, and all the work she and Roland had done to thwart them would be for nothing. She knew that Brigadier M. would say that the safety of the realm must come before the search for her. If she had to be sacrificed for the greater good — well, such were the fortunes of war.

Kim paced the small cellar until she suddenly realized that her feet were wet. The floor of the cellar was awash in water.

*How is the rain getting in?* she asked herself.

She looped the blanket around her neck to keep it out of the water and paddled round the cellar, feeling for water dripping in. There was nothing. The roof seemed intact, with no sign of any leaks.

Eventually she realized that the rising water was coming from the middle of the floor. It was bubbling up from somewhere below as if forced by pressure from underneath.

Kim dropped to her knees and cupped her hands in the fountain, drinking in great gulps of vile-tasting water.

From lapping about her ankles, the water soon rose up her shins. She took refuge on the steps. It struck her that this was probably why this street was called Flood Walk. It was low-lying and not far from the Thames. Probably at one time it had regularly flooded when the river overflowed its banks.

The water was bubbling up through a drain, created presumably to carry away flood water. But flooding had stopped since the building of the Embankment, surely?

Now, watching the water level creep up over the steps on which she sat, she began to wonder how far it would reach. She imagined herself floating against the ceiling, struggling to find an air pocket to allow her to breathe.

* * *

When Roland reached Flood Walk it was still raining, and with the blackout in force, he had to feel his way along. Several of the houses had been badly damaged in the Blitz and the pavement was strewn with bits of rubble. When he guessed that he had reached the house where he had met the conspirators, he risked turning on his torch, cupping his hand over it to reduce the light. Anyone showing a light, even a glimmer from a torch, was likely to hear the shout of an air raid warden: '*Put that light out!*' But there had been no warning of an impending raid and there were apparently no wardens in the vicinity.

It was only a small house, little more than a cottage left over from when this part of London was still almost countryside. Roland reasoned that in most houses of this size the master bedroom was usually at the back. So it made sense to start at the front. He pushed open the front gate and walked silently, on rubber-shod soles, to the front door. Rather than attempting that, he moved sideways to the window of the front room, which was being redecorated. There was a chance the window might have been opened to ventilate the room.

To Roland's relief, the top pane of the sash window had been left open a crack. He climbed onto the sill and inserted his fingers into the gap, pressing down and hoping that the mechanism was well oiled. He was in luck — the window slid downwards almost silently. He reached in, undid the catch and pushed the lower pane up until he could swing his leg over the sill and slide into the room.

As he expected, his torch showed him that the room was empty except for a trestle and various buckets and pots. There was nowhere anyone could be hidden. Nevertheless, he got down on his hands and knees and felt around the floor, looking for any sign of a loose board. There was nothing. He opened the door cautiously and stepped out into the hallway. Oddly, the smell of plaster and wallpaper paste was stronger here than in the room. He decided to try upstairs.

Very carefully, testing each step for a squeaky floorboard, Roland made his way up. Reaching the landing he stood stock still, listening. He could hear no sound of movement or breathing. Following his hunch, he tried the door of the front bedroom. His nose told him that the room was unoccupied. It had the musty smell of a space that not been used for some time. He closed the blackout curtain and risked his torch again. He was in a spare room, sparsely furnished with two single beds, a wardrobe and a chest of drawers. The wardrobe was empty and the drawers in the chest too narrow to hide a body. The beds were divans, too low to the ground to hide anyone underneath. He lifted the mattresses, but all he found was dust.

The next room he tried was little more than a box room. It was cluttered with suitcases and cardboard boxes but it was clear that Kim could not be hidden there.

At the doorway of the master bedroom, he stood still and listened, but there was no sound from inside. Stepping cautiously through the door he realized that this room, like the others, was empty. Had the owner decamped? Unless, of course, he had fallen asleep in his chair downstairs. The blackout curtains were closed so he risked turning on the light, but a quick search showed no sign of Kim.

Roland made his way back down the stairs. There was nothing in the sitting room to arouse his suspicions. He was familiar with this part of the house, as this was where the meetings had taken place. All the furniture was arranged exactly as he remembered it. Here, too, the blackout curtains were closed, enabling him to turn on the light. There were no hiding places, no traces of blood or of a scuffle of any sort. The carpet was fitted and had clearly not been lifted.

That left the kitchen. As he walked down the hallway, he had a sudden impression that something was different. Pausing, he looked along the length towards the front door. It took a moment for him to realize what it was. The framed photograph of the Duke of Windsor with Hitler had been moved from its usual place and rehung on a section of wall that jutted out at right angles. He examined it more closely. The wallpaper on that section was different from the rest of the hallway. Maybe, he thought, Justin was using it as a tester, to decide whether to have the whole area papered like that. Trust him to think of something like that in the middle of a war!

With a shrug, he went into the kitchen. Everything looked normal, except for one chair out of place in the centre of the room. A trace of a scent on the air made his pulse quicken.

Kim!

It was the perfume Kim used. Something carefully pre-served, she had told him, from pre-war travels in France.

He breathed deeply, inhaling it. But even as he did so it seemed to disperse.

He shook himself and checked the larder leading off the room. There were a few tins on a shelf and little more.

Roland stood in the kitchen looking at the chair that was askew. His instincts told him that there was something not right here, but he could not pin it down.

There was one chance remaining. He let himself out of the back door into the small garden. A paved terrace covered part of it. Roland felt around the edges of the flags but there was no sign that any of them had been lifted. Across a strip of lawn with flowerbeds down both sides stood — his heart lifted — a garden shed. He stepped over the grass and tried the door. It was unlocked. The door creaked horribly as he swung it open to find . . . a wheelbarrow and a rack holding gardening tools. But no Kim.

Roland turned away feeling utterly defeated. He retraced his steps to the house. He had been so sure that this was where they would have brought Kim, but now he had to admit she could be anywhere. The chance that her captors had taken the risk of leaving her alive was small and it would not be hard to dispose of a body in the ruins that scarred the city — or to drop it into the Thames. In the blackout, who would be likely to see? He told himself that his relationship with her had never been more than a brief affair, with no prospects, but that did nothing to ease the pain in his heart, or his burning determination to seek revenge. Passing back through the hallway he was tempted to rip the photograph from the wall and smash it, but he remembered that there must be no sign of any intrusion that might alert the conspirators and make them change their plans. Gritting his teeth, he let himself out of the front door and closed it softly behind him.

\* \* \*

As the first faint light showed through the glass panes in the roof Kim became aware that the drumming of the rain had ceased, and after a while the level of the water in the cellar began to drop. She waited until there was barely an inch left and then paddled over to where she had seen it bubbling up.

As she expected, there was a grating in the middle of the floor. Leaning over it, she could hear the sound of rushing water somewhere below. Down there was a sewer, and sewers had manholes leading to the open air. A desperate chance was beginning to suggest itself. She put her fingers into the grating and pulled. Years of accumulating dust and rust had welded it into place. It cost her many broken fingernails and lacerated fingers before she was able to lift it.

The last of the floodwater drained away and Kim found herself gazing down through the grating and into a pipe that disappeared into blackness.

The sides of the pipe were slick with moisture and algae. There were no breaks in the smooth sides, no handholds or anything to give a purchase for feet.

She sat back and considered. Once committed, there would be no way of stopping, and if the far end was blocked by another grating, no way of climbing back. The thought of lowering herself into that black hole, with no guarantee that there was a way out at the bottom made her flesh creep. But the alternative was to sit here, in this prison, in the faint hope that someone would find her. If she got stuck halfway down the pipe she would die like a rat in a drain; if she stayed where she was, she would perish from cold and starvation. There was one chance of survival, and one only.

Kim lowered herself over the edge. She took a deep breath, closed her eyes and stretched her arms above her head.

* * *

Back at the flat after his fruitless search, Roland tried to catch a few hours' sleep but could not shut out the relentless images of Kim, suffering God knew what tortures at Kline's hands, and when he did finally drop off his dreams were full of the same terrors.

He was forcing down a breakfast of stale bread and marge when M. arrived.

'I'm assuming you didn't find her,' said M.

'I searched the place from top to bottom,' Roland admitted, 'but I couldn't see any sign of her. But she must have been there! The cabby was quite sure that's where he took them. There must be clues I didn't pick up. We need to get the police there to do a proper search.'

M. looked at him sadly. 'We can't do that. Not yet. You know that.'

'But we can't just leave her in Kline's hands.'

M. sighed. 'It must have occurred to you that perhaps Kim is no longer alive. The chances are that Kline, or one of his associates, murdered her when they got her to Flood Walk, and they could have disposed of her body anywhere. Bodies are still being dug out of the wreckages of bombed houses. It might be days, weeks even, before she's identified.' He met Roland's eyes with a look of sympathy. 'I'm sorry, Foxy. We have to face facts. You searched the house and she isn't there. We have to concentrate now on pre-empting this coup. I need you to go back to Hackney Downs. It might be tonight that Young and his Blackshirts get the go-ahead to make those phone calls. We can't miss that. If we fail now, all Kim has done, all she has suffered, will be for nothing. We owe it to her to keep going.'

\* \* \*

To Kim, in the pitch darkness of the pipe, the descent seemed endless. She could feel herself accelerating, until suddenly her legs were free and her feet struck a solid surface. She stood, trying to get her bearings. Close to her there was a roaring torrent of water and she knew if she slipped into that she would be carried away, to end up God knew where. The ledge she stood on might only be inches wide. She felt around her and found a brick wall that curved away above her head to a high vault. She turned her head in the direction in which the water was flowing. That way almost certainly led to the Thames, and the outfall was probably guarded by another, much larger grating. She looked the other way and her heart gave a sudden thump. Far away in that direction there was just a hint of a lifting of the blackness. Keeping her hand on the wall beside her she began to feel her way towards the promised light.

* * *

Roland was preparing to set off back to Hackney Downs, when he was stopped by the ringing of the telephone. M. picked it up.

'Brigadier?' It was his secretary's voice.

'Yes. What is it?'

'I've got a Police Sergeant Mayhew from Pimlico on the other line, sir. He says a young woman has been brought into the station and is insisting that he contacts you.'

'A young woman? Does he have a name for her?'

'He says, sir, she's calling herself Lieutenant Maxwell, but he can't verify her identity because she's got nothing on her. I mean literally, sir. Apparently, she was brought in stark naked.'

* * *

They found Kim huddled in a chair in one of the interview rooms at the police station, dressed in what looked like a man's cricketing whites, the only clean garments that could be found in the lost property box to cover her nakedness. She was cradling a mug of tea in hands that shook so badly that every time she tried to take a sip it spilled down onto the white sweater. As M. and Roland entered, she put the mug aside and scrambled to her feet in a semblance of attention.

M.'s 'As you were, as you were' was overtaken by Roland, who pushed past him and gathered Kim into his arms. They clung together, her fingers clutching the fabric of his jacket as if it was a lifeline. He bent his head and whispered, 'Now who stinks? What is that perfume?'

She drew her head back and met his eyes. 'It's called Eau de Sewage Works. Sorry you don't like it.' Then she turned aside to face the brigadier colonel. 'It's the ninth, sir! Tomorrow. That's when it's all going to happen.'

'Are you sure? How do you know?'

'I heard Lyndham tell Harmsworth to hold the front page for the later editions. He promised him the scoop of a lifetime.'

M. stepped forward and drew her hands into his own. His military sangfroid broke down as he said, 'My dear girl, you may have just saved your country from a terrible disaster.' Pulling back, he went on, 'Let's get you somewhere warm and comfortable. Then we can talk.'

With a few words of thanks to the sergeant, who was left no less mystified than before, he led the way out to his car. As they drove, Kim told them how she had been caught and imprisoned and how she had escaped.

'Just as I thought I was home free, I thought it wasn't going to work after all. I got up as far as the manhole cover and no matter what I tried I couldn't shift it. Luckily, a man passing by heard me struggling and lifted it. God knows, he must have got a shock when this naked apparition climbed out. I'm sure he thought I was a mad woman who'd escaped from some asylum somewhere. But to do him justice, he took it all in his stride. He wrapped me in his coat, called a taxi and took me to the police station. The taxi driver wasn't too keen on taking us. I suppose he thought I was drunk. But my knight in shining armour convinced him otherwise. Oh God!' She stopped abruptly. 'I never asked his name. I ought to thank him properly, but I don't know how.'

'On this occasion,' said M., 'the knowledge of a good deed will have to be its own reward. One day, perhaps, he'll realize that he played a small part in a very important event.'

Back at the flat Roland ran a hot bath while M. heated up a can of tomato soup. Kim, wrapped now in a bathrobe, leaned back in her chair and allowed herself to believe that the nightmare was really over.

M., coming back from the kitchen, said, 'Well, we know when but we still don't know what. What's special about tomorrow that makes it the right day for whatever it is they're planning?' He stopped abruptly and clapped a hand to his brow, almost spilling the soup. 'Oh my God! Churchill! They're going to assassinate the prime minister! His ship docks in Greenock tomorrow. They must be intending to kill him. That would certainly trigger alarm and confusion in Whitehall, and all over the country too. But how? Blow up his car? Shoot him?'

'Yes, that's it!' exclaimed Kim. 'Of course! I heard one of them asking if Lyndham was sure he'd got the right man for the job, and he said yes, he was a superb marksman.'

'Right!' M. put down the mug of soup and reverted to his role as commanding officer. 'We're in over our heads here. It's time I took this whole thing upstairs. We need to deploy police and the Home Guard and any troops that can be made available to search all the premises within sniper range of the docks where the PM will land.' He looked at Roland. 'Foxy, I'm sorry to ask this, but I want you back with Young and his lot, so we have eyes on what's happening at that end. Try to identify as many of the ring leaders as you can. I will inform the High Command and get things moving, then I shall get the night train to Glasgow to oversee operations.'

'What about me?' Kim asked. 'What do you want me to do?'

Both men looked at her in silent admiration. 'You, young lady,' M. said, 'are going to stay here and rest. And that's an order. You've already gone above and beyond what anyone could ask of you.'

'But—'

'No buts! There's something useful you can do. You can be the liaison between me and Foxy. We will both phone in at intervals, so you can keep us updated about what's going on.' He moved to the door and paused. 'God willing, by the time we are back together, this whole nightmare will be over.'

# CHAPTER 24

Kim was still in the bath when Roland left. She lay in the warm water, remembering their last lingering embrace and trying to convince herself that nothing could go wrong now. Finally, she pulled herself out of the bath, put on her pyjamas and ate the omelette he had made for her and left keeping warm. It had used their combined egg ration for a week, but she wolfed it down. Then she got into bed and fell at once into a deep sleep. She was aware of Roland slipping in beside her sometime in the small hours, but he was gone again when she woke up at eight o'clock.

She dressed and made herself a pot of tea and some toast and wondered how she would pass the time until she heard from either him or the colonel. She turned on the wireless, half expecting to hear an announcer informing the listeners that the prime minister had survived an assassination attempt — or perhaps had not. But the anodyne broadcast of the Home Service continued uninterrupted. It was in the middle of *Workers' Playtime* that Roland phoned.

'The square's beginning to get busy. People are arriving from all over. I can't be sure, of course, if they are all Blackshirts. Some of them may just be here to see the sights. But my guess is there are several hundred waiting for the signal to move, and more arriving all the time. I know some of the Hackney lot have got banners hidden in shopping bags or inside their coats, ready to unfurl them when they get the word, and I expect the rest have too. Everyone's on edge but trying to look casual, and I can't imagine it will be long before the police realize something's going on. But right now, it's a waiting game.'

M. called a bit later. 'We're expecting the PM to disembark at any moment. I've got men stationed at every vantage point and others combing through all the adjacent buildings, but so far, they've come up with nothing.'

Twenty minutes later he called again, his voice hoarse with frustration.

'Nothing! Nothing has happened and we've not found anyone looking remotely suspicious. I'm beginning to think this whole thing was a gigantic hoax.'

'What about the PM?' Kim queried.

'He's on his way back to London. The RAF are flying him down to Northolt. He should land within the hour.'

Kim put down the receiver without saying goodbye and ran into the bedroom. There she stripped off the casual slacks and sweater she was wearing and struggled into her FANY uniform. Once dressed, she pulled out her case from under the bed and took from it her Webley revolver. She loaded it and pushed it into a shoulder holster under her tunic. She grabbed some cash and her keys and left the flat.

In the road a taxi had just been hailed by a large woman with a small child in tow. Kim sprinted past her with a gasped '*Sorry*' and jumped into the back seat.

'Northolt Aerodrome, as fast as you can! And don't worry about the speed limit.'

'Hang on!' the driver expostulated. 'Who the dickens . . . ?'

The large woman was banging on the door and shouting, '*I was here first!*'

Kim ignored her.

'I work for the security service, and I need to get to Northolt as fast as possible. It's a national emergency.' She had to hope the driver wouldn't ask for some kind of proof.

Instead, she saw a glint come into his eye and guessed that he had fantasized about just such an eventuality, fed by countless films where someone jumps into a taxi and shouts, 'Follow that cab!'

'Right you are!' he said. 'Northolt it is.'

Kim leaned forward. 'Good man! What's your name?'

'It's James. But everyone calls me Jack.'

Driving at any speed along the bomb-cratered streets of London was not for the faint hearted, but Jack knew every side road and back-double and very soon they were out on Western Avenue, the main road leading north-west out of London. At the gates of the aerodrome Kim presented her FANY ID and told the sentry that she had an urgent message for the commanding officer. FANY personnel were often employed as couriers, so she was admitted without query and Jack drove her to the main administration block. As she got out of the taxi Kim heard the unmistakable sound of an aircraft coming in to land and turned to see the Avro York, Churchill's personal aircraft, just about to touch down.

There was no time now to explain things to senior officers. Kim jumped back into the taxi.

'Drive me to the control tower.'

The cab arrived at the foot of the control tower with a squeal of brakes, and Kim was out of it almost before it had stopped moving. She drew her revolver and pounded up the stairs.

Reaching the control room at the top she was met with exactly the sort of scene her imagination had painted. The flight sergeant in command and the airman assisting him were at their desk, but their rigid posture had nothing to do with the operations they were conducting. Behind them stood a man with a revolver pressed into the sergeant's neck.

Kim ignored them and ran on, up an external staircase leading to the roof. There another man was resting a Lee Enfield Mark II rifle, the sniper's favourite weapon, on the surrounding railing and sighting along its barrel to where the portly figure of Winston Churchill, cigar in hand, was descending the aircraft steps.

There was no time to issue a challenge, or even to aim her revolver. Kim hurled herself across the space between them and brought them both crashing to the ground. The rifle went off, the bullet winging its way harmlessly skywards. Kim was on her feet first, kicking the rifle out of reach, but even as she did so boots clattered up the metal staircase and the second gunman appeared, his weapon levelled at her head. There was a moment of suspended time.

Behind her Kim could hear the sniper getting to his feet and she saw the other man's finger tightening on the trigger. There was no time to bring her own weapon to bear. She threw herself flat in time to see the flight sergeant lunge from the top of the stairs and catch the gunman's legs in a rugby tackle. There was another report as the gunman's revolver went off, but the fall had knocked it out of his hand, and Kim, scrambling to her feet for the second time, grabbed it.

'Here!' She threw it to the sergeant. 'Keep him covered.' She turned in time to see the sniper dive for his rifle. She aimed her revolver at his head. 'Drop it or I'll shoot!'

For a split second he hesitated. Then he threw down the rifle with a clatter and raised his hands. From the cabin below Kim could hear the airman frantically calling for help over the radio.

'Down on your knees, both of you. Hands in the air!' She looked beyond them to the sergeant. 'Thanks, chum. That was a great tackle.'

'Well, there.' The accent was unmistakeably Welsh. 'I always knew all that rugger we played would come in useful one day.'

From below came the wail of sirens, and glancing down Kim saw an ambulance and a fire engine plus a truck full of RAF police skid to a halt at the bottom of the tower.

At the same moment, Churchill's Daimler drove sedately past on its way to the main gates.

Kim looked at the two gunmen on their knees and the sergeant standing over them with an ironic grin. 'Oh good, here comes the cavalry!'

# CHAPTER 25

Back at the flat M. poured three generous measures of whisky.

'Here's to the two of you.' He raised his glass. 'It's a sad fact, but probably no one will ever know how close we came to a disaster that would have changed the course of history, or the part you two have played in averting it. Maybe, one day, when this wretched war is over, there will be a chance to recognize your courage and initiative, but for now I'm afraid it will have to remain between ourselves.'

'Not us two,' objected Roland. 'This is all down to Kim.'

'She played a major role, it's true,' agreed M. 'But it was your infiltration of Lyndham's group that gave us the first indication of what was being planned. Without that we would never have understood the full enormity of what might have happened. And now, thanks to your pick-pocketing expertise and your observations among the crowd this morning, we shall be able to arrest and intern a good many of the ringleaders.'

'Tell me about what happened with that crowd,' said Kim. 'The march never got going, did it?'

'No,' said Roland. 'We all stood around for hours, waiting for some kind of signal, and when it didn't come people just got fed up and went home. It was a bit of a damp squib, really.'

'For which we are all truly grateful,' commented M. dryly.

'Presumably the whole idea of springing Mosley from jail never took off either,' said Kim.

'Ah, now there you are wrong,' M. told her with some satisfaction. 'Lyndham and Hastings turned up as arranged. Presumably the word hadn't got through to them that the whole plot had been aborted. But I had pre-warned the governor that they would be carrying a forged letter, so as soon as they presented it, they were arrested. So at least we now have grounds for putting them behind bars. Not that the trial will reveal the full extent of what they were involved in. There are still people who are beyond our reach who ought to bear the responsibility for their crimes, but at least we've got those two.'

'And what about Kline?' asked Kim.

M. shook his head regretfully. 'Disappeared without a trace. We're watching all the ports, of course, but my guess is he had an escape plan ready in case something went wrong. He's probably back in Germany by now.'

'You mean he wasn't Austrian, as he claimed?'

'Oh no. And he wasn't Jewish, either. It was all very carefully contrived, well in advance, by someone.'

'Do we have any idea who?' asked Roland. 'I mean, at Hitler's end.'

'No, we haven't, and I don't expect we ever will. We must just be thankful we managed to thwart it and we all live on to continue the fight.'

'And Raoul?' asked Kim. 'It hurts me to say this, but he was definitely involved. Has he been arrested?'

'No. He must have been prepared for things to go wrong. He took sick leave a couple of days ago and vanished. I've instigated a countrywide search but so far there's no sign of him.'

'What about that chap Justin Verney? It was his house they were using,' said Roland.

'Ah, yes. We picked him up a couple of hours ago boarding a train for Liverpool. My guess, he was hoping to get a berth on a ship going to South America. I fancy he may prove to be quite useful.'

They were silent for a moment, until Kim said, 'I know there can't be any official recognition, and I don't expect any. But there are two people I should like to see get some kind of reward.'

'Who is that?' asked M.

'The taxi driver who got me to Northolt in record time. I've got his full name and address. And the sergeant manning the control tower. He saved my life with a rugby tackle.'

'I'm sure something can be arranged,' the brigadier promised.

There was another silence. Then M. said, 'So, what about the future, where you two are concerned?' They both looked at him in some confusion and he added quickly, 'I'm not asking about your personal affairs. I'm thinking of where you serve next.'

'Ah. I've been giving that some thought too,' said Roland.

'Do you still want to go to France, as an agent?'

'Yes, definitely. But I can't see myself going back to Beaulieu as if nothing had happened.'

'From what I've seen,' said M., 'there's nothing they could teach you there that you don't already know. Don't you agree, Kim?'

'Absolutely,' she said, but her feeling of relief after a job well done had been abruptly shattered.

'So my idea would be to deploy you as soon as a suitable opportunity arises,' went on M.

Roland looked at Kim with a combination of excitement and remorse. 'Great!'

'What about me?' she asked. 'Back to France with him?'

The brigadier shook his head. 'You know we never deploy two agents to the same circuit if they have . . . a personal connection. The dangers of compromise or blackmail are too great. But the plan I have for you will involve going back to France, if you are willing.'

Kim felt a tightening in her stomach but she nodded. 'Of course. Whatever you need me to do.'

'You will not have forgotten that Claudette may not be the only agent subverted by Kline. I have a list of all those who passed through his hands while he was at Beaulieu. It's not extensive, fortunately, but still sufficient to cause grave concern. Several of the names on it are those of women.' He paused and sipped his drink. 'You know Vera Atkins, of course.'

'Maurice Buckmaster's secretary?'

'Much more than that. I sometimes think F Section would fall apart without Vera. The present point is, she takes a special interest in women agents sent to France. I propose to second you to work with her. Under cover of visiting different circuits to find out how women attached to them are faring, you would be able to assess whether they have come under Kline's influence.'

'How would I do that?'

'I leave the precise method to you, but perhaps you might hint that you too believe the twisted philosophy he perpetrates. More generally, you will be able to assess the success of operations carried out by that circuit, and whether they had any suspicion that the Germans knew in advance what they were planning. In other words, is there a mole in the group? There are men on that list too, of course. Your cover story would not prevent you from watching out for any suspicious activity connected with them. In short, I want you to play the detective, just as you have been doing for the last few weeks. What do you think?'

'I can see it's important. But I don't feel happy spying on our own people.'

'I understand that. But when you weigh the damage someone like Claudette was able to do, I think it's justified.'

'Yes, of course.' Kim was remembering Lucien dying so close to freedom. 'You're right. I'll do whatever I can.'

'Excellent!' The brigadier looked from Kim to Roland with a smile. 'But first, I think you both deserve some leave. Two weeks seems about right. I can arrange travel warrants for you. Where do you want to go?'

Roland looked at Kim and raised his eyebrows, leaving the choice to her. She thought for a moment. Her instinct was always to head for the mountains, but there were no real mountains in England, and she'd had enough of the Scottish ones. There was no point in heading for the seaside when all the beaches were closed off with barbed wire in case of an invasion. She shook her head.

'I don't know.'

M. said, 'I have a friend who owns a little B and B in Montgomeryshire, not far from Ross-on-Wye. It's a beautiful area and I think you would find it very peaceful. No air raids, no barbed wire. Just cows and sheep in lush meadows. What do you think?'

Kim sought Roland's gaze and he smiled. 'It sounds ideal,' she said.

'Good. I'll contact my friend and make the arrangements.' He drained his glass and got up. 'Now, I think it's time to say goodnight. It's been quite a day.'

Later, in bed after they had made love, Roland voiced a thought that had been in Kim's mind for some days.

'When this is all over, do you see any future for us?'

She hedged. 'How do you mean?'

'Well, I find myself wondering why a respectable lady should want to . . . to associate herself with a disreputable old con.'

Kim considered. 'Let me think. Perhaps because the old con turned out to be not as disreputable as first appearances might suggest. And because the lady in question didn't find the idea of respectability all that alluring?'

'So you think that perhaps, after the war . . .'

'If we both survive that long.'

'There is that, of course. But if we do . . . ?'

'Then I think the future looks very hopeful, for both of us.'

He smiled and kissed her tenderly. 'Wonderful! But there's just one thing . . .'

'What?'

'Please could you stop calling me Roland? It's not my name. I'll be Roland in France, but when I'm at home I'll want to forget that.'

She ran her hand through his thick russet hair.

'All right, Foxy.'

## THE END

**Thank you for reading this book.**

If you enjoyed it please leave feedback on Amazon or Goodreads, and if there is anything we missed or you have a question about, then please get in touch. We appreciate you choosing our book.

Founded in 2014 in Shoreditch, London, we at Joffe Books pride ourselves on our history of innovative publishing. We were thrilled to be shortlisted for Independent Publisher of the Year at the British Book Awards.

www.joffebooks.com

We're very grateful to eagle-eyed readers who take the time to contact us. Please send any errors you find to corrections@joffebooks.com. We'll get them fixed ASAP.